M000189826

His hand was almost to the flap when the first blow came: something fell hard on the hammock rope above his head. Matt brought his knees up and actually had his legs outside the tent flap when a second blow succeeded in severing the rope, instantly dropping the head end of the hammock to the ground. He took the force of the fall on his right shoulder and cheek but managed to scramble to his feet, arms flailing inside the muslin tent. Then something heavy caught him across the shoulders and sent him to his bare knees; he doubled over, desperate hands through the opening now, searching the ground for the Colima's plastic grip. But the next blow put an end to it: his skull took the impact. The world turned blizzard white before darkness prevailed; he fell and dreamed of snow. . . .

# RÍO PASIÓN

## James Luceno

IVY BOOKS • NEW YORK

Ivy Books
Published by Ballantine Books
Copyright © 1988 by James Luceno

All rights reserved under International and Pan-American Copyright
Conventions. Published in the United States by Ballantine Books, a
division of Random House, Inc., New York, and simultaneously in
Canada by Random House of Canada Limited, Toronto.

Library of Congress Catalog Card Number: 88-91134

ISBN - 0-8041-0263-5

Manufactured in the United States of America

First Edition: November 1988

*For Conrado Linga and the Sayaxche boatmen;
for Francisco Amezqua and the guides of
Palenque;
and in memory of Alberto Gilly, who drowned
in Petex Batun, El Petén, Guatemala, in 1985.*

## Acknowledgements

Thanks to Mayanist and archeoastronomer John Carlson of the University of Maryland; botanist Dennis Breedlove of the California Academy of Sciences; Tom Pierce of High Country Passage, which specializes in adventure and educational travel; Mary Evans of the Ginger Barber Agency for her critique; and Owen Lock, for his keen judgment.

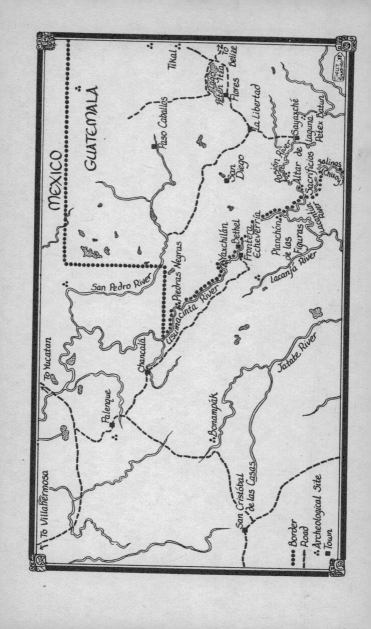

# Bed Of The Year

The year was off to a vague start, with rains well into February and the jungle full of excited calls—ghostly echoes and the sounds of chase. Blood seemed to cover the land, a crimson tide washed in from the past; a tectonic shift, all hell released. The humid air reeked of its presence, and the swollen rivers were tainted—but oh, how these forests had thrived!

He knew he would have to walk softly here, no false steps this decade. A hoped-for turning point, armed now with a solitary purpose to keep some safe distance.

*Bodacious cowboy*, the music mocked him.

At the same time, dead on the downbeat, Matt heard two shots explode from the palm forest behind the lodge. He reached over to drop the volume on the cassette player, set aside his tools, and began to work his way along the thatch toward the peak of the roof. Out of the western sky came mated parrots, protesting raucously as they rode a breeze out over the lagoon. Matt turned and raised himself somewhat, straddling the peak to watch them disappear into the sun.

Reading a new dinner menu in the rifle fire, his stomach gave a low growl—venison or forest pig, anything that promised a change from the diet of *blancos* and *robalos* Silvio had been serving up. He sat still for a moment squinting into the light and listening for further reports. Maybe the old man had missed.

The notion brought on a smile. The colony man, as Silvio referred to himself, was in seventh heaven now with the rifle Matt had brought in. The owner of the lodge, a lawyer from the capital, had refused the old man's request, afraid that Silvio would blow a foot off one drunken night. But given the political climate of Guatemala that spring of 1982, Matt thought it a good idea to have a decent weapon around.

He scanned the high forest for signs of his friend, then returned to work on the roof, Steely Dan on tape while he wove new *redondo* fronds into a water-damaged section of thatch. Two kinkajous—pandalike creatures with coats as velvety as the tropical night—called the roof home and Matt thought himself as much repairman as environmentalist.

Two hours later he was at work on one of the veranda stairways pumping a crosscut blade through a two-and-a-half-inch-thick mahogany plank he and Silvio had ripped with a two-man saw. The plank came from the same stick they'd dragged out six months ago; most of it had since become Matt's near-dugout.

He stopped several times to wipe sweat from his eyes, waving a hand perfunctorily through a nimbus of insects. The mahogany would make for fine stair treads, he decided, but it would be a gift if the stringers held up much longer. Less than a year and they were already going to rot, the jungle calling in its loan, the world at work. Decay was something to look forward to, a constant in revolutionary times.

He replaced a broken handrail next, foraging down near the water's edge for just the right branch, then moved on to what Silvio referred to as the *moza negocio*—the maid's business. Swabbing out the rooms with diluted kerosene, hauling water up from the lagoon, grinding corn. He had to come to a decision about the outdoor latrines as well: bats were in the pits again, and Jake had left it to him to second-guess whether the next group would prefer dealing with the bats or the beefworm-carrying mosquitoes they fed on. Matt was inclined to leave them be. Travel was supposed to be about new experiences, and what better place to recognize this than in a wooden outhouse in the middle of a Central American rain forest, squatting in a latrine with the sound of fluttering wings beneath you.

The lodge was a rustic Guatemalan longhouse partitioned into half a dozen very basic rooms, surrounded by fruit trees, graceful *corozo* palms, and flowering hibiscus. It sat on a rise above the lagoon, some two sinuous hours by *canoa* from the town of Sayaxche on the Pasión River, the tangled heart of Petén province. The territory had originally been cleared and settled by the Maya, who by A.D. 1000 had for the most part abandoned it. The Petén had since played host to loggers, chicle gatherers, scientists, colonists from the highlands, and most recently to tourists, insurgents, and smugglers. The lagoon itself would have been of little interest to anyone outside of a few die-hard sportsmen were it not for the archeological sites that lay scattered along its western shore.

The arrival of each group had been a mixed blessing for the Petén, but it was the guerrillas and smugglers who had most influenced the current state of affairs, having driven out some of the settlers, many of the archeologists, and almost all of the tourists. Problematic for the territory and of growing concern to Matt. A wilderness guide in the employ of Puma Tours, tourists had become something like his life's blood.

The company ran adventure-oriented trips through the Petén, and Matt headed up Puma's Mexico office in nearby Palenque. Puma's clients had a two-day stopover at the lodge before embarking on the downriver portion of the "Classic Maya" tour. Silvio, the Belizian caretaker, could always be relied on for fresh fish and exaggerated tales, but seldom for general upkeep. He preferred fishing, drinking, or smoking the weed—the *donajuana*—he cultivated in a patch of cleared land behind the main house. Consequently, the place had become a kind of second home for Matt.

By midafternoon he had put the final check on his list and had even managed to fit in an hour's work on the dugout. He was in the kitchen when Silvio returned, dragging in a butchered brocket on a makeshift litter.

Hummingbirds were feeding at the hibiscus, and a stiff wind had come in off the lagoon to enliven the palms.

The colony man, his aged brown face lit up, gestured proudly to the deer, Coco barking his own delight. When the mutt stopped to sniff at the litter, Silvio gave him a light whack on the rump with the flat of his machete and sent him skulking away, scarred ears pinned back and shaggy tail dragging.

The kitchen was a dirt-floored, lattice enclosure beneath an elevated section of the lodge. Three long tables with benches knocked together from rough-hewn cedar planks, foodstuffs stacked high on hardwood shelves. Central to the space was a Petén cooktop—a firewood-heated mud stove—and above it, dangling from inverted umbrellas of natural growth, an assortment of cookware, calabash gourd containers, lanterns, and tortilla presses. A few plump hens could usually be found wandering about, along with Silvio's one-eyed, seven-toed cat and the lodge's clipped-tail parrot, Lorita Chula—the flashy dame.

"We got us some meat," Silvio called out. "I tol you, mon: you bring me de right rifle and I provide, to be sure."

"Just don't string that thing too close," Matt said. "We've got enough flies in here to stock Calcutta, and I don't want to hear Jake's complaining."

"Mon, I take care of Jake. 'Sides, dere's gon to be nuttin left to hang. We gon to use all this critter to good purpose."

Matt's stomach talked to him. "Anything'd be better than more fish."

The old man waved dismissively and began to untie the carcass. He claimed to be sixty, but rumor and speculation put him closer to eighty. Perhaps five foot six before he'd shrunk, he was thin but wiry, with broadly callused hands and feet and skin the color of walnut stain. His hair and what there was of his beard had gone pure white, but he had clear eyes, all his teeth, and more knowledge of the *selva* than any ten of his neighbors along the lagoon. He had fished off the cays for most of his life but had left Belize for reasons that remained uncertain—some claimed he had murdered a man, but that was all but a given in the territory. Most Peténeros were disinterested in Guatemala's continuing dispute with Belize and had welcomed Silvio into the frontier fold. He had helped raise the lodge, but the hunters and fishermen it was built to accommodate never arrived. In their place came tourists and tour operators, like Jake Welles, the founder of Puma Tours.

Matt helped him lay the meat out to smoke, and later they prepared a victory feast for themselves, trading insults at the mud stove and sharing swigs from a bottle of Jamaican dark rum. Silvio tolerated Matt's frequent visits and the havoc they wreaked on his personal routines, but even that begrudging acceptance was more than he normally doled out to the guests. He counted on Matt to keep things from becoming too businesslike in their little corner of the woods, and Matt relied on him in a similar way. For a long while theirs had been a kind of partnership in paradise, but lately things were beginning to slip from their grasp.

They were just sitting down to supper when Coco went on alert, padding off into the evening, barking up a storm. When two male voices called a cheery greeting a moment later, Silvio dropped his fork to the table and threw up his hands in elaborate concern. "Dey can smell my cooking all de way to Sayaxche."

The dog returned, tail wagging, followed in by Paolo and Emil, two boatmen from Sayaxche. With a mischievous smile, Paolo produced a bottle of *aguardiente* and set it on the table. "A treat," he announced in Spanish.

Silvio relaxed, a glint of gold in his smile. "Well, why dint you say so straight off, mon? Grab a stool up."

Matt shook hands with the two men and rotated the bottle to read its crude hand-lettered label.

"Mexican. Where'd you find it?"

"Ramon brought it up from Echeverría," Emil explained. "He has two cases of Superior in Sayaxche."

Guatemalan Gallo was the Pasión's mainstay, an inferior brew by any standards. "That's trouble," Matt said.

"He says he's going to bury it, but everyone's been following him around."

Paolo laughed. "The same thing happened last time,

and he ended up drinking all of it just to be rid of it. He was *borracho*, man, no good for a week!''

Paolo was Matt's closest friend in the Petén, a sturdy five-eight, with a fine-featured Castilian face, a thick mustache, and a Vandyke beard. He had been born and raised in Sayaxche and had worked as a hunters' guide until fifteen, when a gringo client accidently shot him, leaving him with the limp that had since become a trademark. But he had made the switch to river pilot without a glance back. Husband and father now, he owned and operated the cargo and tourist launches Puma hired for its trips downriver. His younger brother, Emil, was slight and sinister by comparison but an able pilot and an avid pursuer of amorous intrigues.

Silvio had fetched four *copitas* and arranged them around the bottle of highland firewater. Paolo did the honors and offered the first *salud*.

Matt downed the colorless drink and got up to place the untouched meals on the edge of the cooktop to warm. He wondered what had brought Paolo out to the lodge; if it were something important, the boatman would have used the radio in Sayaxche. Not that casual visits were unheard of, but they were uncommon. Politeness demanded, however, that the rituals be honored before the purpose of the visit was broached.

So they exchanged bits of news while they drank, in a pidgin of their own devising. Silvio, for all his twenty-five years in Guatemala, was still not fluent in Spanish, and Paolo and Emil had only a beginner's grasp of English. The local dialect put an *ng* on words ending in *n*; thus *Petén*—which in Mayan meant "Isolated places"—came out sounding more like *Peténg. Guatemala* was *Huatemala*.

There were disappearances and killings to discuss in the violent wake of the March 7 elections that had landed Brigadier General Aníbal Guevara Rodriguez in the driver's seat, with half the country screaming fraud. The father of a man they all knew had been gunned down in Guat City by the ESA—the Secret Anti-Communist Army—at the behest, many believed, of a general who had since come to La Libertad in the Petén. Politics was involved, but everyone understood that the revolution had afforded convenient excuses for the handling of personal vendettas as well. Matt felt comfortable enough with Paolo and Emil to discuss that, but Silvio grew sullen, so they switched to less inflammatory issues.

The Tikal jetport project was a hot issue still. Flores hotel owners were worried about losing all their business to the park lodges, and engineers were concerned about the effects of vibration on the site's limestone structures. A North American contractor had lost all his road-building heavy equipment to the same torrential rains that were keeping the Mayan International in San Benito inundated.

But the big news was that an archeologist had been kidnapped and held prisoner for several days by a local insurgent group after having wandered into a remote Mayan site the guerrillas were plundering. The two policemen who had accompanied the archeologist from La Libertad had been murdered. There was speculation that the same rebel band was responsible for recent depredations at Río Azul and El Mirador and an attack on the *colonia* of El Arbolito the previous year. The guerrilla leader was a highland Indian who went by the name Raphael Aguilar, a dangerous Marxist revolutionary to some, a kind of jungle Robin Hood to others.

Murders and kidnappings of that sort were nothing new, Matt reminded himself: The Mayanist Sylvanus Morley had been mistaken for a Guatemalan revolutionary back in 1916 when he and his party were traveling to the ruins at Uaxactún. Matt had yet to cross paths with Raphael Aguilar or any of his band, but he had known other men like Aguilar. Years ago and another story.

"De ancient tings belong to dees people," Silvio was saying, commenting on the burgeoning market in Mayan antiquities. "Da priests back den seein dat dey reach de right hands is all."

The four men fell into an uneasy silence that had less to do with the Belizian's homespun wisdom than with the vicissitudes of conversation. The wind picked up, whipping at the kerosene-fed flames that lit the kitchen, and Paolo finally came to the point of his visit: It seemed that he had two American tourists waiting down in the boat, a married couple who had turned up in Sayaxche looking for someone to guide them downriver into Mexico.

"They want to see the ruins," the boatman said leadingly. "And since you are going back to Palenque anyway . . ."

"You figured you'd volunteer my services."

Paolo shook his head. "No, *mano*, they're willing to pay."

"So?"

"So we all go together. We take beers and flour to sell in the *colonias*. It can be a good time."

Matt poured another round and sipped at his glass. "What are they like?"

"*Amistosos,*" Emil said. "Friendly. But *sencillio*, you know—down on earth."

Matt cracked a smile. "Down *to* earth. Down *on* earth makes them sound like angry aliens."

"*Alien!*" Emil repeated excitedly. A grainy print of the movie had recently reached the Cine Norita in Sayaxche and had caused quite a stir.

Matt thought over Paolo's proposal. Things were slow just then, and money was scarce. Jake had only one group lined up for a trip that was still weeks off, which put any hope of tips effectively out of reach. But more than that, things were a bit dull, and in the past side jobs had been known to change that.

"Like old times, huh?"

"*Sí pues.*"

Paolo flicked his fingers together with an audible snap.

Matt leaned into the table and hoisted his glass. "Then let's do it." The two boatmen followed suit.

"*Pico de Oro,*" Paolo toasted, showing a roguish grin.

"*Hijo del Gran Palenque,*" Matt said.

Emil answered with an off-color toast of his own. "*Hijo del Gran Tortuga!*"

Matt suggested to Silvio that he get two more meals ready while Emil went down to fetch the couple. Solo travelers had become a rare sight along the river, and it occurred to Matt that the Americans might be Seventh Day Adventists or journalists, but one glance dissuaded him of either view.

They were in their early thirties, he guessed, with a

West Coast look about them. He was handsome and deeply tanned, with pale eyes and thinning brown hair. Matt put him at six-one, but his muscular physique made him seem even larger. He had on khaki shorts, a Hawaiian shirt, huaraches. She was as lovely as Paolo had described her, dressed in an *ikat* wraparound skirt and a T-shirt from the Tikal Lodge. Five-nine, slender, athletic-looking, she had a broad forehead and strong chin, Mayan blue eyes, and long auburn hair under a paisley kerchief knotted behind her head.

"Billie Westphal," she said, extending her hand to Matt. "My husband, Neil."

"Matt Terry," he said, glancing at her left hand. The ring was simple but elegant-looking, gold, diamonds, and sapphires. "Silvio. We don't know his last name."

Billie's firm grip took him by surprise. He offered them some food, but they declined. They had been traveling for six weeks now, she began to explain, through the Yucatán and Belize. Then, in Tikal, they had heard it was possible to go downriver into Mexico from Sayaxche. It was their first trip to the region, and they were enchanted, their interest in Mayan sites lying somewhere between Coe and Castaneda. And they were enthusiastic about the prospect of Matt's helping them get downriver to Altar de los Sacrificios, Yaxchilan, and Piedras Negras.

He listened attentively while he ate, Coco on haunches beside him awaiting a handout. "I haven't decided to take you yet," he confessed between forkfuls of lukewarm fish. "First off, I'm not leaving here for another two days. And even if we all agree, it wouldn't be a quick trip. Paolo would want to do some trading along the river." He shrugged. "It could take us five days to reach Palenque."

Billie and Neil traded looks. She said, "It sounds great. We've certainly got a week to spare for the trip of a lifetime."

Matt almost winced. Out of the corner of his eye he saw Emil's eyebrows bob in a display of amusement. "Course you'd have to pay for some of the boat expenses. Plus my fee," he added, looking at her again, "if we're going to traipse around in the ruins."

"How much are we talking about?" Neil asked.

Matt did some mental arithmetic. "Say, three hundred dollars for both of you, including meals for the full week. But Piedras Negras is out. We'd need an inflatable, and I don't have one up here right now."

Billie nodded. "That's okay. Yaxchilan's the big one, isn't it?"

Matt grunted noncommittally, still unconvinced he was making the right decision. He wasn't certain he could handle for six or seven days running the excess of enthusiasm going around. But Billie's smile was another matter; she was staring at him when he looked over at her.

Neil asked if they could enter Mexico without a tourist card. Matt told him there was no problem.

"Then you've got a deal," Neil said, and reached for Matt's hand.

Billie was watching the two of them. "Can we park here till we leave?"

Matt puzzled over it. "You mean stay here?"

"Yeah."

He looked over at Silvio, who was already grumbling to himself. "What d'ya say, boss?"

The old man frowned at him. "I guess I don min it, to a certain extent."

Billie grinned at Matt, showing white, even teeth. "Does that mean yes?"

Her nose was hooked ever so slightly to one side, but it was a terrific nose, Matt decided. He looked away, telling himself he'd been in the woods too long, and, businesslike, slid his stool back from the table and stood up. "Emil will bring your things up. I'll get one of the rooms ready."

"This is really nice of you."

"There's water to wash up over there, and the latrines are out back. I'll leave a flashlight in your room." He started off but stopped at the wattle wall. "Oh, and don't worry about the bats. They're harmless."

Matt stepped outside and took the path that ran along the front of the lodge. It was a gentle evening, full of soft sounds, rustling movement, and starlight. He climbed the stairway to the veranda and collected sheets, pillowcases, towels, and soap from the supply closet.

Then he made up the two single beds in room six and lit the lantern. Each bed had a comfortable foam mattress; a small table between them held wooden matches and a stub of candle in a ceramic holder.

He could hear Billie's sometimes husky voice rising through the wide-plank floorboards. She was talking about the Belize cays in broken Spanish and telling Paolo about places in the Yucatán. Her sentences were simple yet well articulated, but what impressed Matt most was her accent: she even said *Peténg*.

# 2

# Neighborhood Of The Heart

**M**att had his hammock strung in the kitchen area. Gradually he came around to feeling all right with the job he'd taken on, and managed to sleep through the rooster's predawn alarms, Lorita Chula's repertoire of calls and curses, even Silvio's early-morning banging around. He roused himself at six thirty, parted the mosquito net, and took a look around. The old man had gone fishing, but there were fresh eggs and papayas on the table and a skillet of black beans on the mud stove. Matt figured he would have to do most of the cooking for the lodge's unexpected guests and decided to take a swim before getting into it. He climbed out of the hammock, pulled on his trunks, slipped into a pair of rubber thongs, and headed for the lagoon. Ten steps across the front lawn he heard his name called.

"Morning," Billie said from the balcony rail outside her room. "Just another beautiful day in paradise, huh?"

He looked up at her, rubbing sleep from one eye. She was barefoot, wearing denim cutoffs and a white halter top, revealing in the golden light. "You two sleep okay?"

"Better than we have in weeks. Where you off to?"

"Quick swim." He pointed to the trailhead. "Then I'll rustle up something to eat."

"There's a place to swim? Wait for me," she said, disappearing into the room.

Matt took the trail at a leisurely pace. She caught up with him, still barefoot, wearing a football jersey by then. The path was stony, but she didn't complain; it dropped through a thicket of bamboo to an earthen beach where the limb of a submerged tree rose from the lagoon's green waters like the neck and head of a sea serpent. Matt kicked off his thongs, waded in, and took the cool plunge. A few long strokes carried him to a water-smoothed section of trunk where he pulled himself up and pushed the hair from his face.

Billie stood on the shore smiling, tying her hair back; then she peeled off the jersey and gave him a wave. She had on a patterned one-piece suit that hugged her shape. Her breasts were high; the muscles of her arms and legs were long and well defined. Matt realized he was staring and turned away.

She swam out into the lagoon with practiced technique, and he joined her after a moment. Schools of minnows gathered around, staying with them as they made for shore. She sat in the sunlight to dry herself, arms wrapped around her knees. Her skin was cream-colored and freckled, but not for want of the sun, Matt suspected. On her right inner thigh was a tattoo—a molet arrangement of marijuana leaves.

"This place is the tits," she said all at once. "Who built it?"

He hadn't heard the expression before; it struck him as crude, but he laughed it off. "Silvio and a few of the locals. But the money came from Guatemala City."

"Doesn't it always. So how long have you been coming here?"

"On and off for two years. Since Puma opened the office in Palenque."

Billie's eyes roamed over him while he spoke, taking in his tanned hands and dark eyes and settling on the circular scar on the left side of his abdomen.

"You know who you look like? Tom Selleck—*Magnum, P.I.*"

"Is that good?"

Billie rocked her head from side to side. "Could be worse. So you learned Spanish down here?"

"South America," he told her. "Peace Corps."

Billie's eyebrows went up. "Peace Corps? How's it go? 'If you want to change the world, start small.' I thought maybe you were in Nam."

Absently, Matt fingered the wrinkled scar tissue on his side. "No, different campaign. You a nurse, or you just happen to know your way around bullet holes?"

"I used to live with a vet," she said in an offhanded way. "He had a couple of those . . . I'll bet he's camped out at that ground-breaking in Washington right now." She was quiet for a moment, untangling her hair. "How do you like working as a guide? You don't mind nurse-maiding tourists? Everybody smelling like Muskol, *ooh*-ing and *aah*ing about everything."

"Deet's my favorite scent," Matt said straight-faced. "Actually I don't have much to do with the groups. I'm more the advance man—the *ayudante adelantado*, as Paolo says. I make sure the boats and mules and planes get where they're supposed to be. On time, if I can help it. It's not too bad."

Billie's blue eyes opened wide. "Not too bad? It sounds cush."

"Used to be. But everything's shutting down. It's not Central America's finest hour."

Billie nodded. "I noticed. So how often do you make it back?"

"To the States? I've been trying to get back for a long time now."

"You know John Belushi died. *Saturday Night Live*," she added, seeing his puzzlement.

"Oh, right. I'm out of touch."

She cocked her head and appraised him. "Sure you're not on the lam, Matt Terry? Running from the mob, or the police . . . some angry wife maybe?"

"Nothing that romantic. I only work here."

"In the middle of a revolution . . ."

"It didn't keep you and Neil away."

"Yeah, but we're just passing through."

Matt shrugged. "Maybe I am, too. Just a different pace."

"And you miss the States."

"Maybe. But I don't play video games, and I'm not computer-literate. Besides, Reagan and Red Brigades,

Libyan death squads—there's not much to miss, is there?''

"Death squads?" She made a face at him. "Yeah, and the miniskirt's making a comeback. Where are you getting your news—*Time* magazine? Qaddafi doesn't have any juice in the States. That's a lot of smoke. He's lucky he's been able to hang on to that sandbox he calls a country.''

Again Matt couldn't place the vernacular and asked where she was from.

"Tahoe," she told him.

"Heard you're having a rough winter."

"It's rough year-round." Billie laughed. "I went there thinking I was going to make astrobucks in real estate, but the market went tits up. Now I'm serving drinks and pulling arms like every other glamour girl in town."

Matt said. "Beautiful country, though. What's Neil do?''

Billie looked back toward the lodge. "This and that. He's got a carpentry business." She stood up and stretched without a hint of self-consciousness, tossing her hair in the light. "I'm going to see if he's up."

Matt picked up his thongs without taking his eyes off her. "You ready for some breakfast?''

"I'm always ready for breakfast."

Matt smiled. "Eggs, papaya, beans?''

She watched him for a moment. "You've got a great smile. Too bad you don't bring it out more often."

Matt left it alone and fell in behind her on the path, feeling as though he'd just gone a few hands of cards and come up short.

By nine A.M. Silvio had returned with his daily catch of peacock bass, perch, and snook, along with a sackful of grapefruits he'd bartered for smoked venison across the lagoon. He agreed to ferry Billie and Neil down to the Mayan sites of Aguateca and Tamarandito at the lagoon's south end, leaving Matt an undisturbed day to complete his chores and work on the dugout before Paolo returned with the launch. The day's list was short, and it wasn't long before he had adze in hand and was down at the water's edge standing over the beached log he had already christened *La Perla*. Silvio had found the fallen tree six months earlier on a piece of high ground two miles west of the lodge, and it had taken the help of two oxen to drag it out. Most of the new bread of Peténeros took the quick route through the mahogany or Santa Maria with chain saws, but Matt was doing it by fire and hand and had logged countless hours with his machete and shapers. The *cayuco* was still far from complete, but he was in no particular rush to see it finished.

Morley, the Mayanist, was believed to have said that only liars and damn fools liked the jungle but Matt considered himself neither one nor the other yet loved the place. Not so much the winter dry season but the late rains, when the rivers were running fast and high and the forest was dazzlingly alive. Indeed, if six inches could have been trimmed from Matt's six-foot-three frame, he might have passed for a native himself. Years in the Latin American sun had rendered his coloring right, and his face, if not exactly handsome, was full of the same planes and contours that characterized many a Peténero's countenance. He wore his curly black hair on the long side and had a thick but well-trimmed mustache, long arms, and a lean frame that looked almost as good at thirty-five as it had when he'd pitched high school hardball at seventeen. Ten years of drifting had landed him at the lodge, which reminded him of the Bitterroot wilderness camps of his Montana youth—his father's notion of paradise. For a while he had tried to make the lodge's natural simplicity a way of life, only the world kept seeking him out, complicating things, infringing on his plans.

It pained him to see what was happening in the Petén and throughout much of Guatemala now that there were no peaceful solutions left. But his feeling went beyond any selfish attachment to the lodge: The nation was tearing itself apart, and Matt often felt like a spectator to its self-destruction, an uncomfortable guest at a violent family argument. His presence as an American involved with tourism placed him in a curious double bind. While a representative of an industry capable of benefiting the entire country, he found himself caught between the privileged, who were trying their best to woo Reagan's America, and the disenfranchised, who viewed U.S. involvement in their affairs as a violation of the country's right to self-determination.

Puma nevertheless had continued to run trips on a limited basis through some of the worst violence Guatemala had known in over a decade. Soldiers in flak jackets were a common enough sight, and each day brought reports of new mutilations and disappearances. Some 13,000 people had lost their lives since 1977, but tourism was largely a matter of how much the American press chose to make of these incidents.

And of course there were always the profiteers and thrill seekers who didn't care one way or another.

Matt went at the dugout with a vengeance, working up a drenching sweat if only to take his mind off Billie for a while. Over breakfast, while they'd discussed details of the downriver trip, she had been probing and flirtatious, much to Neil's obvious amusement. They seemed as anxious to visit Palenque as anywhere else, and Matt had promised to show them around.

That he was attracted to her was understandable enough, he told himself, but what intrigued him was the teasing deceptiveness she employed as a kind of lure. He couldn't decide whether she had an exceptionally fine ear for languages and dialect or whether she had actually been south before. But why hide the fact? He wondered if she was just keeping something from Neil. And he was as much an enigma—quiet, preoccupied, a member of the Tarzan brotherhood, into push-ups and squat thrusts on the lodge's small square of front lawn and bo palms. Matt had nothing to go on but his instincts and a few harmless contradictions, and he asked himself why it should matter one way or another. So Billie had a knack for subtleties and liked to play the woman of mystery? Neil was the one who had to live at the other end of it; Matt only had to put up with it for a few more days.

He had dinner waiting when Silvio returned the couple from the ruins. Neil was talkative at the table, going on about the lagoon and its small population of caimans, about the Maya and the baffling legacy they'd left behind: their abandoned cities, their bizarre practices and once-puzzling inscriptions. He had shot three rolls of film in an attempt to capture the beauty of Aguateca's ravine and natural bridges.

Matt opened a bottle of wine he had been saving for a special occasion, and among the four of them they not only finished it but managed to polish off the last of Paolo's *aguardiente* as well. Silvio entertained them with tales from what he and Matt called "the favorites list." He told the one about the birder who stumbled upon two mating jaguars, the newlywed couple and their experience with the leaf cutters. And then somehow the topic swung back to the Maya.

"A lot of people like Tikal just because it's so damned impressive," Billie said.

"Lucas must be one of them," Neil offered. "He used it in *Star Wars*."

Matt saw Silvio's perplexed expression and explained about the movie.

Billie continued. "That's exactly what I'm talking about. It's a *huge* site. You come away from it understanding that the Maya weren't just some flash-in-the-pan culture but the big kids on the block."

Matt settled back with his drink to hear her out.

If you had to choose an ancient culture that had been at the receiving end of everyone's projected fantasies, you couldn't go wrong by naming the Maya, and Matt had found that people who were interested in the Maya were often obsessed with them. Depending on how you looked at it, they had either developed or refined a system of hieroglyphic writing that could still be read on their stelae and standing stones, on their pottery, and on the pages of the few bark books that had survived the Spaniards' fanatical attempts to expunge the "barbarians'" recorded history. It was a system of glyphic writing that had been studied tirelessly by professionals and interested amateurs throughout the world and had remained elusive for more than a century. But epigraphers and linguists had recently cracked the code and demonstrated that the abstract, animal-profiled, and geometric glyphs were logographs, the phonetic and semantic signs of a spoken language.

The Maya were related to the Asiatic wanderers who had crossed the Siberian land bridge and spread them-

selves into every corner of the Americas, a fact accepted
by all but the fringe groups who liked to tie them in with
Sumerians or Atlanteans. They perfected a vigesimal numerical system, reckoned time in millions of years,
tapped the sapodilla tree for chicle resin, and measured
wealth in terms of cacao beans. But what elicited more
interest than the tracing of their origins were the theories
regarding their demise. Sometime between the seventh
and tenth centuries A.D., they had abandoned the cities
they had carved out of some of the lushest of North
America's rain forests and vanished, or at the very least
dispersed to such an extent that no collective example of
their classical culture had managed to survive intact. The
decline of a people that had produced cities like Copan,
Tikal, Palenque, and Yaxchilan was explained away by a
score of causes—earthquakes, epidemic disease, over-
population, invasion, and climatic changes—but despite
evidence that favored one over the other, there remained
groups of loyal followers who kept each theory alive.

Their legacy, however, was to be found among the cities and temples the jungle had been doing its best to
dismantle and reclaim for ten centuries. And though some
might question the claims of mystics who saw in those
ruins evidence of a culture more highly evolved than any
on earth, one couldn't dispute that the sites had brought
more money into Mexico and Guatemala than any tourist
program yet devised by either government. Consequently
Matt seldom said anything to discourage the romantic
theorizing he often heard discussed on Puma's tours.

For a time Jake worried that the truth would come out,
that the Maya were just as confused as the rest of us—
just as politically incorrect and environmentally unconcerned—and the bottom would drop out of the tourist
trade, leaving Puma all dressed up with nowhere to go.
But when that happened—when new evidence and interpretation began to paint a different picture of the Maya—
just the opposite occurred: the appeal was greater than
ever before, working wonders for Puma and tripling the
value of black market antiquities that happened to find
their way north. No longer noble savages and ethereal
astronomers, the Maya were understood to have been a
warring culture, obsessed with death and entirely given

over to the belief that the world turned on blood, sacrifice, and self-mutilation.

It struck Matt that such reappraisals were the perfect stuff for the eighties.

"Neighborhood gangs is more like it," Neil was saying. "Blood fetishists."

Billie threw Neil a look. "Whatever gets you wet."

"Even I draw the line at tobacco enemas and beribboned glands," Neil said in an affected voice, draining his glass of *aguardiente*. "Not that that's so radical anymore."

Billie threw her head back and laughed. "San Francisco here we come. Loaded down with penis-piercing pre-Columbian lancets. Now there's a new import scam."

Matt studied them while they traded one-liners, wondering how he was ever going to catch up with the States. There were people out there trying to gun down the Pope, float their way to freedom, aerobicize themselves. Lycra spandex, megadeath and megatrends . . .

Billie said, "But Palenque was the crowning achievement. Pacal and his whole clan, they refined it all. You just have to set foot on the Temple of Inscriptions to know what I'm talking about." She stopped herself and reached for Neil's glass to cover her slip, tipping it to her mouth even though it was empty. "That's what I've been told, anyway."

Matt kept quiet. That was what she'd been told. Peripherally he was aware of her gaze; she was watching him, divining his suspicions. So he turned to give her the briefest glance, but no more.

# 3

# Rió Pasión

**A** day's journey west of the lodge, the Pasión River joined the north-flowing Usumacinta, once the central inland trade route of the ancient Maya. The Pasión-Usumacinta system served as the heartline of the Petén, 13,000 square miles of forest-covered undulating karst, savanna, and seasonal lowland swamps known as *bajos*. It boasted 600 species of birds and received up to 160 inches of rainfall annually. But March was not the best month to travel the Pasión; its café-au-lait waters were low, sluggish, sullied with clusters of discomforting yellow foam and odd bits of jungle detritus. The sun was merciless, the forest dry and somewhat lifeless. Billie and Neil seemed perfectly content nonetheless, and Matt was beginning to relax into the trip, as Paolo and Emil already had.

They had departed from the lodge at sunrise, after warm good-byes to Silvio, who was happy to see them go. He was free to return to his normal routines, with no tourists plying him for details about his life and no badgering from Matt about the condition of the lodge or the patch of marijuana that was growing more conspicuous every day. Matt pictured the old man waving *"Que les vayan bien!"* from atop the steep bank, gnarled fingers in the breeze, that permanent but lovable scowl on his dark face. *An don hasten your journey, mon.*

The flat-bottomed boat was six feet wide gunwale to gunwale and thirty feet long. Last year Paolo had repainted it turquoise, but the color was already beginning to fade. It was powered by a reliable forty-horsepower Johnson and roofed amidship by a thatch canopy that provided shade as well as photogenic color. Astern, for backup, a *canoa* was attached to a short length of tow line. Two wooden benches ran the length of the launch, but they and a good portion of the hull spaces were piled high with burlap and plastic bags stuffed with sundry trade goods: rice, grapefruits, watermelons, soap, and salt. Two drums of gasoline, three cases of chocolate-flavored milk of magnesia, and several crates of Fanta sodas and Gallo beers made up the rest of the cargo.

Billie rode in the bow, arms over the sides and legs stretched out across a narrow bench, her bare back cushioned against sacks of white flour. She wore her one-piece suit under jogger's shorts and a wide-brimmed straw sombrero Emil had bought for her in Sayaxche. Paolo, in cutoffs and a visored cap, had the helm, while Emil rode forward watching for tricky currents, signaling his brother with a hand code only the two of them knew. Neil, also in shorts, had abandoned the sun for the shelter of the *caseta*. Matt had taken it as a good sign that Neil had done so on his own, because it meant that he wasn't going to have to play the constant overseer. He recalled Puma's first trips in that same boat, crowded then with retired professionals from the States, most of whom would refuse to listen to advice about jungle travel and would wind up at the trip's end outraged, sunburned, chiggered, and covered with welts. He remembered, too, those wild nights in Sayaxche before Jake had secured the lodge, the surreal atmosphere of that frontier town with its impromptu all-night fiestas and mad midnight shows at the Cine Norita to the accompaniment of yapping dogs.

But the current trip had a different feel, and just maybe, Matt thought, it would turn out to be the carefree jaunt Paolo had promised. It was obvious that Billie and Neil had done their share of traveling. They were relaxed and patient, even in the face of the Pasión's sinuous course and the Petén's slower-than-laid-back pace. Perhaps almost too savvy, Matt told himself—too *acostumbrado*. But he was trying not to push too hard for explanations; he was being paid to guide them downriver, not snoop into their private pasts and presents.

He had spent most of the morning talking with Neil, who turned out to be a lot more than the pumped-up marine Matt had first thought. Neil had a sharp wit and a fine eye for visual detail. He shied away from discussing his carpentry business but seemed determined to learn the local names for the forest's flora and fauna. The dry season didn't offer much color, but Matt did what he could, pointing to trees and riverside vegetation: stately ceibas, strangler figs, and oaks; *cana brava, jimba, camalote* . . . There were loons, herons, snowy egrets, kingfishers, and cormorants in abundance, but one had to leave the river to find the real game, and even that was becoming something of a quest. Cleared tracts and milpas had replaced much of what had been virgin forest fifteen years ago, the jaguars, peccaries, and tapirs that had once roamed the Petén growing more scarce every year. Guatemala had opened up the territory to all takers, most of whom had little or no knowledge of the *selva*. The universal practice of slash and burn had taken its toll, as logging had before it and cattle raising would in the future. But Matt did spot several ridge-back turtles and a *tayra* that had slipped down to the shore for a drink, and Neil caught sight of an iguana as it was slithering back into dense riverside foliage.

When Paolo put in at settlements to sell his goods, Matt took his clients on a tour through dirt streets, meager fields, and wattle homes with corrugated roofs. He liked the fact that they weren't asking the usually inappropriate how-long, how-far questions, because the Petén just didn't work that way. News as well as goods had to be exchanged, and fixed price was an unknown concept. Paolo's bargaining sessions often went back and forth for an hour or more.

Matt didn't need to remind them to be respectful of

local mores and traditions, either; Billie never failed to pull a shirt over her swimsuit, and Neil was careful when and how he photographed. Matt encouraged them to sample the indigenous fruits and vegetables the settlers brought down to the boat. In the meantime, he got to touch base with people he hadn't seen in some time. The river was a linear neighborhood, and everyone thrived on gossip. Word and reputation spread quickly, and secrets were hard to keep.

For Matt these trading excursions brought back memories of his Peace Corps work in the Andes, the years of volunteer service and his short stint as field supervisor following Susan's death. His involvement in the lives of the Pasión settlers was hardly as intense and feverish as it had been among similar displaced groups along the rivers of Peru and, later, eastern Ecuador, but there was the same sense of simple joy and stoicism, an almost mystical resignation to hardship and disappointment. He and Susan and dozens of others had been out to change the world then, to ease some of the suffering through America's exported benevolence and unabashed optimism. Peace had a chance, so they all believed. But it all had come unglued after a while, and Susan's death had become Matt's personal tragedy, the one he had carried around for years and was quick to flash when anyone spoke naively of the rewards of commitment.

Paolo took on a Mam Indian couple and their ragamuffin brood for a short stretch, conveying them downriver free of charge. The father wore a perpetual smile. He was a small leathery man in campesino garb and tall rubber boots, a sheathed chicle machete tied around his waist and a water gourd with a corncob stopper over one shoulder. The children were wary and feral-looking, dark eyes fixed on Billie while they lapped at the *pozole* their *huipil*-clad mother dished out to their cupped hands.

It was just after noon when Matt worked his way up to the bow of the launch to see if Billie wanted any lunch. She had her head back, eyes closed and long hair free in the breeze. She squinted up at him when he called her name, wiping sweat from her brow as she reached for the sombrero.

"Whew . . . hot."

"And then some." Matt handed her a thick slice of watermelon. "You're not worried about getting burned?"

She laughed and pushed her forefinger against the bare skin of her shoulder. "Believe it or not, I'm tan. This is about as dark as I get. Pretty poor, huh?"

Matt was tempted to leave his own mark but thought better of it. "Those kids thought you were some kind of goddess."

"What was that they were eating?"

"It's called *pozole*. Ground maize and cold water. Better than Gatorade."

"They were so cute. I wish something could be done," she started to say.

"About what?"

"This," she said gesturing about. "The fact that we can afford to ride downriver when that man could barely keep his family fed." Billie laughed at herself. "Maybe I missed my calling. I should give up my lucrative waitressing for some serious volunteer work. Is the Peace Corps still around?"

"Not so you'd notice," Matt said. "Silvio packed a couple of things for us," he added after a moment. "We've got hard-boiled eggs, empanadas, and fruit." He indicated the cargo. "And of course there's plenty of warm beer and orange soda."

"I'll pass." she said, draping one arm in the water. "Not exactly ideal for swimming, is it?"

"You missed the dead cow a ways back."

"Just my luck."

Matt bent down to accept a bite from the watermelon. Billie's eyes held his until he straightened up. "There's clear water ahead," he said, scanning the north shoreline. "You can swim there if you want."

"Don't go to any trouble."

Matt said, "It's a service we're happy to provide." He made a theatrical bow he immediately regretted.

He called back to Paolo and motioned to the shore; the pilot waved, indicating that he understood, and reangled the launch. Soon they were navigating the mouth of a calm spring, and fifteen minutes later they had reached a point where the water was crystal-clear twenty feet down to a sandy and stone-strewn bottom. Paolo cut the engine then, and Emil threw a crudely fashioned anchor overboard. Forest towered over their tranquil pool, Muscovy ducks and Wilson's plovers playing across its lambent surface.

Billie climbed up onto the launch's triangular section of bow decking and stepped out of her shorts. She tossed the straw sombrero into the water, dove in, and, frog-stroking underwater, surfaced with the hat perfectly centered on her head.

Paolo and Emil applauded their delight.

*"Caprichosa, verdad?"* Paolo said to Matt.

He nodded without comment. Capricious: yes, she certainly is that, he thought. Neil wore a bemused smile, and Matt regarded him from a distance. Not once had he seen any demonstration of physical affection between them. That in itself wasn't exactly news, but it had left him wondering. There was that wedding ring, however.

He tried to shake the thought from his head. Maybe it was just that he wanted to see *someone* touch her.

Paolo had removed his visored cap and was scratching his head thoughtfully. "Saber, Matt, I'm thinking I've seen her before."

Matt looked over at him. "When, recently?"

"No, not exactly. Before—maybe months ago."

"In Sayaxche?"

Paolo nodded, absently stroking his Vandyke. *"Sí, por allí,"* he said. "Thereabouts."

To make up for lost time Paolo increased the pace after lunch, eager to make the mission at Nueva Vida before dusk. A short distance downstream the Pasión merged with the Chixoy-Salinas to form the Usumacinta proper and Guatemala's western border with Mexico. Matt explained as much to Neil and Billie in the shade of the *caseta*.

"There's a *garita* on the Guatemalan side—a border post. They're going to want to check us out, so I'm going to need your passports."

They exchanged dubious looks. "Check us out how?" Neil asked.

Matt indicated the sacks and crates. "All this. They'll wave their Uzis around and ask some questions, but it's more formality than anything else."

Billie said, "Are they police or military?"

"Military. Red Berets—the Kaibil commandos. They took their name from Kaibil Balan, an Indian warrior. Used to be just a dozen *federales*, but not since the guerrillas moved in."

"I thought the guerrillas were mostly in the western part of the country—in the mountains."

"They were. But now Petén's got a few contingents of its own. They sacked a *colonia* on the Usumacinta a year and a half ago, and they've been pretty active lately."

"Ever see them?"

Matt shook his head. "Silvio claims some of them came by the lodge once, but they left everything alone. They make the rounds, then the army spreads its own brand of terror around. We'll be all right. But it'll make things easier if you let me deal with the officer in charge."

Billie showed a strained smile. "Be our guest."

Matt moved to the back of the boat, uneasy all of a sudden. No one liked having to deal with the military, but there was no way around it. He and Paolo were well known to the group at Pipiles, but Billie and Neil's presence was certain to kindle a bit of dramatic thoroughness on the part of the rangers. If they'd learned anything from the tourists Jake led downriver six months of the year, it was that gringos were easily impressed and often just as easy to intimidate.

Billie walked back with the passports a few minutes later and handed them over. Matt took a cursory look at them. A Mexican entry stamp had been issued at Mérida six weeks ago; another page showed that they had entered Guatemala at Melchor on the Belizian border, a fact that jibed with Billie's story.

"We need to talk," she said in low tones, sitting beside him on the wooden bench.

He turned to her, expectant and curiously apprehensive. " Go ahead."

She bit her lower lip. "Suppose there was something I didn't want them to find—something private?"

Matt sat back and folded his arms. "Is there?"

"Yes," she said, meeting his eyes.

"I won't have anything to do with guns or antiquities," Matt told her. "Maybe I'll be willing to work around the rest, but they've been coming down hard on smuggling." He saw her eyes dart away from his and hastened to add, "We can turn around right here and head back to Sayaxche, no questions asked."

"No guns, no antiquities. What else is there?"

Matt slipped annoyance into his voice. "How do I know what you're into? Maybe you bought a couple of ounces of blow in Belize City."

"What, in this heat?"

"Okay. So someone sold you a piece of pre-Columbian jade in Flores. Or you just had to have those pottery shards you picked up in Tikal."

"It's nothing like that. It's just personal stuff I don't want them fooling with."

"So put it in your pocket," Matt told her. "They're not going to do a body search."

"I suppose I could . . . but I'd feel a lot better about it if we could just keep it out of sight."

Matt mulled it over for a moment. "Get it together and give it to me," he said without looking at her.

Billie put her hand on his and squeezed. "Thanks, Matt."

She left his side and began to dig some things out of her leather shoulder bag. The small package she handed him five minutes later was wrapped in newspaper. It was about the size of a Michener paperback, maybe a bit thicker, but heavier than Matt would have liked. Maybe it was coke after all, or maybe it was nothing at all; he had the feeling she was testing him, trying to determine just how far he would go for her.

There was a storage space under the forward deck, accessible by a small door. Matt placed the package on a ledge that would feel like the underside of the decking to untrained fingers.

A queer sense of self-satisfaction overcame him as he was returning to the shade—possibly the knowledge that she had secrets to hide, but more likely, he thought, the desire to play the coconspirator in her designs, however dark they were.

Three soldiers in full fatigues trotted down the wooden stairway as Paolo pulled the launch alongside the *garita* quay; the oldest, the only Red Beret among them, was no more than twenty, and all three carried Israeli-made assault rifles. Emil leaped into the quay to tie up as they stepped aboard. Neither Matt nor Paolo recognized any of them, but someone at the top of the stairs was calling Paolo's name.

The boatman looked up and waved his cap at the soldier; Matt saw that it was Lieutenant Guttierez, an acquaintance of sorts from previous crossings.

*"El equipaje,"* one of the soldiers was barking, motioning to Neil's backpack and Billie's bag with the muzzle of his rifle. *"Abra la mochila."*

Matt nodded for them to comply. "Let them look at whatever they want, but watch out they don't pocket anything. They're just curious and want to impress you a bit."

As the search commenced, Matt placed his own passport with the other two and started for the steps. Paolo left Emil behind to handle the guards, cautioning him to go around and untie all the burlap sacks before the soldiers got to them with their bayonets.

"Let them have as much Fanta and Spur as they want," Paolo added in English. "But no beer."

It was always the same routine, Matt thought as he and Paolo took the long flight: youngsters with weapons and plenty of macho posturing. But no *mordida* system operated here—that cultural "tipping" ritual that was the rule in Mexico. Things along the Pasión were black and white; you were either clear or you weren't, and no bribe was going to alter the fact.

At the top of the stairs, Paolo and the lieutenant exchanged greetings. Matt asked Guttierez how he'd been.

*"Dos, la semana pasada,"* the solid-looking ranger replied, and went on to explain how he'd killed two insurgents the previous week. Pointing to a row of notches

in his leather belt, he threw Matt a malicious smile. A single gold tooth gleamed in the afternoon sun.

"You're a regular John Wayne," Matt said, trying to sound sincere.

The lieutenant showed Matt a clip with Raphael Aguilar's name etched along its length. He patted the magazine lovingly. "These are for that bastard. His men killed my cousin near Pasos Caballos."

Matt recalled what Paolo had told him about the kidnapped archeologist and the two policemen. He told Guttierez he was sorry to hear about the cousin's passing.

"Tell your president that when he talks about human rights," Guttierez said.

Reagan, who had recently told Central America, "We are all Americans," was busy strutting his stuff in El Salvador, showing Guatemala's leaders the tanks and helicopters that could be theirs if they would only clean up their act.

Matt said, "I'll be sure to mention it."

"And where's the Sandinista lover now, that Carter?"

"Fly-fishing, I think." As if he knew.

The *garita* was seven thatched-roof buildings set on a bluff overlooking the Pasión-Salinas confluence. A corporal escorted Paolo and Matt to the office of Colonel Reyes, where Matt surrendered the three passports, along with Emil and Paolo's *cédulas*.

Reyes impressed one as a man of few words, but that was only until he decided whether you were worth talking to. He was the lean and mean military ideal, with close-cropped hair, a clipped mustache, and pristine fatigues, shirtsleeves rolled up above powerful-looking forearms. He sat straight-backed at his desk in the still heat of his small headquarters, leafing through the pages of the passports and jotting down names and pertinent information into an enormous black ledger.

But once the duties of office had been dispensed with, Reyes swiveled in his chair and turned a broad grin up to Matt and Paolo, motioning them to sit down and ordering one of his men to fetch coffee and tortillas. He offered Matt some cold green beans from the colander on his desk. Matt took a handful and passed the strainer to Paolo; then he reached into his pants pocket for the batteries he had brought with him from Palenque.

The colonel was appreciative: these were not the usual half-dead Everyreadys from Sayaxche, but copper-tops Matt had had Jake bring down from the States. Reyes didn't lose a minute loading the batteries into his cassette player.

The aide returned with *totopostes* and steaming cups of black coffee sweetened with cuts of sugarcane, and Matt spent the next forty-five minutes talking about Reagan and translating lyrics from American disco songs. Twice Reyes mentioned how fond he was of Donna Summer, and Matt promised to see what he could do about having Jake deliver a tape when he came through with the next group. He didn't think of the gifts as bribes; Reyes had always played fair and square and had once helped him out of a tight spot involving the Flores *policía*. He tried not to think about the man's position or his politics, or the war that Reyes and his kind were waging against their own sons and brothers.

Down below, Neil and Billie were in good spirits; it was apparent that Billie had been entertaining the troops. She was handing back the Uzi one of the soldiers had let her use as a visual aid when Matt and Paolo stepped onto the quay. Matt only caught the end of her story, but whatever it was, it had the guards doubled over. Everyone shook hands like old friends.

Matt exchanged an astonished look with Paolo as they reboarded the launch. Emil was still laughing after he had untied from the quay and jumped in. *"Traymoyista,"* he said, shaking his head and gesturing to Billie.

It was an affectionate way of calling someone an imposter.

"I suppose you're wondering about all that?" Billie asked later.

"Wondering about what?" Matt said, pretending to busy himself with the launch's front line.

"My paranoia—about hiding those things."

He turned to look up at her. "You're not paying me to

wonder.'' He felt angry for no discernible reason. Her silence told him he'd been too harsh.

"Right. You're just taking us to Palenque. I keep forgetting.''

They were on the opposite shore of the river, at the trailhead to the ruins at Altar de los Sacrificios; technically they were back in Guatemala, but who was looking. The Pipiles *garita* was visible across the gurgling Pasión; the swift Salinas a dull background roar.

Two Guatemalan *guardianos* in brown pants and beige epauletted shirts had appeared to lead Neil off to search for pottery shards and photograph the unusual reddish sandstone stelae the site was known for. Paolo and Emil had gone along for the walk. The afternoon light was waning, and soft gray clouds hung above the Usumacinta, brilliantly underlit by the low sun.

"No weapons, no antiquities,'' Billie resumed after a moment. "Is that where you draw the line?'' She jumped from the bow to Altar's tiny seasonal sand beach, allowing Matt to secure the line to the exposed roots of a riverside tree.

"It just doesn't pay to tempt the fates down here. Guns are an evil trip right now. And it's just as bad with antiquities. Besides, I figure things should stay where they belong. It's bad enough the guerrillas have gotten into looting sites without tourists lending a hand.''

"You're a loyalist, then. You side with 'Benny,' Rios Montt, and the rest of those cutthroats.''

Matt leaned back against the hull of the launch and fixed her with a stare. "I'm not anything. I love this country, and I'd hate to see it go either way. But I'm not taking sides, if that's what you mean.''

"The guerrillas are looting Mayan sites to finance the revolution,'' Billie said. "You think Reagan's any better than they are? He's got the CIA hiring Argentine contras to help Guatemala rid itself of insurgents and stop the Sandinistas' arms shipments to El Salvador. But they aren't military advisers, Matt—they're specialists in fucking urban counterterrorism. Which in Latin America translates as torture and disappearances. You know that.'' She laughed bitterly. "Reagan talks about human rights violations. Have you ever heard of the 'Dry Submarine' or the 'Hook'? Real cute stuff. He's supporting the torture he wants stopped. That's what we export now—bad news. Go see *Missing*.''

Matt made a fatigued sound. ''I know: all the Indians are socialists without knowing a thing about politics. We should arm the Miskitos, the contras, the Maya. And then I tell you about how the guerrillas sacked and burned a settlement around the bend, or the policemen they executed. It goes on and on. They're wrong, Guevara's wrong, everybody's wrong. It's all grays, Billie. It's twilight time.''

She walked over to stand toe to toe with him and look up into his face. ''Suppose you *had* to choose sides, Matt. Which would it be?'' She laughed before he could answer and tapped her forefinger lightly into his left side above the waistband of his pants. ''Where'd you get that scar, anyway?''

Matt restrained her hand.

''Can't you quit being a tour guide for five minutes? What are you really doing down here? Neil thinks you might be CIA.''

Matt sniggered at the suggestion, but more at the easy way she had moved the conversation from her own court to his. ''Now we're talking about me all of a sudden. And I thought you were going to tell me all about yourself.''

Billie made an exasperated sound and sat down, her fists grasping handfuls of sand. ''You caught that slip I made about Palenque, and you didn't say anything about it.''

''What was I supposed to say?'' he asked, squatting down in front of her. ''So you're not telling the whole truth and nothing but the truth. You're not the first to play that game on the road.''

Billie's jaw came up. ''Don't be so arrogant.''

''I'm not trying to be, but I don't know what you—''

''Did it occur to you that I wanted to slip up? Why did you decide to help me hide those things? Or is that just another service you're happy to provide?''

Matt said nothing.

She frowned as though disappointed. "You don't make it very easy, do you?"

"You've gotta let me know what kind of game we're playing; then maybe I'll know where to start."

Billie leaned forward and kissed him lightly on the mouth. "Right here," she said, getting to her feet.

Matt looked up at her without a word. By the time he had collected his thoughts, she was already walking up the trail.

# Tropical Ice

They overnighted on a point-bar beach four clicks up the Salinas near a midriver island known locally as La Culebra. Matt, a miner's lamp strapped around his head, prepared a simple meal, and the five of them drank rum and fresh-squeezed orange juice, laughing together around a windblown fire. The river roared at their backs, a chilling current driven out of the Guatemalan heartland, and around midnight a jaguar called out. Paolo answered it by blowing across the mouth of a bottle-shaped gourd the Mam Indio had left behind; the jungle cat responded once and was gone.

Later, Matt and Neil struggled against a constant wind to spread tarps on the sand and erect two tents while Paolo and Emil wrapped themselves in cotton blankets and huddled down in the launch. There was mist in the morning, a radiant silver glow fallen over the world. Venus shone brilliantly in the east; the planet whose helical rise the ancient Maya had timed to ritual warfare and the capture of sacrificial victims.

Paolo had them under way by seven o'clock, back to the Pasión confluence and north into the Usumacinta River, with Mexico on the left and Guatemala on the right. The land was rugged and thickly forested on both banks; the river wide and turbulent, with whirlpools treacherous enough to foil the most experienced swimmer. To the west were the foothills of the Lacandon *selva*, a vast rain forest basin that stretched to the highlands of Chiapas. North—downriver—were the Mayan sites of Yaxchilan and Piedras Negras, and below them a white-water canyon through which the Usumacinta plunged before assuming a meandering course across the Tabasco plains to the gulf. The past seemed to linger here, ghost-like, and more than one traveler spoke of the river's almost palpable aura of sinister enchantment.

The original plan called for them to put in at Bethel and Frontera Echeverría and make Yaxchilan by sunset, but Neil asked if they couldn't manage a side trip to Planchon de las Figuros, a graffitied slab of rock a short distance up the Lancantún River, one of the Usumacinta's major tributaries. Matt talked it over with Paolo, and the boatman agreed to postpone his trading stops until the return trip from Yaxchilan. Matt hadn't decided yet how he and his clients would enter Mexico.

One option was the logging road that had been pushed through from Echeverría to Palenque. Alternatively, they could continue downriver to Anaite, where a bush pilot put down once a week to ferry out loads of *xate* brought in by local gatherers. *Xate* was an indigenous palm that had become something of a decorative staple in Stateside florist shops, but along the river it had gained nearly legendary status as a secret ingredient used by the U.S. in the manufacture of atomic-powered submarines. The gatherers received about seventy-five cents per hundred stems. *Xate* cargos were being used to smuggle out shipments of cocaine, marijuana, and antiquities.

Matt had no problem with Neil's request; in fact, there was a plus side to it, for rather than try for Yaxchilan that night, they could make camp upriver at La Garganta, avoiding hassles that could crop up at the site. March typically saw an influx of *obreros* from Tuxtla, who were flown in to clear the ruins and attend to Yaxchilan's grass strip. Most of the *palapas* would be taken up by their hammocks and gear. And there was no guarantee of space on the beach below the ruins, either—with the Usumacinta running higher than normal, there was no guarantee of a beach at all.

So Planchon de las Figuras it was.

They arrived before noon and tied up along the shore. Paolo and Neil hurried off to view the rock's incised figures and petroglyphs, and Emil wandered off to shoot the breeze with some local fisherman. Matt stayed behind to keep an eye on the cargo, and Billie elected to join him.

They remained on board after the others left, taking sun and sharing a bottle of warm beer. There had been no private conversation between them since the beach at Altar, but they had exchanged more than a few meaningful glances, brazen on Billie's part, awkward on Matt's. The fact that Neil had remained amiable and somehow detached from all this coquettish behavior had only contributed to the problem. Matt liked him and didn't know whether to feel grateful or sympathetic. He knew that Paolo and Emil shared his feelings, although both had decided that there was nothing between Billie and Neil. But even if that were true, Matt decided, he wasn't comfortable with the idea of making love to Billie with Neil smiling on from the sidelines, eighties or not. Affairs had a way of complicating matters, and Matt sensed that he was just too old for threesomes. Still, his curiosity about Billie was not to be denied. He gave her a sidelong glance and found her staring at him. Paolo and Neil were out of sight.

"Think somebody'll be walking around in our ruins one day wondering what happened, Matt?"

"I'm already wondering."

She gave him a suspicious look. "What about the past, then? You give that much thought?"

"Only when it starts repeating itself."

"Then what do you do?"

He shrugged. "I go fishing."

Billie snorted. "Maybe I'll try that next time. Just forget about the wrong turns, shine it on . . . ."

"You figure you've cornered the market?"

"Did you get that scar from a wrong turn?"

"An accident."

"What kind of accident?"

"I was accidentally in the wrong place at the wrong time."

Billie was quiet a moment, watching the river. "Are

you going to kiss me or not?'' she said without looking at him. ''Because if you're not, then I'm going to find Neil and Paolo.''

Matt looked up into some imaginary space and laughed wryly. ''How come I feel like I'm about to shoplift something?''

''Because you fancy yourself the only moral man left in the Petén, that's why. Matt Terry, ecologist and wilderness guide, who believes that things should stay where they belong, including married women.''

''There's something wrong with that?''

She heard the harshness in his voice and changed her tone. ''No, Matt, there's nothing wrong with it. Maybe I even like it.''

''Then what's with all this flirtation?''

Billie fell silent for a moment. ''I guess I want to believe there's something between us, Matt—I felt it that night we walked into the lodge—even if it's the last thing I need right now.''

Matt made a face.

''I thought I felt something from you, too.''

He said, ''Maybe you did.''

''But you don't like to mix business and pleasure. And this is business, huh?'' She gazed out over the river, her hands flat against the bench top.

''Remember the one about the tour guide and the married couple who went on safari together?''

She turned to him, one hand holding her hair back, and shook her head.

''The husband got shot, the guide lost his license, and I think the woman ended up in prison.''

Billie laughed. ''Is that what you're worried about— losing your license? What'd you do—skip the seventies or something?''

''I survived the seventies, if that's what you mean.''

She folded her arms. ''You like Neil, don't you?''

He told her he did.

''He's my best friend,'' she said absently. ''We've been through a lot of shit together . . . but we're not married, Matt. Does that make a difference?''

Matt felt her eyes examining his face. ''I'd be lying if I said it didn't. But what about the passports?''

Billie walked over to sit beside him. "Listen to me, I'm telling you we're not married. I can't go into the rest of it right now."

"The rest of what?"

She shook her head. "Can you trust me for a day or two more if I promise to tell you then? It's important, Matt—maybe the most important thing I've ever done."

Matt made a disgruntled sound. "I don't know what you're talking about, Billie. Trust you how? And why tell me about anything?"

She said, "Because I want to tell you," touching his arm. "I'm your queen of hearts, desperado, and I think you and I are on the same side."

"In what?"

Billie motioned to the river and forest. "I love this country, too, Matt. But maybe I'm just a little more active about showing it than you are—a little more demonstrative. I see what you've carved out for yourself down here, and I think it's great. You're a survivor, the same as me. You live outside the rules, except the ones you've made for yourself. You've got a personal code and you stick to it. Am I right or not?"

"Everyone's got a code, Billie. That doesn't set me apart."

"No," she said, shaking her head. "You think the dudes that run this country have a personal code? You think they give a shit about this river or the people who are trying to make a life for themselves here? You were in the Peace Corps, for Christ's sake. Do you think we'd need to have a fucking *Peace* Corps if everyone understood the code?"

Matt wanted to interrupt her, to tell her that she had misunderstood, that maybe she was describing herself more than she was him. That he saw himself more as the gringo *perdido*—the stranger at the end of the river—than as the embodiment of any ethical ideal. He had taken a turn off the road to commitment years ago, and all he asked for now was a clear path between the complications and intricacies. But any debate could wait. What he wanted at the moment was another taste of her.

He put his hands around Billie's waist, firm beneath the sheen of the swimsuit, and urged her toward him.

Her hands interlocked behind his neck as their mouths met, softly, then with mounting passion, until the warmth of their embrace seemed to meld into the very heat of the afternoon, the forest folding over them like a dream.

The extensive ruin complex of Yaxchilan—first mapped and explored at the turn of the century by Désiré Charnay, Teobart Mahler, and others—lay within an omega-shaped loop in the Usumacinta an hour or so downriver from the Mexican settlement of Frontera Echeverría. At the narrows of the loop, scarcely three forested miles separated the river from itself, and it had therefore come to be known as La Garganta, the "neck" or "throat." Paolo and Matt knew of a little-used trail that ran between a small patch of beach at the southern side of the loop and the site itself, offering a backdoor approach to the hilltop pyramids and temples that made up the central group.

The launch put in just before sunset. The trip downriver had been leisurely and uneventful. Paolo and Emil were reacting to something joyous in the air, and every so often one of them would shout out, *"Pico de Oro!"* or *"Hijo del Gran Palenque!"* and flash Matt a sly grin.

Billie and Neil had passed most of the trip up front, engaged in some intense conversation, the nature of which Matt could only guess. But there was no indication they'd been arguing; Neil remained as responsive as ever while Matt laid out the Palenque options, and it was agreed that they would spend a day in the ruins, then have Paolo drop them in Echeverría on his way upriver, where Matt would see about arranging transportation.

Matt spent most of the afternoon remembering the kiss and thinking about the complications he was opening himself up to. He knew full well where Billie was leading him, but it was becoming something of a game to ride behind her. Signs reading, GO BACK! were posted every few feet, but Matt kept telling himself one more mile, one more mile. It was the call of an old thrill coming back to haunt him, the need for a periodic excursion into outlaw territory. Not to mention just how wonderful she had felt in his arms and how there was already more between them than he was willing to admit.

Susan was also on his mind. She was one of the intricacies Matt had been negotiating for the past several years, and he found himself thinking about her as the launch neared La Garganta. She was lithe and beautifully black and a sixties volunteer who, like Matt, had ended up in the icy cordilleras of Peru's Callejon de Huaylas trying to teach soil conservation techniques to Quechua-speaking Indians. They had fallen in love with the land, with each other, even with the hopelessness of their tasks, and had been married in the *cabildo* in Ayacucho alongside Indians wearing conical hats and tire-tread sandals, alpaca ponchos and rose-colored colonial skirts. After the Peace Corps it was to have been a weaving cooperative or some other such valiant enterprise, but the earthquake had intervened, the *terremoto*, and it had left Matt shaking ever since. Susan had been set on getting into the areas hardest hit to render what assistance she could, and he had gone along, fighting back a nagging sense of misgiving that rode with him all the way to Huaras. But things got off to a good start there, and he had all but forgotten the omens by the time Susan stepped aboard the old bus she and two dozen Indians would ride to their deaths at the bottom of an impossibly steep gorge. Twenty-seven white crosses marked the spot where the bus had edged off the road, and Matt was never able to figure out just what had gone wrong. There was still a lot of suffering attached to her loss, and now unexpectedly came Billie, offering hope of a new alliance. But where Susan had been open and unremarkable, Billie was covert and dangerous in ways he was at a loss to understand.

The first snag in the travel plan had coincided with the launch's arrival at La Garganta: there was no beach. So Paolo, Emil, and Matt had gone to work with machetes, clearing two small spaces just large enough to accommodate the hammocks. Matt strung his close to the boat and set up Billie and Neil's Yucatecan *matromonia* inland about thirty feet away. After a cold supper, the boatmen excused themselves and returned to the launch, promising to alternate the watch. This hadn't been necessary along the Salinas, but the Usumacinta had seen a rash of incidents during the past six months, most of them involving thieves working the Guatemalan refugee camps upriver or gunrunners who were supplying rebel groups on the opposite bank. Matt told Paolo to wake him for the final watch. Neil, too, had turned in.

Matt was sitting on a portion of tree stump now, sipping at the lemon grass tea they had brewed. He set the enamel cup down as Billie approached him. She straddled his lap, put her arms around his neck, and began to kiss his face and lips. He slid his hands around to the small of her back and encouraged her with the gentle motion of his head, deliciously lost in her soft hair and fragrance. Again he experienced a sense of connectedness, the urgent sounds of their breath commingling with the incessant call of the river, the steady chorus of life.

"You feel so good," she whispered, her voice a low rasp of pleasure.

"You, too," he murmured back, sinking his mouth into the hollow of her neck.

"And you don't even mind the repellent."

"As long as it's only for mosquitoes."

"I want to know all about you. Were you married?"

"Once." Matt nodded, his lips at her ear.

"And it's over? There's no one else in your life now?"

"No one I want to share straws with."

They kissed deeply, but she broke it off, holding his face between her strong hands. "Suppose I came back down here in a month or so . . . could you get away? We could go to Costa Rica or Belize, just hang out on the beach drinking margaritas and making love. . . ."

"Sounds great. Backpackers, sea urchins, and sand fleas."

She laughed. "You make it sound so romantic."

"Do you have to leave Palenque right away?" he asked, more serious now.

He saw the glint of her teeth in moonlight, a crooked smile. "Neil and I have business in New York. But I'll write to you, and I'll come back if you want me to."

"What kind of business, Billie?"

She put her fingertips to his lips to shush him. "Not now, Matt."

She brought her mouth hard against his, her tongue probing the corners of his lips. She slid her hand along his arm and brought his hand to the softness of her breast, her breath coming in quick pants. Matt's fingers found the top button of her shirt, his palm the warmth of her flesh. She leaned into him, head raised, offering her neck and breasts to his mouth, her fingers in his hair. He kissed and caressed her, working the shirt free of her shoulders, all but pinioning her arms. Their bodies began to seek a mutual rhythm, her groin pressed to his, her legs wrapped around him.

At the same moment they pulled away and looked right and left, searching for space to stretch out; then they saw the curiously comical desperateness on each other's faces and laughed.

"Guess Paolo and I were a bit hasty with our machetes," Matt said. "But there's always my hammock."

Billie grinned. "I'm fine right here." She reached down between Matt's legs to stroke him. He kissed her lightly, and she stood up and stepped out of her pants.

Matt dropped his fatigues to his ankles; she straddled him again, easing him into her. He was aware of their strong mutual scent, mixing with the profusion of night odors, some sweet and redolent, others musky, hinting at death and decay. Billie was grinding against him, wet and supple.

"It's all right, you can come in me," she told him, sensing his reluctance.

Matt put his hands behind him on the tree stump to change the angle of his thrusts. She put her hands lightly on his shoulders and leaned her damp forehead against his. She came a moment before he did, her body rigid, legs taut and quivering. Matt moaned; a brilliant light show flared behind his closed lids. Wordlessly, they collapsed into each other, chests heaving, hearts pounding, and remained that way for a time, the steamy hothouse sounds of the forest riotous and sublime.

It was well after midnight when Matt climbed into his hammock; much to his disappointment, Billie had decided to sleep with Neil. But he understood: she didn't want Paolo and Emil to find them together in the morning, even if they already sensed that something was going on. As far as they knew, Billie and Neil were married, and she didn't want to come across as a wanton gringa, cuckolding her husband for a quick piece of the guide. Billie said she didn't feel like going into an explanation, but she told Matt that he was free to tell them as much as he cared to. Besides, by tomorrow or the next day they would be in Palenque, and things would change.

Matt's hammock was not one of the lightweight cotton types from Yucatán but an unusual one of his own design: a boldly striped length of highland Guatemalan weave—coral, reds, and blues—with an attached tent of muslin netting held aloft by separate guy lines. The muslin, in addition to keeping out mosquitoes, helped contain body warmth, which was especially beneficial in the sometimes chilled morning air of the Petén dry season. But the cream-colored cloth had the disadvantage of effectively sealing out the visible world. Sounds, too, were somewhat muffled. Matt, however, had keen hearing.

He awoke at first light with a sudden start, remaining motionless while his ears adapted to the cacophony surrounding the camp. Emil hadn't roused him for the final watch. He took a moment to isolate and catalogue the sounds, screening out the rush of the river and the stridulation of insect life to focus in on particulars: the throaty bellowing of frogs, the bark of distant howlers, an owl's Halloween call. And something else: a slight rustling, the crunch of dry underbrush. Matt closed his eyes to eliminate all but the auditory, all the while edging his hand along the tight fabric of the hammock to the muslin flap of the netting tent. His Colima machete lay on the ground two feet below the curve of his ass.

The stalking sound was more pronounced now. Matt thought it might be nothing more than a small animal on the prowl, but he stopped lying to himself as he began to feel the sweat trickle down his face.

His hand was almost to the flap when the first blow came: something fell hard on the hammock rope above his head. Matt brought his knees up and actually had his legs outside the tent flap when a second blow succeeded in severing the rope, instantly dropping the head end of the hammock to the ground. He took the force of the fall on his right shoulder and cheek, but managed to scramble to his feet, arms flailing inside the muslin tent. Then something heavy caught him across the shoulders and sent him to his bare knees; he doubled over, desperate hands through the opening now, searching the ground for the Colima's plastic grip. But the next blow put an end to it: his skull took the impact. The world turned blizzard-white before darkness prevailed; he fell and dreamed of snow.

# ⬅⬅ 5 ➡➡

## *La Noche Triste*

The boatmen brought Matt around; it was just before dawn, and he could see their breath clouds in the cool air. The forest was strangely still, enshrouded by a luminescence that seemed to have silenced the camp and all life around it. Only the river was speaking, gray eddies gurgling, waves popping against the mud bank.

Matt knew that he hadn't been unconscious for long; he had a fogged memory of coming to and plunging into a fitful sleep where screams were mixed into his winter dreams, rambling thoughts and nonsense that had left his head pounding.

*Turn that jungle music down*, the singer of the band kept saying.

He had put a hand to the back of his head when Paolo had cut through the ropes and found his curly hair matted with blood. His right knee was sliced open where he'd apparently caught the blade of the machete on the way down.

Emil was saying, "*Lo siento*, Matt, *lo siento*," over and over again, "I'm sorry, I'm sorry." He had a piece of damp rag tied around his head, and there was blood at his left ear. Matt sat up and gave a confused look around. He had been dragged unconscious a good distance from the clearing and left bound hand and foot. A cotton flour sack from the launch had been pulled down

46

over his head and shoulders, saving his face from suffering as his bare legs had.

Paolo was down on his haunches, his stiff leg thrust out to one side, offering him a water bottle. Dried blood was caked under the boatman's nose, and his face looked puffy and discolored.

"*Ladrones*, Matt. *Desconocidos*."

He thought there might have been four men involved, but he didn't get a good look at any of them. They were armed with handguns and had worn bandannas. Surprised them on the boat, hit them before they could respond. . . . He and Emil had been bound and gagged; he showed Matt the rope burns on his wrists and ankles. After the men had left, Emil had managed to move himself to one of the machetes and free his feet and hands.

Matt took a sip from the bottle and splashed some water on the back of his neck while his friends helped him to his feet. He stood dazed and nauseous, waiting for the world to come into focus, unable to discern when dreams and reality had parted company.

He asked, "You didn't hear a motor—anything?"

"Matt, I fell asleep," Emil said ashamedly.

"Yeah, but—" Matt stopped himself and put his hand on the boatman's shoulder in a gesture of understanding; then Paolo's words seemed to sear into his awareness: *Thieves, murderers!*

Paolo saw Matt's expression and said, "*Ven, rápido!*"

Matt stumbled toward the clearing where his hammock lay in a heap on the ground; he kicked at the thing, then pulled on his trousers and followed the boatmen into the second clearing. He was relieved to see that the *matrimonia* was still strung, but it was empty, the cleared area around it strewn with things that had come from Neil's pack: clothes, paperback books, and toiletry items. He noticed Billie then, lying on her side, naked legs drawn up to her belly. One arm was pillowing her head, and the other was outstretched; her long hair swept across her face. For a moment it looked as though she might be sleeping. She had on a pair of bikini panties; the Tikal shirt was pulled up to the underside of her breasts, revealing the soft curve of her hip.

Matt knelt beside her and took her limp hand in his,

feeling for the pulse he knew he wouldn't find. He gathered her hair in his hand and gently moved it away from her face. Her neck was girdled with purple bruises and angry red marks—from a rope, Matt guessed. He stood up, staring down at her. She had soiled herself, and her body was already beginning to discolor. It would get much worse. Matt's stomach convulsed, and he turned away, supporting himself stiff-armed against a strangler fig while he vomited. He was no stranger to death, but he was not immune to it, either.

Paolo and Emil were across the clearing, standing over Neil's body. Matt took reluctant steps toward them, his eyes brimming with tears. Neil was propped up against the buttressed gray-green trunk of a ceiba. His entire shirtfront was so drenched in blood, there was no telling whether he had been shot or stabbed to death. Ants and flies had found him before the boatmen, and Paolo did what he could now to cover the body with a tarp Emil brought from the boat. Matt did the same to Billie.

He felt himself beginning to come apart and tried to let rage fill him instead. Time for grieving would come later, but just then he convinced himself, it was more important to learn what he could about the crime. He instructed Emil and Paolo to help him comb the clearing. The three of them went down on their knees and picked through the discarded items, trying not to disturb anything. Matt knew that the police investigators weren't likely to be Kojaks, but reasoned it was best to let things lie if only to underscore the credibility of their story. Several items had been torn apart, including the frame pack itself, but there were no signs of just how many assailants had been involved. In one of Neil's paperbacks Matt found a telex addressed to a Lauren Riordan. He pocketed the paper and began to search the surrounding forest. Gradually they worked their way back to the launch.

Billie's bag, as well as Matt's, had been rifled and dumped on the shore. His passport, cash, and cassette player were gone, along with Neil's camera and the couple's jewelry, cash, passports, and traveler's checks. Almost every sack in the launch had been opened, but nothing was missing.

Matt inspected Emil's head wound and told him to get rid of the bandage and wash away any traces of blood. There was a good-sized bump above his ear, but most of it was concealed by the young man's thick hair. When he had done that, Matt asked him if he was well enough to take the *canoa* up to Echeverría and return with the police. Emil said that he was.

He was simply to tell them that there'd been two murders committed downriver, Matt emphasized. It was imperative that Emil maintain that he and Paolo had spent the night on the Guatemalan side of the river; otherwise they were bound to be drawn into the crime and perhaps held by the Mexican authorities. The police wouldn't buy any of it, but Matt was certain that he could buy some understanding from them.

Matt said, "You only learned about the murders *after* you crossed over to pick us up."

When Emil had motored off, Matt did what he could to mask Paolo's bruises; it was possible that the bridge of Paolo's nose was fractured and obvious that he would end up with two shiners, but at the moment there was little more than some swelling and a cut under his left eyebrow. The two of them then began putting the launch back together, closing up the crates and doing their best with the sacks. Four were beyond repair, so they dumped the contents and buried the shredded bags downriver. In two hours most of the work had been completed. The sun was out by then, burning off the mist, and river pilots in cargo-laden *canoas* were waving to them as they sped by.

Daylight had a way of rendering the night's horrors even more unreal. Matt found his thoughts clouded; even yesterday's events were difficult to recall.

It was conceivable that the thieves—whether they were rebels, smugglers, or everyday *mapache* scum—hadn't initially had murder on their minds. Perhaps they had decided as an afterthought to rape Billie, and Neil had tried to do the heroic thing. They had murdered him for it and inadvertently killed her during the struggle. Matt found that he could only examine the possibilities objectively, from a distance; when he sought details, his mind seized up on him, trapped between terror and a profound sense of desolation. Paolo, too, was horrified beyond words, but the boatman was quick to reject Matt's talk of guerrillas or smugglers despite the use of the bandannas and the sacks, which were calling cards on the Usumacinta. Paolo was certain that the murderers had come by boat and that either group would have emptied the launch of supplies. Nor would he buy the idea that they were mere *mapaches*—"racoons," literally, but bandannaed thieves in the river patois. The assault had been too professional: It was as though Billie and Neil's murderers had been looking for something specific.

Matt felt a weariness begin to descend on him: the onset of shock and the recognition of truth. He wanted to keep it all to himself, much as Billie had done, deny that whoever had sneaked into their camp had had a single purpose in mind.

Then he remembered the package Billie had asked him to stash.

Matt and Paolo rushed to the bow of the launch. Matt threw open the small door below the decking and reached in. His fingers found the edge of the hidden shelf and walked their way to the top; the small package was still there. He brought it out into the sunlight, hefted it once, and hurriedly began to unfold the newspaper Billie had used as wrapping. Paolo stood beside him, one hand tugging at his beard. There were two U.S. passports on top, and beneath them was a three-inch-thick sheaf of pesos, quetzales, and dollars bound by a rubber band.

He sat down on the gunwale rail and opened the top passport. It had been issued in Los Angeles in 1978 to one Michael DeLuca. The photo, however, was Neil's. There were several pages of entry and exit stamps—for Honduras, Guatemala, Mexico, Colombia, Peru, India, and Nepal—but only two from the States, and they both dated back to 1979. The second passport showed a somewhat younger Billie, with shorter hair and a bright smile. It, too, had been issued in L.A., to Lauren Riordan, whose address was given as Stateline, Nevada. The entry and exit stamps were all but identical to those in Neil's passport, and neither listed next of kin or persons to contact in case of death or accident.

Matt put the documents aside and dug into his pocket

for the telex. He tapped the envelope against his palm, deliberating, then opened it and began to read:

> RELIEVED TO HEAR THAT YOU TWO ARE BACK ON SCHEDULE. THANKS, BOTH OF YOU, FOR THE ADDED HASSLE; I'M SOMEWHERE BETWEEN DREAD AND ELATION OVER THE WHOLE THING. DONE WHAT YOU ASKED AND HAVE TICKETS AND ALL IN HAND. IT SEEMS TO ME A COMPLICATED PROPOSAL, BUT I WILL DEFER TO YOUR JUDGEMENT AND EXPERIENCE. PLEASE BE CAREFUL. I HAVE BEEN A NERVOUS WRECK AT WORK.

It was signed Sis and had been received by the Tikal Lodge more than two weeks ago. Matt studied the telex numbers but couldn't begin to guess at the source of the note. He jumped down from the bow of the launch and once more began to pick through the rifled contents of Billie's bag. Then he and Paolo made their way to the clearing, where they searched through Neil's things. Ultimately Matt located a small, fabric-bound traveler's address book. He looked under *W* for a Westphal but found none. Under *D* for DeLuca, he found a Ricky, in La Jolla, California. And under *R* he found the name Rachel Riordan and a New York City address.

Matt memorized the address and returned to the launch. He realized it would be easy enough to scatter the passports among Billie and Neil's effects and plead ignorance, but the cash was another matter. Found, it was unlikely the money would make it as far as Echeverría, let alone to the district headquarters at Tenosique or Villahermosa.

Matt took another look at the telex and destroyed it, aware that by doing so he was following Billie deeper still into the intricacies she had tried to lay out for him. But in Matt's mind the complicity was already there— there when he had accepted the package, there when he'd hidden it and sealed their deal with a kiss.

Maybe it had something to do with loyalty, he told himself, or the promise of love. He watched as the current carried the bits of paper downriver and began to wonder what Billie and Neil could have been into that was worth dying for. Something way off the mark of Susan's lofty ideals. And something just as alien from the white-water solo-ascent deaths Matt had encountered along the adventurer's circuit.

Worse than all of it was the dead-ahead fact that he had failed them. He had been hired to guide them, to steer them clear of trouble and protect them from the river and its currents, and yet someone who knew the maps better than he did had managed to track them down and kill them.

Paolo asked him what it all meant, but Matt could only shake his head. He leafed through the cash, peeled off the pesos, and rewrapped the rest of it in the newspaper. He shoved the pesos into the pocket of his fatigues and placed the package back under the bow decking of the launch.

There was blue sky by ten-thirty when Emil returned to camp with two of Echeverría's finest, Sergeants Jorge Colunga and Sicorro Delgado. The Mexicans were almost carbon copies of each other. Both stood a wiry five-six, were dark-complexioned and somber, and were proud of their positions. They wore khaki uniforms, creased trousers, and short-sleeve shirts with button-down epaulets. Each wore a holstered revolver, and Delgado, who had a trace of mustache, was equipped with a camera and tape recorder as well. It had already flashed through Matt's mind that they would be open to bribes, but he also knew that he would have to walk carefully. Billie and Neil's movements would be easy to trace from Tikal on, so any lies would now serve only as temporary stopgaps.

The sergeants squared away their police caps and jumped from the bow of the *canoa* to the shoreline. Matt and Paolo greeted them with handshakes. Delgado asked whether Matt wanted to make a statement; Matt said that he did, and the policeman switched on the recorder. Matt gave their names as Billie and Neil Westphal and explained how they had showed up at the lodge five days earlier and how he had agreed to take them downriver and on into Palenque. They had planned to hike into Yaxchilan, Matt told Delgado, but someone had attacked them during the night, stolen their valuables, and killed the man and woman. Paolo and Emil had come over from Agua Azul on the Guatemalan side shortly before dawn and found Matt bound and sacked.

Colunga asked whether anyone could corroborate the story. Matt listed the stops they had made along the Pasión and Lacantún and named some of the people they'd dealt with. Delgado chose to focus on Emil and Paolo. Matt understood that the sergeant had seen through his ploy to keep the boatmen out of the picture, but he was encouraged when Delgado suggested they discuss those details later on. Matt wondered how much of a bite the sergeants would put on him and felt for the wad of bills in his pocket.

Reentering the clearing was like going back into a nightmare; he could recall the horror, but with an element of detachment that hadn't been present before. He could at least bring himself to look at the bodies. Delgado announced that the woman had been strangled; the man, he speculated, had been stabbed repeatedly with a large knife or machete. Colunga had forgotten to bring film for the camera, and Neil's unexposed rolls weren't suitable, so no photos were taken. The two of them began to poke around, and in a few minutes they had discovered the passports where Matt had asked Paolo to place them. The find brought on self-satisfied smiles and feigned surprise, but only until the sergeants realized that the names didn't match the ones Matt had given them. Delgado was willing to concede that it could have played as Matt suggested—that robbery and rape had been the original motives and murder had entered into it only when the woman had resisted—but the false identities had the cop wondering whether Matt had been entirely straight with him.

Matt helped them rewrap Neil's body in the larger of the two tarps; they placed Billie in Matt's hammock, which made for a gruesome body bag. The effects were gathered in a pile and stuffed into one of Paolo's plastic cargo sacks. Matt was allowed to repack his own things.

Two hours later the clearing was clean, with only the blood, trampled underbrush, and macheted stalks to betray evidence of its brief occupation. After the bodies and effects were carried onto the launch, Delgado said that he had a few more questions. Matt flashed Paolo a signal, and the boatman broke out five Gallos he had left to cool in the river.

"Perhaps we should go across to Agua Azul," the sergeant began. "Someone there may have seen something. . . ."

Matt understood the implication and suggested that it might be more profitable to return to Echeverría as soon as possible. After all, he pointed out, the murders had taken place on the Mexican side.

Colunga said, "Then we may have to go later on. It means added work for us."

"I'd like to cover the costs," Matt told him. "In the interest of expediency."

"Well . . ." Delgado said, thinking it over. "It's going to cost ten thousand pesos—*each*. And you are still going to have to accompany us to the authorities in Tenosique."

"Understood," Matt said. "If we can agree that Paolo and Emil passed the night on the other side."

Ultimately the policemen agreed to the terms. Matt paid them with Billie's pesos; the amount was more than either policeman earned in a month.

Colunga and Delgado hopped aboard the *canoa* while Emil brought the boat's small outboard to life. They shouted for Paolo to follow them up to Echeverría. Matt untied the forward line, shoved the launch into the current, and threw himself into the bow. Paolo swung wide to make the turn and slowly nosed the boat upriver, the two corpses laid out on the benches in the shade beneath the thatch *caseta*.

# 6

## Abuse Of Corpse

The Indian women were wringing their hands over the bodies. Matt watched them from a square of shade in front of the Echeverría police post. At Delgado's behest, the corpses had been removed from their crude body bags and rewrapped in cotton sheets the sergeant himself had provided. Normally superstitious about such things, the Indian women—Mayan refugees from Guatemala's embattled central highlands—had insisted on washing the bodies. A few of them were keening now, their shrill songs contrapuntal to the midday sounds of the high jungle surrounding the settlement.

Unlike the *ejídos* along the Usumacinta, Echeverría had been carved out of the forest by loggers and planned and built with federal money. It was not just another collective farm trying to survive, but a bustling frontier town of houses and shops that was rapidly becoming a commercial center for the area, especially since the completion of the all-weather road that linked it to Chancala and Palenque. Matt had no fondness for the place; what could have been a small city of verdant parks and wooden homes was little more than a sunbaked grid of dirt streets and a scattering of lifeless buildings captured in corrugated glare. The Guatemalan refugees were confined to a cramped area of tents and thatched-roof *champas* north

55

of town along the river. Delgado had permitted a few of the women to leave the camp to assist with the bodies.

Matt tried to shut out the sound of their incessant chatter and ululations. He had gulped down a half grain of codeine on the ride up from La Garganta, but while the drug had helped to calm him, it had left his headache untouched. Sunglasses helped some, but the stabbing pain behind his eyes was less a creation of Echeverría's harsh light than of the horrors of the previous night.

He was massaging his neck when one of the Indian women approached him, round-faced, barefoot, and petite, dressed in a dark-colored skirt of highland weave and a white embroidered blouse. Matt's hammock was bunched up in her dark hands.

Matt lifted the sunglasses to his brow to regard her. The one-eyed dog that had decided to sprawl alongside him on the veranda was suddenly alert, struggling up to meet the woman halfway and sniffing at the hammock while she spoke to Matt in Mayan. He realized that she was offering to wash the thing out in the river, and he gave her the go-ahead. Even clean, the hammock was going to be a fulsome reminder, but Matt saw some purpose in that.

The boatmen were on their way upriver to Sayaxche. Matt had instructed them to find out if anyone had been nosing around town for Billie or Neil. If it was true they had been followed into Mexico, the killers would have had to have learned about the arrangements the couple had made with Matt. He had given Paolo some of the quetzales from the hidden cache of bills to cover damages and expenses; the rest of the money was stashed in his boot. He continued to grapple with the events, but thinking about the telex addressed to Lauren Riordan only ended up fueling his headache.

Delgado had warned him to stick close to the police post and had left instructions with his desk man to keep an eye out. Matt could feel the corporal's attention every so often, when the young man's gaze strayed from the Kaliman comic book he was reading. Delgado and Colunga, meanwhile, were off in search of transport. The police post had its own four-wheel-drive vehicle, but an early morning tree-felling accident at the edge of town had complicated matters.

The tree was an enormous outlaw hardwood that had somehow survived decades of logging; it had barber-chaired and toppled across the only road out of town, effectively cutting Echeverría off from the outside world. Matt had once seen a topper killed when a big tree had refused to obey a chain saw command. It had been the summer before he joined the Peace Corps, when he'd worked as a lumberman in Idaho and Montana, rigging platforms and setting chokers on slopes full of felled trees. The accident that had killed the topper had been his first real exposure to death after his mother's protracted illness and slow demise, and the memory had stayed with him in vivid detail through the years.

The sergeants had allowed Matt to accompany them to the resultant blockade shortly after Billie and Neil's bodies had been taken off the launch and carried up the steep riverbank into town. One man was at work on the tree then, a tough Indian *maderero* chopping his way through ten feet of trunk, while a dozen others stood around counting blows. It was apparent that wagers had been made. The ax man was beaming, soaked in sweat but enjoying all the attention. Delgado and Colunga took the incident in stride and put down some of the money Matt had given them earlier.

Palenque had been notified of the murders via radio. The police there had ordered that the bodies be delivered to Villahermosa. But with the road temporarily closed, the sergeants were stymied. Delgado had suggested that a plane be called in, but the closest airstrip was Yaxchilan, and Colunga, much to Matt's relief, nixed the idea. It would have entailed another trip downriver and an inevitable sequence of delays.

The Indian woman was hustling off with his hammock, the dog trailing behind her, playful and curious. Matt got up and walked inside, positioning himself in front of the small room's modest table fan. The corporal had left his desk, which was layered with official paperwork and men's magazines. The wall behind it was an odd mixture of religious art and pop culture, as Mexico itself so often was.

The corporal was carrying a lemon Fanta when he returned, the bottle glazed with ice, and he handed it to Matt without comment. Matt offered him a silent toast, pressing the base of the bottle to his forehead and neck before indulging in a drink.

A moment later the police vehicle pulled up sharply out front, sending a brief dust storm into the room, and Matt heard Colunga shouting orders to the Indian women. Delgado came in removing his shades.

"Let's go," he told Matt.

Matt took a final swallow of soda and set the bottle down, thanking the corporal. "Who won?" he asked Delgado.

The sergeant snorted. "Not yet." He splayed the fingers of his right hand. "Five thirty this afternoon, I'm certain of it."

Outside, the Indian women were delivering the washed and rewrapped bodies to the Jeep, with Colunga hurrying them along like an impatient parent. Matt took one look at the height of the vehicle on its oversized knobby tires and knew it wasn't going to work. He started to say something to Delgado, but the sergeant was already throwing open the Jeep's tailgate and reaching for Neil's feet. The women, diminutive pallbearers, were supporting the body on their heads and raised hands. Their hold, however, was a reverent one, making it appear as though the body were floating above them, and Delgado's efforts lacked sufficient subtlety to maintain the spell. The corpse slipped from everyone's grasp and hit the dry ground with a muffled thud, raising a rust-colored explosion of dust. Delgado cursed, and the women commenced their lament once more, doing what they could to brush dirt from the sheets and reposition Neil inside his wrappings.

Matt muttered "Christ," biting the word out and turning away from the scene.

The policemen had sense enough to let the women get Billie's body into the back of the jeep unassisted. After that, Matt squeezed into the shotgun seat alongside Colunga, and the jeep sped out of the square.

He was surprised to see that the ax man had already chopped a V-shaped notch more than halfway through the tree trunk, but in place of a smile the logger now wore a look of weary determination. Half of Echeverría was gathered around. Matt was still wondering how Delgado meant to negotiate the tree, when he spied a blue Japanese pickup on the other side of the trunk. He recognized it as one of the vehicles owned by the Lacandon Indian community of nearby Lacanjá, one of several gifts the federal government had bestowed on the group several years ago.

Matt stood on the jeep's running board to scan the crowd, and in a moment he had located the truck's drivers, two slight young men with jet-black hair that fell well below their shoulders. They were dressed in cotton shirts and polyester slacks rather than the homespun shifts still worn by many of the group. The Lacandons were regarded by some as the twentieth century's last link with the ancient Maya. There were perhaps one hundred pure Lacandons left, self-confined to three villages— *caribales*—in the jungle that bore their name. They referred to themselves as Caribs and continued to practice a kind of pre-Christian pantheism. Until recently they had been known to travel as far as Yaxchilan to burn copal incense to their ancestor gods.

Delgado explained that he had commandeered their truck for official use. *"Brutos"* was the word he used for the two Indians.

Interest was momentarily diverted from the woodchopper when Colunga dropped open the gate of the Jeep and announced his plan to everyone within earshot. The bodies were to be conveyed to the other side of the tree and laid out in the back of the pickup, the sergeant said, choosing volunteers when no one willingly stepped forth. Matt assumed that they would take advantage of the wide notch in the trunk to ease the task, but they all were so bent on adhering to Colunga's orders that they failed to take the notch into account. As a result, the policeman's reluctant band of assistants began to pass the corpses over the top of the coarse trunk to an equally reluctant group on the far side.

Matt stormed away from the noisy scene, hoping to separate himself from the ignominy of the moment; by the time he had made it clear around to the waiting truck,

the hopelessly soiled and abraded sheets that cocooned
Billie's body were partially undone, revealing a single
discolored hand.

He wanted to scream. Instead, he climbed into the back
of the pickup and tried to put matters right, much as the
Indian women had done in the plaza. Gently, he forced
Billie's cold and rigid hand back into the folds of fabric,
then hunkered down on the bed alongside her corpse and
effects, his back pressed to the pickup's cab.

"Quickly, quickly," Delgado was saying, a black
briefcase in hand. "We're leaving." He and Colunga
wedged themselves into the cab with the two Lacandons.

Matt exchanged a brief expressionless look with the
sergeant through the rear window as a dozen people
scampered up into the bed, jostling one another for space.
Matt thought for one horrified minute that someone was
actually going to sit down on the bodies, but it never
came to that. The corpses were afforded a certain respect, even in the tightness of the situation, and the kind
of nonchalant acceptance Matt had grown accustomed to
in Central and South America. He yielded a bit of his
own space to a woman and her tiny child; she in turn
yielded some of hers to a hunter with an ancient-looking
firearm slung across his back and two dead parrots dangling from leather ties looped over a broad cartridge belt.
At the last minute one of the Mayan women padded up
to the truck with Matt's hammock. He thanked her and
paid her a quetzal.

"Let's go, let's go," Colunga shouted, reaching out
the passenger-side window to slam his hand on the roof
of the cab.

The Indian behind the wheel leaned on the horn once
or twice to part the crowd, and the ax man went back to
work. Matt thought he caught the logger's eye as the
pickup left the fallen tree, something indecipherable attending the moment.

The road ran north through the forest, a red-brown
wound that had stained the trees and foliage along its
length. Every so often the truck would stop at solitary
*fincas* or crossroads *tiendas* stocked with hardtack, tins
of condensed milk, and Vienna sausages. The passengers

in the bed had become a merry group, exchanging bits
of local news while the pickup bounced closer and closer
to Palenque. Everyone realized that Matt had some connection with the corpses, but no one questioned him
about it, speculation being preferable to clear understanding in any case. So by and large he was left to his
own thoughts, which seemed to grow more ordered with
each passing kilometer. Perhaps, he told himself, through
nothing more than the recognition of what lay ahead.

There had been several close calls in his Puma Tours
past, but they had all been of the hairy-moment variety
in that none had ended in death for either staff or clients.
An incident on the Inca Trail to Machu Picchu two years
earlier when a Stanford professor had come down with
altitude sickness—what the Andeans called *soroche*—only
it wasn't the garden-variety headache and nausea but the
one that everyone feared, a textbook case of pulmonary
edema. Even the physicians who were part of the group
had failed to diagnose it as such. But Matt and Jake had
stayed up all night, a few hundred feet shy of the high
pass, monitoring the woman's symptoms and leafing back
and forth through Wilkerson's *Medicine for Mountaineer-
ing*, until they were certain they had called it right. Jake
had run down the trail in the dark and returned by sunrise
with a swaybacked horse from the village below, and
Matt had taken the woman out, waved the Quillabamba
milk train to a stop, and delivered her to Cuzco's small
hospital in time.

More recently, there had been a case of bleeding ulcers
at the lodge; a client had doubled over in pain on the
floor of the bat-infested latrine, his wife unhinged by the
massive spill of blood, the stench of death.

But there had always been some benevolent force on
their side, some patron saint of tourism watching over
them. For Puma, at least, although Matt knew of several
other operators who had lost clients to rapids, ava-
lanches, and bee stings. But never *murder*.

Fixing his gaze on the bodies of his two clients, his
two friends, he took a kind of perverse satisfaction in
blaming himself for their deaths. If only he had maintained a professional distance, he berated himself; if only
he had secured the watch that night at La Garganta. . . .

In a way it had been the same with Susan's death: he had failed to secure the watch. He had already climbed onto the bus that day when she had stepped on to take his place, literally pulling him down off the steps, saying, "You need some rest, I can handle this." So he had ignored the omens, surrendered the watch, and returned to the makeshift camp the volunteers had set up in Huaras. And he had slept while she died.

*The husband got shot, the guide lost his license, and the woman ended up in prison,* he heard himself telling Billie. Or Lauren. Only now there was no telling the fate of the guide. The police in Villahermosa were going to come down on him a lot heavier than Delgado and Colunga had. And of course there was Puma Tours' reputation to consider.

Matt suddenly realized how exhausted he was, got to his feet, and stood for a moment with his face in the wind, staring out over the top of the pickup's cab. Two hitchhikers were walking in the road up ahead, a man and a woman, young foreigners toting unwieldy frame packs. The Lacandon slowed the truck just enough to say, "*No hay campo*"—there wasn't enough space. The woman was good-natured about it and motioned the truck by with an elaborate wave of her arm. Matt noted that she had brown hair as long and fine as Billie's. She caught his look and gave him a radiant smile as the pickup passed them by.

# 7

# Interrogation of the Officials

It was six in the evening when the truck pulled into Palenque. The bodies were carried into police headquarters and turned over to the custody of enforcement agents who dealt almost exclusively with tourist-related incidents. Delgado had been led to understand that the bodies of the two *norteamericanos* would be driven on to Villahermosa, but soon learned that Lieutenant Escobar of the Palenque division had been placed in charge of the investigation. Unlike the sergeants from the Echeverría post, who were both judicial police, Escobar was a *federale*.

Matt had good reason to be less than thrilled by the news. Without much in the way of preliminaries, he had been ushered into a foul-smelling and dilapidated two-story building behind the district headquarters and left in a holding cell on the ground floor. He had often glanced at the place from the street and knew at least half a dozen people who had spent a night or two inside. The cell was long and narrow, empty except for two chairs, with heavy, rolled-stock doors at either end; one of those opened to a dimly lit hallway, the second to an adjacent cell occupied by a young man seated on a wooden stool, his head in his hands. A rusting awning window sat high up in the concrete wall at Matt's back; the front wall was fully barred. The kid in the cell was weeping.

There was nothing like bars to rid a person's mind of extraneous thoughts, Matt decided. He had seen rooms like that one before, but not for several years, and he was beginning to wonder just how long Escobar planned to keep him guessing. He and the lieutenant were acquaintances of a sort in that they would occasionally find themselves at the same bar in the late hours of a Saturday night. But it was Puma business that had brought them together initially. Early on, Escobar had fought hard against the company's acceptance in Palenque, where, the lieutenant had argued, there was a surfeit of capable local guides. But Jake had gone around him by taking in a Mexican partner, a man named Coco Sinagua, who owned one of the village's most popular night spots, Xibalba. In the end Puma had triumphed over everyone's misgivings—the company always worked in close cooperation with the Mexican guides—but Escobar had never really forgiven Jake the insult.

The lieutenant was from Jalisco, near Guadalajara, and was known around Palenque as the wrong man to cross. He was tough, troubled, driven, and not above going outside the law to serve the needs of justice. His unofficial escapades had likewise captured the town's imagination. For mistresses, he favored gringas, and more than once he had hit on Matt's blond second in command at Puma.

But at the same time, Matt judged that things would have been worse if the case had gone to Villahermosa. The city was so layered in corruption that even the Gulf mob bosses couldn't find their way through it. It was easy for Matt to imagine himself locked away and forgotten, a mere oversight on the part of 'Hermosa's blend of opportunism and bureaucracy. Palenque, on the other hand, was scarcely more than a pueblo. Though it antedated the discovery of the ruins that were its namesake and had once served as an important conduit between Guatemala and Mexico, the village now relied on tourism and cattle raising. The name meant "palisade" or "enclosure" and was often used in reference to cockfights. Escobar notwithstanding, Matt liked to think of the place as his town—to a certain extent—and was confident the lieutenant would at least give him a fair shake.

Still, he didn't see anyone rushing in to spring him.

And jails in Central America were full of people waking up to just that. Serving time often had less to do with judicial procedure than it did with the weather or the mood of the arresting officer. Maybe Escobar had had a bad day. Or maybe his wife had caught him with the ticket vendor from the Cine Twilite again.

Matt was picturing himself curled up on the floor, a bed of paint chips and exterminated flies, when a plain-clothesman appeared at the door to the cell, a sturdily built agent from the DEA in wraparound shades and an olive-green suit. Matt stood up and made a move for the door, but the man locked it behind him and stormed past Matt to the door of the adjacent cell. He threw it open, startling the teenager inside, then without warning began to beat the kid about the head and torso, kicking him senseless as he slipped from the stool to the filthy floor.

Matt felt each of the agent's carefully placed blows and had to fight down an urge to break a chair over the guy's head. The anger was misguided, born of a champion-of-the-underdog instinct that had gotten him into more than one fix, but it remained a gut-level response. He tried to keep a glower from his face as the agent emerged, grinning and attending to the collar of his jacket.

"Drug trafficker," the man said after a moment, gesturing to the youth. "Colombian garbage." He showed Matt an enigmatic smile. "Sit down. Wait awhile longer. We're taking care of everything."

The kid was on the floor, moaning now, and Matt asked him if he was badly hurt but got no answer. The brief face-to-face with the agent had left Matt disturbed and thinking vaguely about Mexico, about his own ambivalent attachments to a culture where such posturings were the norm. He reached out and took hold of the bars. Perhaps it was a mistake to judge the States so harshly.

An hour went by, and a young boy approached the cell to inquire if Matt needed anything. Matt recognized him as one of the urchins who sometimes played soccer in the street outside Puma's office. The boy knew Matt as well, but there was nothing in his dark eyes or soft voice to suggest any surprise at finding him in jail. Matt dug into his pocket for pesos and told the boy to bring him and the Colombian some fried chicken with *habanero* sauce from the restaurant on the plaza. The young smuggler had recovered but was scared shitless that the agent was going to return for a repeat performance. The two of them ate in silence when the food arrived, for all the Colombian knew, Matt was a DEA plant. Shortly before nine o'clock Escobar sent for him.

The lieutenant was perhaps ten years older than Matt and a couple of inches shorter. Where Matt was lean and long-limbed, Escobar was barrel-chested, beefy, and powerful-looking. He liked boldly colored suits and garish ties but was in shirtsleeves when Matt was shown into the office. An overhead fan was stirring Palenque's thick heat, and Escobar had his tie loosened. From his desk, he motioned Matt to a torn but padded chair. A uniformed sergeant was seated at a second desk, his fingers poised over the keys of an old Royal typewriter.

The lieutenant asked Matt to give his account of the events leading up to the murder, and Matt began to lay it all out. Escobar was pensive, saying little in return, swiveling slightly in his chair.

"So we have a mystery on our hands," he said in Spanish when Matt finished. "False identities, murder, theft, the stuff of intrigue, no?" Escobar glanced at Delgado's hastily prepared report and the tape of Matt's statement. "Officially the North Americans had not entered Mexico when they were killed, and yet they *had* exited Guatemala. This could place them in a kind of political no-man's-land. But in reality they were on Mexican soil, and it therefore falls upon us to deal with this most unfortunate affair—unravel it, if you will. In any case, the *selva* refuses to recognize borders, is it not true?"

Matt felt his jaw and nodded, wondering what Escobar was getting at. Ranchero music and laughter were wafting in through shutters that opened onto Palenque's central plaza, a pleasing mix of multinational sounds Matt was anxious to immerse himself in.

"Do you know why I have decided to investigate this case, Matt? Because you and I are known to each other, and because I am confident that you are going to tell me exactly what happened out there."

Matt shifted his gaze from the shutters to Escobar's

heavy-lidded eyes. "It happened exactly like I told Delgado. Our camp was attacked during the night. My clients were killed."

"Yes, of course. And it encourages me to hear you refer to them as your 'clients.' " The lieutenant placed his hands flat on the desk and leaned forward in a conspiratorial way. "After all, Matt, we are both men of the world. I understand the . . . *intrigues* a man can find himself involved in, especially in the *selva*, where the rules don't always apply."

Matt realized he was staring at the fat ring on Escobar's right hand; it was of the same Masonic design as that worn by some of the local guides who worked the ruins, a kind of framing square encompassing an all-seeing eye. He felt the lieutenant's eyes and redirected his attention. "As I said, Sergeant Delgado has the full story."

Escobar's grin collapsed. "I understand why you had to tell them that story. But you are not talking to some *rurale* now. How much did you pay them?" The lieutenant made a dismissive gesture before Matt could respond. "Two people are killed along an isolated stretch of river. You claim that some money, some passports, and some cameras are stolen. But the man guiding the couple escapes with a bump on the head. And when the police arrive on the scene, what do they find but a *second* set of passports, somehow overlooked by the thieves." Escobar picked up Delgado's typed report and slapped it with the back of his fingers. "You expect me to believe this? Why did they leave you alone? Why did they leave the passports?"

"You'll have to ask the killers, Lieutenant."

Escobar thrust a thick forefinger at Matt. "I am asking you—why?"

"Maybe they panicked." Matt held Escobar's gaze. "Or maybe the gods are saving me for something special. You think I haven't been asking myself the same question since last night? You think I wouldn't rather be dressed up in some body bag than have to sit here listening to you dream up stories?"

Escobar flipped open the report. "How do I know that

they gave their name as . . . Westphal? Maybe you have a reason for telling me this.''

Matt tightened his jaw. ''We passed through the *garita* at Pipiles, and there are no exit stamps in those passports.''

''How do I know you came in from Guatemala? You have no papers that bear out your claim.''

Matt let Escobar work on him for a while; it was the only way, really. ''Are you charging me with something, Lieutenant?'' he asked finally.

He wasn't surprised to see the lieutenant's grin return. Steepling his fingers, Escobar leaned back in his chair and told the desk sergeant to go get himself a cup of coffee.

Escobar tapped a cigarette onto the desk and struck a wooden match. ''Who said anything about charging you?'' He offered the pack to Matt. ''I'm interested to hear your side of it. Does it make sense to you, these theories about thieves and guerrillas?''

''Not really,'' Matt confessed. ''But fill me in if you've got a better one.''

Escobar's thick eyebrows went up, and he exhaled smoke toward the ceiling fan. ''Oh, I do, Matt. In fact, I have several.'' He held up a finger. ''One: The gringos were involved with drugs. *Mota*, no? Or *cocaina*. The false identities suggest this, no?'' Escobar's middle finger joined the first. ''Two: Someone, some unknown third party, knew the gringos were carrying drugs, perhaps cash, and decided to rob them. Consider the fact that the man was stabbed and the woman was strangled. Why would they strangle her? Enraged husbands or lovers strangle their women. But so do murderers who are looking for information. How do you like things so far?''

''You're still not telling me anything I haven't already thought of, Lieutenant. Either one makes sense. But if it was drugs or cash, it was so well hidden that the sentries at Pipiles couldn't find it.''

Escobar's smile was tolerant. ''Is this anything new? These passports weren't found. Guns and drugs move through that checkpoint every day.'' He shook his head. ''I have one last theory that lays all these complications to rest.''

"Go ahead," Matt said, leading with his chin.

"You and the woman—what shall we call her, Billie or Lauren?"

Matt said, "Billie's the only name I knew her by."

"Fine. You and this Billie became close friends during the trip downriver. The husband grew jealous of your friendship. The two of you fought. . . ." Escobar shrugged. "This is Mexico, and the three of you were alone in the *selva*."

Matt regarded Escobar for a long moment. "That's crazy. I kill some guy, then report his murder when it would have been just as easy to bury his body out there?"

Again, Escobar shrugged. "You had no choice. There were plenty of witnesses who could place the three of you together. People would begin to ask questions when the couple didn't show up, here or wherever they were going. And just exactly where were they going?"

"Palenque," Matt answered absently. "On to the States, I don't know. And why would I kill the girl if we were lovers? What purpose would that serve?"

Escobar stubbed out the cigarette. "She was repulsed by your violence. Now, instead of love it was rape. And you got carried away with yourself."

"Are you charging me or not?"

"You're not telling us everything, Matt." Escobar pointed to his heart. "Something in here tells me. And unfortunately the boatmen weren't there, so they can't confirm your story." He paused a moment, then added: "But no, we're not making any charges. Consider this, though: I think your two boatmen from Sayaxche would corroborate the fact that there was more between you and the woman than an agreement to travel. And I also think that an autopsy of the woman might reveal the presence of your juices."

Matt frowned. Tough-cop talk. He smirked but said nothing.

"Who knows?" Escobar grinned. "It might jar your memory some."

Matt was released shortly before ten o'clock. He stood for a moment at the edge of Palenque's elevated *zócalo* feeling renewed if not entirely reborn, then shouldered his hammock and lightened rucksack and crossed the cobblestone street. Escobar's investigation had taken an unexpected turn, but Matt refused to allow himself to worry just yet. It wasn't likely that Paolo and Emil would be dragged in, and even if it came to that, Matt was certain the boatmen would stick to their story. He likewise dismissed the lieutenant's mention of an impossible autopsy; Escobar was merely trying to put the fear in him.

Activity around the plaza was not as riotous as it had been an hour before, but there were still plenty of locals and visitors milling about, with rock, ranchero, and mariachi music filtering out from bars and cafés. At one of the *zócalo*'s iron benches, three young Mexican Rastas were hassling two women travelers. Matt figured them for Europeans and thought he could detect mild amusement under all the gestures of annoyance. A vendor with a cartful of cigarettes, Chiclets, and candy had stopped to watch the exchange. Elsewhere, two Lacandons in native garb were conversing with the driver of the pickup, all three of them standing in Mayan fashion, with their arms folded across their chests, fingertips tucked beneath forearms. Lacandons from Mensabok and Naja, the more traditional of the villages, would frequently make the trip to Palenque to sell bows and arrows or clay god pots.

A long line of taxis had formed along the south side of the square, most of the drivers busy polishing their cars. Two defeated-looking shoeshine boys were sitting on the high curb watching the passing parade of sneakers and jogging shoes. Heat lightning lit the sky west of town.

Matt recalled telling Billie that fishing was his own response to trouble and thought about Rachel Riordan and the letter she had written to her sister. Perhaps big-game fishing this go-round, Matt told himself as he set off for the office.

Shops were shutting down along the *Calle Central*, the southern terminus of the two-lane paved road that linked Palenque with the Villahermosa-Mérida highway. Trucks and a few motorcycles cruised by, but it was mostly pedestrian traffic at that hour: tourists in groups of three or four lazily fingering the weave of Yucatecan hammocks or highland serapes, street boys with lottery tickets or evening-edition newspapers, the odd drunk staggering off to urinate against a wall. The restaurants were crowded with bored-looking budget travelers swapping grapevine information while they waited to be served. Two more weeks and Palenque would begin gearing up for Semana Santa, but just then the town was quiet.

The pueblo didn't offer much in the way of comfort, shopping, or entertainment, so for most travelers it was little more than a brief side trip, a stopover on the way to San Cristóbal and the highlands or Yucatán's postclassic sites and Caribbean beaches. Only the hard core lingered there—professional and amateur Mayanists and psychedelic mushroom aficionados—but what magic there was didn't begin until one reached the ruins themselves, which were some six miles outside of town in the lush foothills of the Chiapatecan range. As little as ten years back it had been possible to wander those forests for days without coming upon a settlement, but more and more Tzeltal- and Chol-speaking highlanders were finding their way into the *selva*, and the area was succumbing fast to the same slash-and-burn techniques that had leveled much of the Petén.

Jake had chosen Palenque as the site of Puma's Mexico office because of the crossroads nature of the town. The ruins afforded a magnificent wrap-up for the downriver tour, and within half an hour's hop by small plane were a dozen equally rewarding sites and destinations. But the office was more than a mere coordinating center; it was a way to keep the company's name in the public eye, and Puma could always count on a decent amount of walk-in trade: travelers who were interested in arranging custom-tailored local trips or who were just curious to see what treks Puma offered in other parts of the world.

The office was on the main street a few blocks north of the *zócalo* in a well-kept building with a red tile roof near the town's only movie theater, the Cine Twilite. A plate-glass window advertised PUMA TOURS, INC.— WILDERNESS TRIPS AND INTERNATIONAL ADVENTURE- TRAVEL. Below, was a fanciful depiction of a prone cougar toying with a world globe as a house cat might play with a ball of catnip. Matt was surprised to find the lights on; he rapped his knuckles against the picture window before he entered, stooping to ease himself under the office's partially lowered security grate.

Natalie, Matt's cheerful, honey-blond partner, was on her feet when he walked in, coming around the desk to give him a welcome-home hug. He held on to her longer than she had anticipated, one arm around her waist while he waved to Ángel with his free hand.

Born and raised in the Yucatán, Ángel had classical Mayan features: dark epicanthic eyes, a long, broad-based nose, and a copper-brown complexion. From his father, a noted sculptor from Mani, he'd inherited an intuitive grasp of the art and the mind-set of his ancestors. Experts claimed that the untrained eye couldn't distinguish one of Jesus's Jaina replicas from the real items, and Matt had heard it said that several of the man's pieces were on display in the museum in Villahermosa, the originals having been sold off to private collectors.

Ángel wore a sheepish grin now; a ledger was open on the desk in front of him. Natalie disengaged herself from Matt's hold and gently pushed him to arm's length.

"What're you two doing here so late?" he asked.

"Working," she said flatly. "We've got all sorts of problems with the Yucatán trip. I don't know how Jake expects to take eighty people on this thing." She stopped herself and regarded Matt with a puzzled expression.

Matt ran a hand over his face and tried to imagine how he must have looked. He hadn't shaved since the lodge; his hair was matted and impenetrable, his clothes and boots caked with road grit.

"Jeez, who died?" Natalie asked laughing.

Matt turned around to close the door and walked to his desk. He opened a bottom drawer and reached inside, but came up empty-handed. "Ángel!" he said harshly.

When he looked up, Natalie was hurrying over to him with bottle and glass in hand. "Don't get crazy. He was just about to put it back when you came in."

"It's true, Matt," Ángel said from his desk, Mayan eyes wide under a comma of raven-black hair.

Natalie poured an ounce of bourbon into the glass. "Here. Relax. Tell your overworked and underpaid staff all about it."

Matt drained the glass at a toss and sat down. Natalie perched herself on the edge of his desk, arms folded across her chest. She had hazel eyes and wavy sun-streaked hair cut short for the dry season. She was tan and lovely, and she and Matt had once thought they were in love. Now she lived with a mushroom collector named Kit in a small house outside of town. Matt still adored her; her crooked-tooth smile would always leave him lovestruck and weak in the knees.

She seemed to sense some of this now and reached out for his hand. "What's going on, light of my life?"

Matt exhaled, slapped his hands on his knees, and stood up. "I need to talk to Jake as soon as we can get him."

Natalie slid off the desk. "I just spoke to him an hour ago."

"Was he at the office or at home?"

"At the office. But on his way out."

Matt glanced at the wall clock. "An hour ago . . . Try and get a line through to the States and call him at home. If you get the machine, leave a message for him to get back to us as soon as he gets in."

"But Matt—"

"I'll be in the back." He was three steps away from the desk when he swung around. She was standing arms akimbo, a Puma T-shirt that read THE WILDERNESS EXPERIENCE stretched tight across her breasts. Ángel, too, was staring at him. "Look, I'll explain everything when Jake's on the phone. I just don't want to go through it twice."

He exited the office through a narrow hallway and a hardwood door that led to his apartment in the rear of the building. There were two high-ceilinged rooms there, with a cramped *baño* and a tiny kitchen. A month had passed since he installed a paddle fan in the ceiling and completed work on a loft in the rear room, but he had yet to get around to moving his bed up there. A second door in the front room opened onto a wooden veranda overlooking a deep, steep-sided ravine that undercut the *Calle Central* and was crisscrossed with footpaths. A long but trustworthy flight of stairs led from the veranda directly into the tangled growth at the lip of the barranca.

Matt dropped himself onto an arrangement of cushions that passed for a couch, unlacing his boots and kicking them off. He pulled the compressed wad of currency from his sock and placed it in front of him on a wooden trunk he had disguised under a red and black Bolivian manta. He contemplated the money for a moment and wondered whether he would let Jake in on *all* the details. Proceeding as he was, one foot in front of the other along an unmarked trail, he was unsure just what he intended to say. Jake was a good boss and a trusted friend, but he was also a worrier.

Puma operated tours in half a dozen countries in Central and South America in addition to running occasional excursions to Nepal, east Africa, and New Zealand. The company employed more than a dozen guides worldwide and a staff of eight in the Denver home office. But primarily Puma had always been a one-man show headed by Jake Welles, its founder and guiding spirit, a modern American red-haired cowboy more at home with horses, small planes, and big skies than the sometimes prosaic world of international travel. But Jake possessed an uncanny business sense and could play travel trends the way some people played the stock market. Puma catered to a new breed of tourist, the one who had "done" Europe and was looking for trips that combined clean-living travel fun with moderate amounts of exercise and adventure.

Jake and Matt had crossed paths five years before in Peru, where Jake had trailblazed Puma's future, leading small groups on hikes into the Apurimac or doing the Inca Trail by way of Salcantay. They both shared an enthusiasm for maps, hard-to-reach places, and the logistics of getting people there. Matt's Peace Corps training and subsequent position as field coordinator had taken him from one end of South America to the other and into remote areas Jake dreamed of opening up for tourism. So Jake had proposed a partnership of sorts, but back then Matt couldn't grasp the notion of packaging adventure. They had kept in touch nevertheless, and two years later—after Matt had had a change of heart and gained a bullet hole in his side—Jake had hired him to scout out new trips in Central America and guide some of the ones

Puma had already pioneered and perfected. By then the company had become a force in the travel industry.

The bourbon had left his throat parched, and Matt was on his way to the sink when the office phone rang. Natalie had her hand raised to knock when Matt threw open the door.

"Jake," she announced as Matt brushed past her.

He grabbed the handset, beckoning Natalie and Ángel to the desk at the same time. The connection was bad, so he pressed a hand to his ear, straining to understand Jake's rush of words. Once through the formalities, Matt dove right in, beginning with the day Billie and Neil had showed up at the lodge.

As the line cleared somewhat, Matt sat down, taking a breath before he brought the story to its evil climax. Jake, who had been listening without comment, was suddenly saying, "Are you kidding me, Matt, this is unbelievable, this is unbelievable." Matt had heard Natalie gasp; she had her fingertips to her lips now, a shocked expression on her face. Ángel was shaking his head, mumbling to himself. Matt thought it best to include Escobar's theories as well as the lieutenant's veiled threats. Jake had a hundred questions ready when he was through: Did Escobar understand that Matt had been hired by the couple? Had Matt received any word from Paolo and Emil? Had the newspapers gotten hold of the story yet?

"I didn't see any reporters at the station," Matt said. "But I was out back for a good three hours. I don't know what went down in the meantime."

Jake made an agitated sound and fell silent for a moment. "Matt, I don't want to seem mercenary about this—"

"You don't have to say it, Jake," Matt interrupted.

The political situation in Guatemala had made the Usumacinta trips a risky venture at best, but once word got out that tourists had been murdered on the river, there would be a slew of cancellations for the upcoming tours. *A river of no financial return*, Matt thought, recalling an outfitter friend's lament. Worse still, Puma's reputation could be damaged across the board. Matt said as much, but it seemed that Jake's concerns were of a more personal order.

"Puma can take care of itself," he told Matt evenly. "It's your reputation I'm worried about."

Matt uttered a short, ironic laugh. *The guide loses his license.* "There's more," he told Jake on impulse, moved by his friend's concern, and went on to explain about the telex and the cash. Natalie's look changed from one of horror to one of stark disapproval, and Matt thought he could discern the same thing in Jake's silence.

"I don't understand, Matt. Why didn't you just hand everything over to the police?"

Natalie was holding up a scribbled note that read: WHY?!! The word was underlined three times.

"Because I want to know why they were killed," Matt answered him, meeting Natalie's eyes. "I think the sister knows something, and I want to talk to her before the police get to her. I can still dump all this into Escobar's lap later on, say I found out a couple of things after the fact, from Paolo maybe."

"But you said Rachel addressed the telex to Lauren Riordan," Jake pointed out. "Maybe she doesn't know anything about the false identities."

"That's one of the things I want to find out."

Natalie was tight-lipped, shaking her head; Ángel appeared to be considering it.

"You sure you know what you're getting into, *compadre*?"

"I'm not off the map yet, Jake."

Jake took a moment to respond. "How can I help?"

"I want you to send a telegram to Rachel Riordan. Something like: 'It has fallen on me to inform you that Lauren and her companion, Michael, have met with a tragic accident in Mexico. There are aspects of this I must discuss with you personally. . . .' Include the phone and telex numbers here and mention that I want her to contact me as soon as possible."

Jake asked Matt to run through it again while he jotted everything down. Matt gave him the address he had memorized.

Jake said, "I'll confirm it with information. Maybe I'll be able to get a phone number."

Matt thanked him, and talk turned to the next Classic Maya trip. "And see if you can bring down a couple of

Donna Summer cassettes for Colonel Reyes,'' Matt thought to add.

"This is horrible, Matt,'' Natalie said after Matt had hung up.

He came around the desk and draped an arm over her shoulder; then he took Ángel by the elbow and steered the two of them toward the door. "Get out of here and get some sleep. I'll lock up behind you.''

"Are you going to be all right?'' Natalie asked.

"Go.'' He kissed her lightly.

Matt lowered the grate, shut the door, and poured himself another drink at the desk, carrying it back to the cushions in his apartment. He sat and thought about Billie, and suddenly he was hurting all over, cold clear through to the inside. A small animal moan seemed to escape him, tears and a prickling sensation in his face. In five minutes he was fast asleep.

# 8

## The Road to Ruin

The phone rang at five thirty in the morning, wrenching Matt from an unpleasant dream. He stumbled into the office and answered on the seventh ring, switching on the desk lamp as he sat down. Rachel Riordan was on the line, calling from New York City. Matt's ears pricked up when she asked for him in Spanish.

He identified himself, and they switched over to English; then he recounted the events, keeping things brief and to the point, making certain to say "Lauren" and "Michael" and to make no mention of the money or the telex. Rachel's voice grew more and more panicked, filled initially with a kind of angry disbelief that gave way to anguished cries. Matt held the handset away from his ear, helpless in his need to comfort her. He was trying to sympathize, to apologize, when once more Rachel changed course on him.

"Something's wrong about this," she said, suddenly composed. "Why are you the one telling me this? I haven't heard anything from the Mexican embassy or the State Department."

"You will," Matt told her.

"But Laurie didn't say anything about a river trip. They were planning to fly to Guatemala City. And just how did you get my address, Mr. Terry?"

Matt was momentarily fazed. At the same time, her

78

abrupt turn toward suspicion only served to up the alert.
"I don't know why your sister changed plans. They hired
me to take them downriver into Mexico so they could see
the ruins. I found your address among her things."

"What right did you have to go through her property?" Rachel snapped. "Isn't that supposed to be police
business?"

Matt's jaw tightened. "Look, Ms. Riordan, I'm sorry,
but your sister's *property* was scattered all over the jungle."

She was crying again, and Matt cursed himself for losing control.

"I don't understand how this could have happened,"
Rachel said after a while. "Why weren't you watching
out for her? Isn't that what they hired you for?"

Matt shut his eyes. "Ms. Riordan, listen—"

"Are the police going to contact me? What am I supposed to do? And what are these 'aspects' you want to
discuss with me?"

"I have something for you." The line went still. "Can
you come down here?"

Rachel took a long time answering, and when she
did, her tone was calculated. "I . . . Frankly, Mr. Terry,
I'm just not sure I believe you. I'll have to get back to
you."

Matt recalled what she'd sent in the cable: *Thanks for
all the added hassle. I've done what you asked . . .* "All
right," he said. "Call me after you've thought about it.
I can attend to the travel arrangements."

"I'll make my own arrangements," she said harshly.
"If I decide to come. I've been in Palenque before. But
I will contact you."

Matt continued to stare at the handset long after he
had recradled it, lost in new concerns. She had been to
Palenque before. Was that a message?

He had a rope around his neck now. Rachel might
choose to involve the embassy or simply show up unannounced. In either case Escobar would learn that
Matt had withheld evidence. He had assumed that Rachel would want to hear what he had to say before
reaching out for official confirmation, but now he wasn't
so sure.

Matt was at his desk three hours later when Natalie threw open the grate and came quietly through the door. He was shaved and showered but was feeling phobic in some unspecified way.

"You make one hell of an advertisement," she said, surprised to find him up and about. "I thought you'd be in bed."

Matt collapsed the steeple he had formed with his fingers. "She called this morning."

Natalie dropped her day pack on Ángel's desk and moved one of the chairs to face Matt's. "Well, spill it," she said, sitting down. "The poor woman."

Matt shrugged and ran a hand down his face. "She didn't believe me. She couldn't understand why the State Department hadn't notified her. Said she'd call back."

"Uh-oh."

"Yeah, uh-oh is right." Matt shook his head. "You better get a hold of what's his name, that lawyer."

"Bustamonte," Natalie said, vexed. "Why, is she going to sue us?"

"I just want to find out where we stand. Does he have a phone yet?"

"Probably not."

"Well, see what you can do. The sooner the better," he added, getting up.

"What happens in the meantime?"

Matt turned to her. "Business as usual." He glanced through the notes on his desk: messages from Jake, telex cables from hotels in Mérida and Cancun, reminders he had written to himself weeks ago. "I've got to pin down Joachim and Emilio. Jake thinks their lectures are getting too esoteric."

Ever since 1973, when the Mesa Redonda group had held its first conference on Mayan studies, Palenque had become something of a center for new schools of thought and interpretation, with modern-day Lords of Tikal often at odds with the Lords of Palenque or some other such site.

"Jake wants them to prune out some of the dynastic stuff."

"What does he expect?"

"Blood and warfare, self-mutilation, the rise and fall."

Natalie made a face. "Is this before dinner or after?"

"With, I think."

The guides Jake wanted Matt to reprimand worked the ruins from sunrise to sunset. Matt could have used Puma's Range Rover but opted to walk, if only to rid himself of what was beginning to feel like a toxic overdose. It was a perfect day for it in the sense that one couldn't move ten steps without breaking out into a full-body sweat. The sky was clear, cerulean save for a dark smudge hanging over the forelands west of town. It might have been smoke, the campesinos setting fire to their fields.

A mile along, the heat began to weigh on him like Atlas's burden. Taxis and tour buses tore by in both directions. Right and left of the road, the savannas were dotted with humpbacked cattle and their companion egrets. Matt observed a couple of gringo headhunters inspecting cow pies for magic mushrooms.

Shit happens, he told himself while he walked, taking the phrase up as a kind of cadence chant. It was a different song from the one he had marched to a decade earlier. Some control over the course of things had seemed possible then, but the world had been running amuck since, and a lot of that he tied to the States. If it was drugs that Billie had died for, he could blame the States. The rich and the well connected had been through the paces, speedballing and freebasing, but cocaine was making its way into the mass market now. And if it was guns, well, he could trace that north as well, because Central America's revolutions had become America's top priority. It all made him wonder why he had set his sights on a return. But nothing was left for him here; Billie's death had driven home that much. Was there anywhere left to go, he wondered.

The paved, unshaded road ran straight for almost six miles before climbing steeply into the hills through a series of switchbacks that culminated at the ruins. He arrived in just under two hours and downed a *refresco* at the outdoor café near the entrance to the site, where tourists were already beginning to queue up for lunch. A couple of local guides were lounging in the shade of a *palapa* playing cards; Matt went over to say hello and inquire after Joachim and Emilio Cortes. He took it as an encouraging sign that no one mentioned the murders or the few hours he had spent in "*la Cantina Escobar*," as some of the pueblo referred to Planeque's jail.

Twenty minutes later he was sitting at the top of the site's pyramidal Temple of Inscriptions waiting for Emilio and his fold to emerge from the internal stairway that led down to Pacal's burial crypt. Two uniformed *guardia civil* were seated nearby, sharing a smoke.

A Mexican archeologist by the name of Dr. Alberto Ruz Lhuillier had discovered the tomb in 1951 while searching for tunnels believed to connect the temple to other structures in the site. The find had set the archeological world on its ear. But even without it, the ruins at Palenque stood apart, for it was there that the ancient builders had erected their masterpieces, transforming limestone and plaster to high art. Off to Matt's right, across a narrow stream shaded by fruit trees and spanned by vaulted bridges, stood the cross group, a courtyard arrangement of small but stately temples with graceful roof combs and corbel-arched interior rooms whose walls were adorned with bas-relief panels of glyphs and dynastic portraiture. Fronting the temple was a complex of quadrangles and galleries known as the Palace, from the center of which rose a tall, roofed tower unlike any other building thus far unearthed in Mesoamerica. The site was walled in on three sides by high jungle, but from atop the temple or tower one could look north across the steamy plains of Tabasco almost clear to the Gulf.

Gangs of schoolchildren dressed in bright colors were scrambling up and down the exposed stairways, running in and out of temple doorways, laughter echoing back and forth and erupting from a dozen different openings in the labyrinth beneath the Palace. For Mexicans, Palenque wasn't an archeological site but a park to be explored and enjoyed, a commingling of past and present, of life and death.

Matt recalled Billie's first mention of Palenque and

remembered how they had talked about going up to Agua Azul's travertine cascades to swim. The memory touched off dark thoughts, and for a moment the site seemed to reveal its real face to him. The buildings, mausoleums really, began to take on a bleached and dazzling midday directness that was more sinister than enchanting. Just then something down below caught his eye: a woman dancing jubilantly in the clipped-grass plaza near an unreconstructed mound; she was singing, throwing her arms wide and twirling about, her long skirt flowing. Matt brought his hand to his brow and recognized her as one of the Europeans he had seen in the *zócalo* the night before. A small crowd was gathering to watch her gyrations: children, tourists, and two *obreros* with machetes who had been working close by. One of the *guardia civil* soldiers laughed and said, "*Hongos.*"

When Matt returned his attention to the plaza, he saw that the woman had stripped off her blouse and seemed to be fumbling with the rear zipper of her skirt.

The mushrooms were known to elicit far worse than impromptu nudity. It was considered quite normal, in fact, to expect several deaths by suicide, drowning, or automobile accidents during the dry high season, when caravans of freaks would show up in town, turning the campground into the closest approximation of a *Star Wars* bar scene this side of Kathmandu.

Matt thought about the expanded endorphin states the Maya had shot for with techniques of self-mutilation. Maybe part of the problem with contemporary drug journeys was just that there were no signposted roads, no maps detailing the manifold demonic places one could stumble into.

The woman seemed to catch sight of herself for an instant and collapsed to her knees, desperate to cover her nakedness and, Matt suspected, crying. The soldiers were angry, neither of them enthusiastic about having to descend the temple's three hundred-odd stairs to deal with the situation. Matt was contemplating going to her rescue when he spied the woman's friend shouldering her way through the crowd. In any case, Emilio and his group were just emerging from the stairway, and Matt didn't want to miss him. The guide wore his usual Buddha grin, offering a helpful hand to members of his breathless flock while he fielded questions about the symbols on the sarcophagus lid. Erich von Däniken had taken the bas-relief to be a pilot at the controls of a spacecraft, but it was more likely a representation of clubfooted Pacal suspended between Mayan depictions of heaven and hell.

Matt gave a look back to the plaza, saw that the woman was being well cared for, and waved to Emilio. Catching sight of Matt, he smiled and excused himself from his group of elderly Americans, warning them to be careful of the stairs. "Soon we'll have the escalator built," he said with a thick accent, eliciting laughs from everyone. He and Matt exchanged a brief *abrazo*. "So, how is El Petén?"

"Good, for the most part," Matt told him, and they began to talk of local matters. Emilio was bighearted and avuncular and had worked the ruins for most of his life.

"You see that smoke?" Emilio said, indicating the smudge Matt had observed from the road.

"Yeah, what's going on? They burning early in Cristóbal?"

Emilio's eyebrows made a rakish movement. "El Chichón. The mountain is getting hot. You know the *Comisión Federal de Electricidad*—they want everyone in El Naranjo to move out."

"They're Zoque up there, aren't they? Do they really think it's going to blow?"

Emilio shrugged his round shoulders. "They claim that even the rivers are warming. But who can say for sure? It is in the hands of the gods who rule the day, no?" Again, the Buddha smile.

"Which reminds me," Matt said, getting to the point. "Are we all set for Semana Santa?"

"Sure."

"Good. But Jake's got one request: He wants you to cut back on some of the details when you talk to the group."

Emilio snorted. "Jake thinks we're being too academic." Jake came out sounding more like "Jackie."

"Just save all that Mesa Redonda stuff for the Stanford groups. What Jake wants is a little more sensationalism, more about bloodletting and sacrifices. You know, the *new* Maya. And I'd appreciate it if you'd pass the word to Joachim and the rest of the guys."

Reluctantly, Emilio agreed to edit the lectures somewhat. As they shook hands, Matt could feel Emilio's Masonic ring pressed against his own flesh.

"Oh, by the way," Emilio said, a few steps down the stairway to rejoin his group. "Our friend Lieutenant Escobar was up here early this morning asking after you. Is anything wrong?"

Matt considered it and said, "I'll let you know."

"The gods that rule the day," the guide remarked cheerfully, sidestepping his way down the pyramid.

Matt lingered at the top for another fifteen minutes, soaking up the light and wondering if Rachel would call. The red-hot coil in his chest had Billie's name on it, and he couldn't put down a feeling that his life was soon to be crowded with people who weren't always what they seemed, with unexpected events and risky business he thought he had grown beyond, or at least outrun. In some ways, it was like coming out of retirement.

He picked his way down the stairway, but instead of walking back to the road and suffering through the trapped heat of the switchbacks, he headed north across the grass plaza toward the museum. Behind the small building was a steep and seldom-used forest trail that paralleled the river and came out at the foot of the switchbacks across the street from El Templo, Palenque's only four-star accommodation. A five-star hotel—part of the Misión group—was under construction in town, but until that was completed El Templo would continue to serve as a base for Puma's guests. The swimming pool, however, had been under repair for over a month now, and Jake was growing concerned. Eight of ten recent trip evaluations had made mention of this, and Jake had asked Matt to check on the situation.

The jungle was refreshingly quiet. Matt stopped once to drink from the river and watch a group of birds thrash about in the shallows. The sun found its way through the canopy here and there, dragonflies, butterflies, and sting-less bees moving about in the shafts of light. It was a beautiful patch of forest, and the river's cascades and azure pools had once been a well-known collecting spot for freaks, a place for visions or skinny-dipping before the *policía* had put a stop to it. Matt had this in mind while he was scampering down alongside one of the larger falls where the river plunged over the maw of a limestone cave into a deep clear-water basin. And so he was quite surprised to find someone sunbathing naked on the smoothed travertine lip of the pool below him. But as he drew nearer, the scene his eye had composed began to rearrange itself, and all at once it wasn't a naked sun-bather at all, but a hairless, bloated corpse that had somehow misplaced its head.

Matt stood still, frozen in midstride ten feet from the body. The man's swollen feet dangled in the agitated wa-ter; the rest of him was on shore; a dark stain on the ground led from his neck. The body was mottled, the color of cream cheese in the light and deep purple below. It was bloodless and artificial looking, like a thing half-glanced in a nightmare.

Matt looked around, worried he might find the man's missing part. The jungle was serenely still, save for the flies bombinating around the corpse and the comforting rush of the waterfall. He forced his eyes shut, as though by doing so he could make the scene disappear, and opened them to the sight of Lieutenant Escobar easing his way out of the poolside thickets. He had a 9-mm automatic gripped in one hand, a walkie-talkie in the other.

"You have a sexual thing for dead bodies, is that it?" Escobar said. "We find a corpse, and we can be sure that el Señor Puma is close by." Escobar thumbed the talk stud on the radio and fired orders into the built-in mike. He had three men with him, one of them in ci-vilian dress.

Matt gave him a blank look.

"He was murdered sometime last night," Escobar continued, gesturing down the trail toward the road. "Beat up first, then dragged up here. Señor Rivera thinks the murderer used a machete."

The civilian nodded gravely, crossing himself as only the superstitious can do in the presence of a mystery that reeks more of black magic than of out-and-out mayhem. Escobar toed the body gently with his boot, then waved away the flies he'd disturbed. "Must have been popular with the women, no?" he said, laughing at his own joke. "Where did you go after you were released?" he asked Matt without looking at him.

"Back to the office," Matt said after a moment. "Why, you think I came out here to lop this guy's head off before I went to sleep? Who the hell is he?"

Escobar turned to him. "We don't know. We haven't found the face yet."

Matt looked around uncomfortably. Two more judicial cops entered the clearing on the trail he had taken from the museum. One of them clutched a field radio. "I told them to let you through," Escobar was saying. "The criminal always returns to the scene of the crime, true?" When Matt didn't respond, he asked if he had given any more thought to their discussion.

"I've barely had time to sleep."

Escobar stepped over the body and brought himself well into Matt's space. "Then go home and get your rest. My men down below will let you pass. You can have the weekend, but we're going to talk on Monday. People are whispering things in my ear. The gringos may have some surprises in store for us."

Matt set off and followed the trail down to the road, where Escobar's men were sharing a fat joint of what they claimed to be sinsemilla. He declined a hit and crossed the street to El Templo, wondering why death was suddenly sending him so many messages.

Constructed to mimic the Palace in some uncertain fashion, the hotel was a modern one-story quadrangle of rooms and suites set well back from the road. The interior courtyard was a combination parking area and lush garden, central to which was a dry trapezoidal concrete and tile pool. Hano Olivar, the hotel's manager, assured Matt that the pool would be filled by the time Jake's group arrived. It would have been filled already had Villahermosa sent the correct replacement parts for the filtration system.

Matt commiserated and asked to use the phone. Natalie told him that there had been no word from Rachel Riordan but that Paolo had radioed from Sayaxche to say that he and Emil had returned without incident. She had also managed to reach Cosmo Bustamonte on his new phone.

"He's willing to see you on Sunday afternoon at four o'clock."

"Call him back," Matt said, "and tell him I'll be there."

Matt drove into Villahermosa on Saturday to apply for a new passport and spent most of Sunday taking care of Puma business. There was still no word from Rachel Riordan when he set off at 3:30 P.M. to keep his appointment with the lawyer.

"They haven't got a shred of evidence," Bustamonte was telling Matt an hour later. "No motive, no murder weapon." The lawyer laughed. "And no matter what Lieutenant Escobar may claim to the contrary, it is not a crime to fuck with a married woman. Not, that is, unless the husband is around to press charges," he added, "and we certainly have no need to concern ourselves with *that* eventuality."

Matt mulled over Bustamonte's appraisal. The lawyer hadn't provided him with any new information, but Matt felt good about hearing his rights read by someone who knew the ins and outs of Mexico's curious and sometimes inconstant legal system. Bustamonte was in his early fifties, a portly man with pale eyes and a fringe of neatly trimmed hair. He was smartly attired in a three-piece white cotton suit he'd had custom-made in Mérida. He favored matching cuff links and tiepins and made frequent use of the gold-fobbed watch he carried in his vest, as if to suggest just how precious his time was.

"Ah, the day has too few hours," he commented, reclining in his chair. "Business, always business. How is a man ever to find the time to enjoy the finer things in life?"

The office was two air-conditioned rooms on the top floor of Palenque's only high-rise commercial building, south of the *zócalo* near the local chapter of Alcoholics

Anonymous and the Mayanesque Masonic lodge. University and law degrees were prominently displayed on a wall of framed photographs featuring Bustamonte in the company of nearly every VIP who had passed through Palenque in the past twenty years. Matt suspected that the lawyer slept in the back room.

He had told Bustamonte the truth about his relationship with Billie but had withheld mention of the cash. By then Matt had all but succeeded in convincing himself that the entire cache was a figment of his imagination. Still, the possibility remained that Rachel would blow everything wide open, and Matt had to be certain about the risks involved.

He said, "Let's just suppose for the sake of argument that I was withholding evidence."

The lawyer regarded him for a moment. "That would be a serious mistake on your part. Although the courts will distinguish between uncooperative and actually *hampering* an investigation, the line is a fine one. It will count for something, however."

"And if Escobar decides to pick me up?"

Bustamonte stuck out his lower lip and rocked his head from side to side. "Three days at the most. Then you will have to be brought before a judge and charged. As long as this case remains in Palenque, there is nothing much to worry about. But should it move to Villahermosa, things will become a little more complicated."

Which Matt understood to mean *expensive*. And he was beginning to wonder whether that was actually the case. *"Pueblo chico, infierno grande,"* Natalie had reminded him. The smaller the town, the busier the devil.

Bustamonte quoted a fee, and Matt agreed to retain him. The lawyer told Matt of a similar case involving a local guide and two tourists who had been robbed and killed in Ocosingo.

"Two women—" The lawyer grinned. "—making tortillas, you understand? Lesbian lovers."

The murderers had never been found, but no charges had been brought against the guide. So Matt was encouraged when he stepped out of the building and was cautiously optimistic for the first time in forty-eight hours.

He was heading off to treat himself to a dinner of the Misol-Ha's *mole poblano* when Escobar's black Dodge Fury screeched to a halt alongside the curb. A plain-clothesman riding shotgun rolled down his window; two more dark suits rode the rear seat. Escobar leaned over from the wheel, took a look past Matt toward Busta-monte's building, and remarked, "Talking to your law-yer, that's good. You are going to need him."

One of the dark suits threw open a rear door, and Matt said, "I thought you were giving me the weekend."

Escobar told Matt to get in. "Your weekend's over," he said over his shoulder, punching the accelerator.

*Rachel*, Matt thought.

At the same time he kept telling himself that there was something about the plainclothesmen that ran counter to the *federale* stereotype. These men weren't wearing shades, and their suits were all wrong for Palenque's tropical climate. The two in the back were soft-spoken, confident, almost casual. They weren't cops, Matt de-cided. They had the look of clandestine services.

At police headquarters, Escobar confirmed the fact.

"This is Captain Segunda," the lieutenant said, intro-ducing the sullen-looking man who had been in the pas-senger seat. "He is with the *Dirección Federal de Seguridad*. Agent Ortiz and Agent Suentes," he added, an impatient edge to his voice. "From Operación Res-cate."

Matt nodded to the two men.

Escobar opened a folder and passed two photographs across the desk to Matt. "Who are these people?"

He wasn't surprised to see Billie and Neil, but he hadn't expected to see official numbers typed across the bottom of their head shots. They weren't police photos, however, but more like telephoto close-ups. "I knew them as Billie and Neil Westphal," he said to the room.

Escobar glanced at Captain Segunda.

"You claim that you didn't know about the second passports."

Matt nodded. "Right, so far."

"But let us suppose for the moment that you did." Escobar tugged at his earlobe. "Let's say you saw the passports, perhaps when the North Americans tried to conceal them from the rangers at Pipiles. Or perhaps the boatmen saw them, it makes no difference. In any case, it aroused your curiosity. And you began to ask yourself just what these two were doing traveling downriver under assumed names. So you decided to look a little more closely at what they were carrying, and surprise!—your search revealed something. Something so valuable that you had to possess it no matter what the cost.''

Matt said, ''So I stage a murder and theft. I throw my own passport away, scatter some things around . . .''

''You see how quick he is?'' Escobar said to Segunda.

Ortiz took it from there. He was the shorter of the two agents, five foot ten, Matt guessed, sturdy and compact, with a significant bulge beneath the left armpit of his jacket.

''Interpol contacted us after Lieutenant Escobar's identity checks with the Mexican DFS and the DEA confirmed his suspicions about the couple.''

''Drugs,'' Matt said, and everyone smiled.

''There are outstanding arrest warrants for Lauren Riordan and Michael DeLuca on drug charges,'' Escobar said. ''But it isn't drugs that have brought Agents Ortiz and Suentes to Palenque.''

''What, then?''

Ortiz said, ''Antiquities.''

So it had nothing to do with Rachel, Matt told himself while he listened, no one in the room recognizing his sigh of relief for what it was.

Rescate was an international agency with police powers that had been organized to stop the flow of illegally obtained antiquities from Central America. Ortiz and Suentes had an official connection with the Prehispanic Monument Department of Guatemala's National Institute of Anthropology and History. And the names Lauren Riordan and Michael DeLuca, alias Billie and Neil Westphal and Linda and Randal Clover, were near the top of Rescate's list of known smugglers who were running Mayan treasures to the United States and western Europe.

Suentes, who wore wide-rimmed glasses, passed two more photos to Matt.

''We do not know precisely when they turned their hand to antiquities. But it is their dealings with these men that first brought them to our attention, and which makes this case one of national interest.'' He gave Matt a moment to study the photos. ''We understand that you have spent considerable time in the Petén, Mr. Terry. Do you recognize either of these men?''

Matt smoothed his mustache and shook his head.

''Rafael Aguilar,'' Suentes said, identifying the one with the pockmarked face. He had a highlander's profile, perhaps pure Indian blood, the name notwithstanding. ''He is the leader of a band of insurgents now based in the Petén. The same rebel band that looted the museum in Tikal. They have plundered dozens of archeological sites in the department.''

''I've heard of him,'' Matt said, trying to downplay his astonishment. He recalled the discussion he'd had with Billie before the launch had reached the Pipiles border post and their talks afterward on the Altar beach and Planchon de las Figuras. *Suppose you had to choose sides?* she had asked him. *I love this country, too, only maybe I'm just a little more active about showing it than you are—a little more demonstrative.*

''Just weeks ago,'' Suentes was saying, ''they held an American archeologist and his assistant hostage at a remote site in the Petén and murdered two police officials.''

Matt glanced at the photographs again. Ortiz saw him puzzling over the second man's face, which was broader than Aguilar's, lantern-jawed and hardened.

''Alejandro Volan. A Honduran. He is the go-between, the middleman, between Aguilar's insurgents and the antiquities runners. His spies work on legitimate digs and supply him with the information Aguilar needs to stage his raids. Volan takes charge of the money from these transactions, and with that money he equips the guerrillas with the weapons they require to continue their fight against democracy in Guatemala.''

Matt wondered precisely what role Billie and Neil could possibly have played in all that. As if reading his mind, Escobar said, ''What were they carrying that was so important?''

*Maybe the most important thing I've ever done . . .*

"Is it possible that they double-crossed Aguilar somehow?" Ortiz asked.

Matt threw him a look. "Sure it's possible. What the hell do I know about it? You snatch me off the street, you dump all this stuff on me. . . . Now you want me to solve the case for you?" He laughed wryly. "I brought Billie and Neil Westphal from Sayaxche to Yaxchilan. Someone killed them. I'd like to see those people hung as much as you would."

Escobar said, "According to Sergeant Delgado's report, the two boatmen returned to Sayaxche after the bodies were delivered upriver to Frontera Echeverría. Whatever the gringos were carrying could have been sent away with them."

"Bring them in if that's what you think," Matt told Ortiz. "Tear Sayaxche apart, search my rooms. You're dreaming."

The two agents fell silent. Escobar stared at him, then grinned. "And the woman told you nothing, because she was simply your client. You have nothing to hide, and yet you visit your lawyer."

"That was business," Matt affirmed.

Escobar folded his arms. "We will see."

Ortiz went on to explain something of Aguilar's past, of his campesino upbringing in Quiche province and subsequent enlistment in the Marxist cause by ORPA leaders, of his indoctrination into insurgency, and of the Cuban training he had received in squad tactics, security, communications, and interrogation. He had risen quickly through the ranks and led his splinter group on a journey out of the mountains into the forested lowlands of Petén, where there were far fewer troops to contend with. The plundering of archeological sites had begun as a temporary means of sustaining themselves, but it had soon become a primary activity. Aguilar had since enlarged his network, assimilating other rebel bands and taking on groups of men experienced in clearing techniques, some of whom had worked on legitimate digs.

Matt listened as though dazed, emerging an hour later into the activity surrounding the *zócalo* as though locked inside some spell that Billie had cast over him. Had she hoped to enlist him, to use him somehow? And still, what was it she had died for?

The plaza seemed unchanged from two nights ago; the *Calle Central* held the same mix of strollers and street boys; *Muñecas a Medianoche* was still showing at the Cine Twilite, and Natalie was at her desk.

"She called," Natalie announced in an exhausted voice as Matt came through the door.

# Rachel's Arrival

The murders made the Monday morning edition of the local and capital newspapers. A front-page article in *El Diario* proclaimed SMUGGLERS FOUND MURDERED IN CHIAPAS. Matt read it aloud from the passenger seat of the Range Rover on his way to the Villahermosa airport. Ángel had the wheel.

Rachel's flight from New York via Mexico City was scheduled to arrive at two P.M. She had asked Matt to meet her at the airport.

According to the article, the Echevarría police had made the gruesome discovery. There was no mention of Matt or of Puma Tours, but Lieutenant Escobar was quoted as saying that his investigation had already turned up several important leads. The story painted a lurid picture of deception and death along the Usumacinta River and used the murders as a springboard for a blanket condemnation of the border situation. Profiteers were operating with impunity—running guns, drugs, and antiquities—and corruption was rampant, murder an everyday affair. Moreover, the refugee camps were viewed by some as an invitation for an incursion by Guatemalan forces. Mexico was practically encouraging an international incident.

The article went on to lambaste the practices of Pemex, the unchecked and criminal deforestation of the

95

*selva* by land barons and settlers, and the CFE's proposals to dam the Usumacinta, which would not only imperil several Mayan sites but flood countless hectares of virgin forest.

The paper was harshly critical of President Lopez Portillo, who had recently called for a forty percent devaluation of the peso in the face of the country's unchecked slide into inflation and unemployment. The lucrative petrodollars days were over. The articles, however, concerned themselves less with economics than with revolution. Portillo wanted Reagan and Mitterand out of Central American affairs, especially with regard to contra aid. But the press was accusing him of waffling on his promise to take a personal hand in matters related to arms smuggling.

"The murders of the North American smugglers," Matt read, "hint at what lurks around the bend for the Usumacinta River and the Lacandon *selva*. Unless the federal government acts soon, the area will be awash in the blood of settlers and visitors alike, and Mexico will find itself culpable and hopelessly dishonored."

Ángel whistled softly.

Matt turned his attention to related articles about smuggling and the growing market in antiquities. Arms dealers were smuggling Belgian-made weapons into Mexico through Cozumel and flying antiquities out of country from hidden airstrips in the scrub-forested lowlands of Quintana Roo. Britten-Normans and Twin Otters would unload their precious cargoes in south Florida or the Caribbean, and from there the looted objects would be moved along well-established drug routes into the hands of black market scammers or wealthy collectors.

The UNESCO Convention of 1970 had tried to institute some control over the illicit import, export, and transfer of cultural property, but few countries had ratified the agreement. America's own Association of Dealers in Ancient, Oriental, and Primitive Art had in fact continued to lobby against the passage of any such import laws. Consequently, according to some reports, as many as a thousand pieces of illegally obtained pre-Columbian objects were reaching the international art market monthly. But in spite of easy availability, prices had skyrocketed. The present situation was in some ways analogous to what had occurred a century earlier in the Egyptian art market, when new insights into the Nile cultures had kindled a collecting craze and looters had learned that a painted pot could be worth more than a bracelet of gold. Now the Maya were in the spotlight, and collectors in the States and western Europe were ravenous.

But people were entering the market for purposes of clear profit as often as they were for the thrill of collecting. Tax deductions based on the donation to museums of even illegally obtained, unprovenanced objects were still allowed in the States, a fact that in itself had influenced market prices and made inflated appraisal a commonplace practice. Arms dealers would frequently retain items for use in international deals, where certain choice pieces were as good as gold in securing credit.

Matt was aware that the market was moving away from monumental art and stone—which was often difficult to authenticate—to more easily transportable items. But this hadn't always been the case. Looters, called *haucheros*, *estileros*, or *moneros*—*huecheros* in El Petén, "tunnelers"—had been known to go after glyph panels, statuary, and stelae as well. Everyone had heard about the carved pedestal base that almost left Puerto Barrios disguised as the floor of a jaguar cage, or the eight- by thirty-foot stucco panel that had been moved out of the Yucatán stone by stone, some believed with the help of Mexico's Institute of Anthropology.

But small pieces dominated the trade now. Ear flares, pendants, and onyx beads; spouted bowls, polychrome vases, and tripod plates; funerary urns, eccentric flints, fushite masks, and animal-bone umbrella handles; engraved antlers, ceramic rattles and ocarinas, abalone and oyster shell necklaces; obsidian-bladed knives, spondylus-shell spindle whorls . . . the market was wide-open. These were relatively easy to move—posing little problem at customs, where agents trained to spot the real goods were hard to come by—and just as easy to place.

Fakes, too, were in the news.

Ángel said, "Sometimes you can apply fresh paint to an authentic monochrome vessel. You can still find the soils and ores the ancients used for their colors. Manganese for black, iron oxides for red.''

There was an attapulgite clay from Agua Azul that his father used to achieve the famous Mayan blue, and another from the Usumacinta he used for yellow. Pressure cracks and root traces on new pieces could be simulated by burying the items for a year or so. And caches of pre-Columbian paper were available for faking texts or codices.

But those were harmless practices compared with the depredations going on in the field. Archeologists would attempt to keep their finds secret or bury newfound stelae, but word frequently leaked out, and statues or carvings would sometimes end up on the black market even before they had been cataloged. Temples would be trenched, bas-reliefs would be defaced by carborundum-tipped blades, tombs would be opened and plundered. In an effort to ''make the gunfighter the sheriff,'' Guatemala had been known to offer a permanent position of *vigilante*—guardian—to a *chiclero* or campesino who reported a new site. But there was no way to see to it that each and every site had police or military protection against looters. Archeologists and *guardianos* had lost their lives by entering remote sites unannounced, and then the guerrillas had gotten into the action, actually *filling* orders, if the Rescate agents could be believed.

If Ortiz was likewise correct in his assumption that Billie and Neil had been carrying something, how much, then, Matt wondered, had their deaths added to the value of the prize?

He felt that his trust had been betrayed. But that had less to do with the emotional politics of the situation than with the disservice Billie's misguided efforts were doing to the archeological world. Even when smuggled items were recovered, it was a nearly impossible task to return them to historical context, and while their artistic value was not necessarily diminished, their worth to the scientific community was compromised.

Matt had spent the previous evening at a side table in Xibalba wondering how Billie would have explained it, and he was hoping that Rachel would be able to supply him with some answers.

He and Ángel had left Palenque at the last possible minute, anticipating that the flight would be delayed. The arrivals monitors confirmed that, so they cruised by the American consulate to pick up Matt's new passport before heading for the airport's oppressively hot waiting area. There they managed to find two plastic seats against the rear wall, which afforded them a view of the arrival gates and the shimmering runway beyond. The flight from Mérida had just deplaned, and the room was crowded and chaotic, filled with American voices grumbling about the heat, the delays, and the in-flight service. Matt was watching two gangly oilmen push their way through the room, when he spotted one of the Palenque's top guides moving against the traffic in the direction of the Mérida gate.

"Humberto is here," Ángel pointed out, motioning with his chin.

"I see him," Matt said.

Humberto Obregone was Ángel's uncle on his mother's side, a short but powerful-looking man with swarthy good looks and an easygoing charm, second only to Emilio Cortes in his knowledge of the ruins and local lore. Matt thought he looked particularly spiffed up, and in a moment he saw the reason for it. The man Humberto had come to greet was wearing enough jewelry to qualify as excess baggage. He had to be midfifties at least, close to five-ten, deeply tanned, and—except for a basketball-size potbelly—of medium build, with long hair too black to be natural tied in a ponytail so high up on his head that it might as well have been a topknot. His hairline was high, accentuating the slope of his brow, and his full-lipped mouth was framed by a Fu Manchu mustache and goatee. The jewelry was gold—rings, bracelets, chains, hair band, and earrings—offsetting a white cotton outfit of drawstring trousers and sleeveless shirt. He wore huaraches, one of which had a built-up sole, and carried a kind of telescoping walking stick.

"Check it out," Matt told Ángel, elbowing him lightly.

"Rico," Ángel said with an appreciative trill. "He looks like a Mayan lord, doesn't he?"

Humberto was giving orders to the man's two servants, directing them off to the baggage claim, Matt guessed.

Both were young boys, one Hispanic, the other southeast Asian, Thai, perhaps. Matt also noticed a fourth member of the party, a tall and professorial-looking sandy-haired man whose accent readily identified him as American. Some pleasantries were exchanged, then the American said something in confidence to the ponytailed noble, and the two traded grave looks before following Humberto out of the area. The man's left leg moved as though it were spring-loaded, jerking up at the knee, toes thrown downward with each step.

As Matt's gaze lingered on them, a woman's voice on the PA announced the arrival of the flight from Mexico City.

Matt had little trouble recognizing Rachel Riordan, she bore such a striking resemblance to Billie. The hair was all wrong of course—cut boyishly short and somewhat darker than Billie's auburn mane—but everything else was so perfectly matched, he began to wonder if he wasn't about to meet Billie's twin. She was dressed in a plain but expensive-looking skirt and a short-sleeved round-necked sweater, light-colored tights, and running shoes. She had a squarish leather bag over her shoulder and a down jacket in one arm, her hand clutching a cloth purse and a sun hat that looked either brand-new or unused.

"Ms. Riordan," Matt called out as she hurried in out of the sun.

Rachel wore a flustered and confused look when she turned around to face him. "Mr. Terry?" she asked uncertainly.

Matt nodded and began to weave his way through the crowd as Rachel did the same. He introduced himself, extending his hand, and she gave him her jacket. Matt hefted it, checking a grin. "Still cold in New York, I guess."

Rachel stared at him a moment, then quickly reached for the jacket, apologizing and offering him her hand. "Rachel," she said. "Rachel Riordan."

She was a few years older and a bit shorter than Billie, not heavier but more curvaceous, with more fullness to her breasts and hips. The cut of her hair imparted an almost severe quality to her face but had fortunately left the handsomeness of her features intact, her deep-blue eyes especially, which were accentuated by a meticulous application of liner and colors. Her mouth, too, was lined and glossed, and her cheeks bore a color that had little to do with the Mexican sun. She wore a thick gold band on the ring finger of her right hand, a turquoise bracelet on her left wrist, and a pair of brightly enameled hoop earrings.

Matt said, "Ángel will get your bags."

"There's just one other."

"Was it a good flight?"

"No, it wasn't," she said, moving off.

At the Rover, opening the back door for her, he asked if she had heard from the embassy. Rachel said she hadn't. Matt was certain that Escobar had learned about her by then. He guessed that somewhere along the way Rachel and a telegram from Mexico City must have crossed paths.

"So what made you decide to trust me?"

Rachel waited for him to throw her bag in the back. "To be honest, I did some checking into Puma Tours." She almost smiled. "I'm sorry for the way I sounded on the phone."

"Nothing to be sorry about," he told her, climbing into the front.

Ángel got the Rover back onto the *carretera*. The day had grown more uncomfortable, the sun a white disk behind threatening clouds piled up around El Chichón. Rachel stared absently out the window. To the southeast, a freak rainstorm was moving across the flatlands.

"How long a drive is it?"

Matt said, "About ninety minutes."

She was tugging at the neck of her sweater and fanning herself with her hand. "I should have changed into something more practical."

"We can stop."

"No, I'll be all right."

"You did say you'd been here before."

"I arrived by plane from San Cristóbal. I was on a buying trip in the highlands."

Matt didn't like the sound of it, but he persevered. "What do you do in New York?"

"I have an imports boutique. Hand-knits, pottery, *molas*, *ruanas* . . . mostly South American crafts. Nothing you're unfamiliar with, I'm sure."

"You travel a lot, then."

She shrugged. "Not as much as I used to. I go to trade shows now and deal with buyers."

Matt turned to gaze at the highway, wondering how long the dance would go on. "Did you and Lauren see a lot of each other?" he asked gravely. "She told me she lived in Tahoe."

Rachel's eyes were filled with tears when she looked up.

"I'm sorry," he started to say. "Maybe you don't want—"

"No," she told him, digging into her pocket for a package of tissues. "Sometimes I can almost forget, then the slightest thing—a word or a flash of memory— and . . ."

Matt and Ángel swapped grim looks in the front seat. Rachel continued to weep. She blew her nose softly and took several deep and shuddering breaths. Matt felt the coil return to his chest, a tightness behind his heart.

She said, "Our parents died a few years ago. Laurie and I were just beginning to grow close again. We had some difficult times."

Matt worked his jaw muscles. "If there's anything I can do—"

"Have the police learned anything?" she asked suddenly.

"Not yet. It's just speculation at this point."

"What about these things you wanted to discuss with me, Mr. Terry? What is all this about?"

"Matt," he told her. "I thought it could wait until you got settled."

"I'm ready to hear it now."

"All right," he said, exhaling. "I guess I should start by telling you that I met Lauren and Michael as Billie and Neil Westphal. I didn't learn their real names until . . . later on. That's when I found your address."

Rachel fell silent. She took out a pack of cigarettes and asked if they would mind if she smoked. Matt reached back to crack open one of the rear windows, and

Rachel blew the smoke toward the opening. He watched her, wondering if she was half the actress Billie had been.

"I knew about the false identities," she said at last. "It's funny. I was the one who was smoking grass in 1966. Joining SDS, taking over student unions, protesting the war, and reading Hesse."

She drew on the cigarette and laughed in a self-mocking way. "Class of sixty-five. But Laurie was the free spirit. She traveled all over the world. Spent six months picking olives in Greece, did she tell you that? Bought jewelry in Afghanistan and sold it in Boston, lived on a commune in Oregon. She could fly and sail, handle a horse or a motorcycle. She lived with a Vietnam veteran who taught her how to shoot and field-strip a machine gun."

Matt asked about Neil.

"They met in Goa and began traveling together. Made a few trips to Peru, started importing weavings and sweaters to the States. Then a few years ago they came back with cocaine and got busted in L.A. Michael was terrified by the very thought of prison. Somehow he got them new birth certificates and passports—he was always good at that sort of thing—and they left while they were out on bail. They didn't have much money left, but they were enterprising, and within a year or so everything was back to normal. Except now they were Billie and Neil Westphal."

Rachel crushed out the cigarette in the armrest ashtray. Tears had drawn two black lines down her right cheek. Matt saw that Ángel was watching her in the rearview mirror. He thought about what Rachel had said and decided it was time she was brought up to date. "I think you'd better have a look at this," he said, showing her the newspaper. "Can you read Spanish?"

She nodded.

A minute later she was crying again. She stopped once to say, "How could you let this happen?"

The rainstorm moved through, fat drops spattering the Rover's windshield, teasing the parched land and passing on without a look behind like a proper Latin señorita. Ángel swung south at the Palenque *cruce* and accelerated on the straightaway to overtake a cattle truck.

"I don't think the finality of Laurie's death hit me until just now," Rachel said with a hint of apology. She dabbed at her eyes. "But how can the police be certain they were involved in anything like this, even if they had a record of smuggling? Couldn't it have been thieves?"

Matt pulled Billie's money from his pants pocket. He tapped the wad against his palm, then handed it back to Rachel. "I don't know why they were killed, Rachel. But I found this among their gear."

Baffled, Rachel leafed through the bills. "Is this what you meant when you said you had something for me?"

Matt said, "There's just over eight thousand dollars."

He spent the remainder of the ride telling her about what Escobar and the Interpol agents had pieced together. And while it was true that there was no hard evidence one way or another to support their suspicions, the investigators were convinced that Billie and Neil's deaths had not been simple homicides but planned executions.

By the time the Rover reached Palenque, Rachel looked lost and overwhelmed. Matt explained that he had booked a room for her in a hotel in town. He cautioned her to wait a day before going to police headquarters and suggested she tell Escobar that a friend of Billie's living in Mexico City had alerted her to the newspaper articles. It was likely that the embassy was trying to contact her now, but Matt encouraged her to follow his advice. She said she understood and agreed to it.

"You're registered as a guest of Puma Tours," Matt said when they reached the Hotel La Cañada. He passed Rachel her hat and bags. "Listen, if you'd like to get together this evening . . ."

Rachel offered him a weak smile and a no thanks. "You've been very kind. But I think I'm better off going it alone from here on in. I want to thank you for everything you've done."

Matt tried to hold her gaze. "I appreciate that, but I didn't do it for thanks."

"Oh, oh, of course," Rachel said, peeling several bills from the wad. "Please take this. I don't know if it's enough to—"

"No," he said, more harshly than he meant to. "You

don't understand.'' Rachel made an embarrassed sound. ''I did it for Billie—for Lauren,'' he went on. ''We became friends.''

Rachel gave him a surprised look. They shook hands, and she walked off toward the hotel office.

# ⬤⟫⟫ 10 ⟪⟪⬤

# Lord of the Mat

The following afternoon, Jake Welles phoned from Denver to say that the international *Herald Tribune* had picked up the story from the Mexico City papers. Matt took the call in the office. Jake was glad that neither Matt nor Puma's name had appeared in connection with the murders. He wasn't surprised to hear that Rachel was in Palenque, he told Matt, because she had spoken to him from New York about Matt's background with the company. Matt filled in him on what the Rescate agents had had to say and what he and Rachel had discussed on the ride in from Villahermosa.

"So you're through with this thing now," Jake said hopefully.

Matt swiveled his chair to face the relief map on the wall behind his desk. He was aware that Natalie and Ángel were staring at his back. "There are still loose ends, Jake."

Jake made an exasperated sound at the other end of the line. "There are always going to be loose ends, amigo. It sounds to me like they were murdered because of some dirty deal."

"I don't think they played dirty, Jake. That's the point." He pivoted around in the chair to throw his partners a disapproving look, and they reluctantly returned to their work.

"So someone played dirty with them. It comes out the same, doesn't it?"

Matt snorted. "Yeah, I suppose it comes out the same in the long run. But I'd rest easier with it if I knew what happened. For starters I'd like to know what they were carrying."

Jake said, "Maybe it was just the money."

"That's a long shot."

Jake was quiet. "How's Escobar treating you?"

"He knows as much as I do now."

"Except about the telex."

"That's the one thing."

"And you still think Rachel knows something?"

Matt didn't for a moment doubt that her grief had been sincere, but he had been fooled once and was wary of taking anything at face value. "She told me she has an import store in New York. Any way we can check on that?"

"I could try," Jake said uncertainly. "But I wish you'd stick to the tour on this one."

"It's the sucker's tour, Jake. I'm not buying it."

Jake let it go and changed the topic to the Cortes brothers and their lectures. They talked business for a few minutes before Matt got back to the paperwork stacked up on his desk. Rachel was still on his mind, but he managed to lose her momentarily in the intricacies of plotting room assignments for the upcoming Yucatán group. Shortly he became so engrossed in the task that he barely stirred when the front doorbell sounded. It took Natalie's voice to bring him around.

He looked up vacantly at the sound of his name. The long-haired eccentric he had seen at the airport was standing by the desk.

"Matt," Natalie repeated, making eye motions toward the man.

"Uh, have a seat," Matt said, getting up and sliding a chair over from Natalie's desk. The man's Asian servant had positioned himself by the door in a cross-armed and vaguely vigilant stance. Ángel was regarding the youth askance from his own desk.

"Allow me to introduce myself," the man said in affected American, proffering a card.

Matt took it in hand, running his thumb over the embossed letters. It read JULES KUL. Phone numbers were given for New York City, Los Angeles, and Rome, but no hint at what Kul was selling. The upper left-hand corner of the card bore a Masonic symbol similar to the one on Escobar and Emilio's rings. Matt gave a quick look at Kul's hands, but there were too many rings to take in at a glance.

"And you are?" Kul was saying.

"Matt Terry."

Kul gave Matt's hand a light touch. He was seated in the chair by then, with his legs apart and his walking stick collapsed to the length of a short cane, dressed much as he had been at the airport. Matt thought that one or two of Kul's beard hairs might measure close to ten inches in length. Otherwise, there was nothing about the man's face that appeared natural from his slightly crossed almond-shaped eyes to the orange cast of his skin. His lips were enormously full above a receding chin, and his left nostril was perforated in three places. The more Matt stared at him, the more Kul came to resemble a kind of demonic Uncle Sam.

"Chocolate, Mr. Terry?" Kul produced a small jade box filled with what looked like bittersweet chips. Matt declined, but Natalie helped herself to one.

"Delicious," she said, smiling at Kul.

Kul said, "Chiclet, then?"

A Mayan lord indeed, Matt told himself, shaking his head and forcing a smile. "What can we do for you, Mr. Kul?" He was leaning back in the chair now, casual but attentive.

Kul extended his stick and rapped it twice against the floor. "Well, I'm interested in a trip, Mr. Terry—Matt, if I may?"

"Shoot."

"But not just one of the run-of-the-mill tourist jaunts," Kul cautioned. "Something special, something that will allow me to experience the wonders of Mayan Mexico to the fullest. And it's my understanding that you are the person to talk to about such things."

Matt smiled pleasantly, ignoring the exaggerated

raised-eyebrow look Natalie was directing his way. "How did you hear about Puma?"

Kul shrugged, momentarily disturbing his pectoral arrangement of gold necklaces and chains. "From Humberto Obregone for one. But don't look so shocked, Matt. Your name is well known in Chiapas."

Matt laughed. "A statue in the *zócalo*, that's all I'm after." Kul returned a patient smile. "Well, what sort of special trip did you have in mind?"

"I have a keen interest in the Maya, as I'm sure you can discern. The cities they left us, the culture their stelae and carvings hint at, the science contained in their calendric and astrological writings, the enigma of their origins and disappearance." Kul was serious all at once, seemingly transfixed by his own musings. "I want to soak up some of the mystery that lingers in these ghost-ridden forests and verdant mountains. Can you sense what I'm after?"

"I think I understand what you mean," Matt said uncertainly. "But do you have somewhere specific in mind?"

"Specific . . ." Kul said, as though mulling it over. "Bonampak and Toniná certainly. And the Lacandon *caribales* at Lake Mensabok and Nahá. Then on to the Usumacinta perhaps. Altar, Yaxchilan, and Piedras Negras." Kul's eyes sparkled. "What a wonderful river, is it not? So many unanswered questions, so many riddles to solve!"

Matt brought his fingertips together and gazed at Kul through narrowed eyes, but the man's face was unreadable.

"Problem, Matt?"

Matt said, "Give me a little more to go on," and Kul did, enumerating the sites he was interested in visiting.

Matt dismissed his misgivings. Kul was well informed about the area, but the trip he was asking for would be a logistical nightmare. They would need the Rover, horses, mules, the motorized raft, a cook staff—he spelled it out for Kul and received the same tolerant smile.

"I am willing, of course, to pay handsomely for a guide who is willing to go out of his way."

Matt exchanged brief looks with Natalie, who was pretending to busy herself with work. He put a few of Puma's color brochures together and slid them across the desk. "I'll work up a few different options," he said. "But in the meantime, why don't you take a look through these?"

Kul accepted the brochures and stood up, telescoping the walking stick as he did so. "Fine, fine. I'm staying at the El Templo. Suppose you come by tomorrow—for lunch, say?"

Matt said he thought he could have something ready by then.

"One more thing," Kul said from the door. "Kim will be accompanying us, along with one of my other servants."

Matt and the Asian youth eyeballed each other. "I'll figure on three, then."

"Why not just figure on half a dozen," Kul told him, as though it were a dinner invitation. "I may decide to invite some friends along."

As soon as Kul was out of earshot, Natalie and Ángel burst out laughing. "What's so funny?" Matt said, laughing along with them.

Natalie had one hand to her mouth. "Just the thought of the two of you out in the woods together for ten days."

Matt snorted. "Go ahead, laugh all you want. I'm bringing you along as a cook."

That evening Matt headed for Xibalba, leaving Natalie to close the office.

The club was on the north side of the barranca, a ten-minute walk from Matt's back door along an overgrown trail through the scrub. He usually arrived around nine o'clock, downed a *cucaracha* at the bar, nursed a few beers through two sets of the house band's Vera Cruz–style salsa, and was back at home by midnight. The club was a potpourri of tropical woods, rambling but well kept, with a mahogany bar and two dozen indoor and outdoor round tables, each of which was candle-lit and could accommodate four at a pinch. Specimens of stuffed forest fauna hung from the rafters and peeked from behind potted plants: monkeys, peccaries, brockets, jaguars, possum, agouti, bushmasters. The food was basic Mexican fast-food fare (although the guacamole was renowned), and the music cooked. The band—keyboard, harp, string bass, sax, flute, and two percussionists—played *cumbia* and *danzon* until two in the morning.

He spent awhile at the bar talking to Xibalba's owner, Coco Sinagua, then moved to a rear table that overlooked the ravine. An American movie company was in town shooting an adventure film about cocaine cowboys, and quite a few of the stunt people and crew were present, loud and wild. Months before, Matt had furnished the location scouts with a number of leads, and both Natalie and her friend Kit had landed small parts. The day's shoot had been out at the grass strip, near the husk of a downed DC-3. It was the most excitement Palenque had seen since a truck loaded down with Tecate had overturned on the *Calle Central* a while back.

Huddled around two tables off to Matt's right were a group of Canadian freaks in jeans and bandannas from the Mayabel campground; near them were three silver-haired women he had noticed among Emilio's group at the ruins. Elsewhere, two well-built travelers were trying to score with the club's frazzled waitresses, Marisol and Elena. Matt finally succeeded in getting the latter's attention and ordered a Tres Equis.

"*Bien fría,*" he added.

"*Nalga de muerte,*" she shouted back, giving him the seductive look she was famous for. It literally meant "the cheeks of death," but translated as "cold as a witch's tit."

Matt was munching on tapas and waiting for the beer to arrive when Rachel Riordan stepped onto the tiled patio from the steps that led down to the barranca trail. She was wearing sandals, a sleeveless T-shirt, and a pair of tight-fitting khaki shorts with large button-down front pockets. Dismayed, Matt took a long look around the room, searching for plainclothesmen. From the way Rachel was scanning the tables, he guessed that she might be looking for him, but he didn't make a move to signal her until she spotted him.

"Hi," she said hesitantly, giving a worried look at the large-toothed animal heads overhanging Matt's table.

Matt got to his feet, talking through clenched teeth. "We just met. I had no idea you were in town. You stopped by the office, and they told me where you could find me."

"It's true."

"Then play it that way. Shake hands with me and sit down."

Rachel did so, apologizing and slipping into the role. "Your secretary told me I would probably find you here."

"My partner," he corrected her. "You want something to drink?"

She shook her head, listening to the sax player's solo for a moment before turning around.

"So how did it go?" Matt asked her, still eyeing the room for *federales*. "I wanted to stop by, but I wasn't sure you'd be ready for company yet."

"It was horrible," she told him, her eyes moist. "I had to see them. . . ."

Matt stopped short of reaching out for her nervous hands. Elena appeared with Matt's beer, and he asked her to return on the double with a brandy.

"*Ratito,*" she said, darting a suspicious glance at Rachel before hurrying off.

Rachel had her head lowered; Matt saw a tear fall on the shellacked tabletop. "I went back to La Cañada and tried to reach Michael's family," she said after a moment. "He has a brother in La Jolla, but I couldn't get a line to reach the States."

"We'll try tomorrow morning from the office. I'll telex Denver and see if they can help."

Elena brought the drink; Rachel sipped at it and pushed it aside. Matt added lime to his beer, watching her. It was plain that Escobar had filled her head with all sorts of doubts, and perhaps he had asked her to see what she could learn on her own.

"What did the lieutenant have to say?"

"Not much more than you told me yesterday," she said, fumbling with a cigarette. She regarded Matt through the smoke. "They suggested that you were keeping something from them. In fact, I think that Lieutenant . . ."

"Escobar."

Rachel nodded. "Escobar wanted me to spy on you."

Matt allowed himself to relax somewhat. "I did know something—I knew about you and the money."

"Yes, but . . . why didn't you tell me about the boatmen, Matt?"

Oh, yeah, Escobar had talked to her all right. Matt said, "What do they have to do with this?"

She averted her eyes and put out the cigarette. "Well, it's just that I thought you were alone."

"I told you we came downriver from Guatemala," he reminded her. "There were five of us altogether. What are you getting at?"

"Escobar let me go through Laurie's effects. I know you said that everything of value had been stolen, but I was wondering if everything you found had been brought to Palenque. I mean, I know how the police can be down here, and I thought they may have kept some of her things for themselves."

Matt caught a glimpse of Billie in Rachel's face and felt the hairs on the back of his neck stand up. Rachel was feeling her way into something. He computed the odds and decided to hold to his course. "Well, that's possible. What was it you were looking for exactly?"

"An heirloom," Rachel said, looking over at the stage. "It would mean a lot to me if I could get it back. I'm not sure how to go about dealing with the police. And if they don't have it, I thought perhaps the boatmen might have found it."

Matt said, "An heirloom. Jewelry, what?"

"I'm sure they'd know it if they found it. And I'd see to it they were well rewarded if the piece could be brought here."

Matt rubbed his chin. "I could ask them. . . . Uh, how much did you say it would mean to you? Just so I can motivate them," he was quick to add.

"Ten thousand dollars," Rachel said evenly.

Matt walked her back to La Cañada, then set off for home along the same trail he had taken to Xibalba. Rachel didn't bring up the "heirloom" again, and Matt didn't ask. It was understood that she had laid at least some of her cards on the table and that the next move was his. Instead they discussed the possibility of having Billie's body cremated in Mexico—years ago Rachel had promised her sister as much. Matt told her he wasn't sure about the legalities involved and said that he would consult Cosmo Bustamonte the following morning. Chances were that the lawyer would be willing to handle everything.

It was a hot, moonlit night that had brought out the worst in Palenque's canines. Rachel had taken Matt's arm during the short walk, and at the door to her room she had kissed his cheek and thanked him for all his help.

Preoccupied, Matt was negotiating the barranca trails by rote. If the question of Rachel's involvement had been answered, there was new cause to wonder why she had assumed that the heirloom—surely an antiquity of considerable value—had not simply fallen into the hands of the killers. Matt tried to think it through a dozen different ways but came up blank each time. It was ridiculous to attempt to piece things together as long as Rachel considered him one of the enemy. He was trying to see a way through that when he first sensed that someone was following him.

Matt was careful not to break stride. He had been moving along at a good clip, shuffling noisily through the undergrowth at the side of the trail, announcing himself to anything living along the route. Recently a fer-de-lance had been spotted in the ravine. Matt had had run-ins with that deadly variety of snake in the Petén, where it was known as the *barba amarilla*. There wasn't much chance of encountering the thing at night, but he had gotten into the habit of loud travel just in case. Some people were walking around with crushed garlic rolled up in the cuffs of their pants.

Matt wasn't sure just how he had managed to hear the stalker, but all his indicators were suddenly registering in the red. He ruled out thieves, knowing that the local types didn't work that way; they were second story men, con artists, and pickpockets. One of Escobar's men, he ventured, assigned to follow Rachel.

Emerging from the barranca, Matt slowed his pace,

sidestepped into an intersecting footpath, and moved quickly into the thickets that bordered the main trail. A moment later a tall, broad-shouldered man rushed into view, his suddenly confused gestures discernible in the moonlight. The man turned and doubled back, taking long strides toward the intersecting trail. Matt kept to the thickets, reentering the main trail when he was certain he had lost him.

Maybe there were peaceful solutions left after all, he told himself as he walked.

As he approached the stairway to his apartment, he stepped off the trail to see if Escobar had planted anyone outside. Instead he glimpsed a flash of light behind one of the windows. Someone was inside. He saw the beam a second time and ducked beneath the stairway to listen. The intruder would have to leave through the rear door at the top of the stairs; there were no windows that opened at ground level, and even if the thief had made it into the office, the security grate at the front door would prevent an exit to the street. Matt considered waiting it out, but the sound of things being overturned and pawed through began to work on his resolve. Ultimately he climbed the staircase, avoiding the treads near the top—which had a tendency to creak in the dry season—and two minutes later he was standing poised at the door, running his fingers along the damage the intruder's pry bar had inflicted on the jamb.

The intruder was rummaging around in the loft; Matt heard the man curse as his head possibly connected with one of the ceiling's exposed rafters. He was tempted to go in but decided to hold off until the man took to the ladder, when his back would be turned to the door.

Matt waited another minute, steeling himself, then shot through the door in a crouch and tackled the man from behind. The two of them hit the wall together and went down, the flashlight striking the floor and failing. The intruder was Matt's size, but the unexpected attack had knocked the wind out of him. Matt had him around the chest and flung him hard against one of the loft supports; the man dropped to the floor with a loud grunt but instantly came up swinging. Matt leaned back and heard the whoosh of a fist near his face. He threw a left straight out and caught flesh and bone, then sent his right up and into his opponent's chest. The man doubled over but caught Matt's legs on the way down; Matt stumbled and rolled, scissoring out of the hold, and managed to plant a foot solidly into the guy's face.

The man spit out a curse in English, backing himself along the floor while he lashed out with his feet. Matt didn't expect him to get up, but he did, windmilling his arms as he advanced. Matt twisted away from grazing blows, landing a crippling kick behind the man's right knee as he whirled past. Confident, he moved in, only to sense the guy execute a kind of squat-thrust rear kick. Matt's raised forearms absorbed the brunt of it, but the force of the kick propelled him back against the wall, allowing ample time for the man to return to his feet.

An enamel pot that had been sitting atop the stove smashed into the wall next to Matt's head, followed by two glasses and a flock of airborne utensils. Matt made a grab for a wooden chair and shielded himself, getting up in a lion tamer's stance. But all at once the man was breaking for the door. Matt threw the chair aside and lunged, just managing to grasp a handful of shirt. The man turned around to rain a few hammer blows on Matt's back while he continued to struggle forward, closing on the door. Matt worked his right hand around to the man's crotch and squeezed. The guy let out a shocked wail and buckled over, collapsing over the threshold.

Matt pushed himself up from the floor and was coming in openhanded when something cracked him violently on the right side of the head. He staggered away, snaking splay-finger jabs into the air with his right hand, but a second blow found its way to his rib cage and dropped him. A starfield erupted behind his eyes as a third punch tagged his jaw. Before he passed out, he had an indistinct vision of the first man getting up and kicking him squarely in the groin.

Matt was unconscious only for a few seconds, but when he came to the men were gone. He remained on the floor for several minutes, wondering if he was going to die or simply vomit. Pleased to have escaped either eventuality, he began a slow crawl toward the couch, stopping once to feed *Magical Mystery Tour* into the cassette player, and fell out somewhere in the middle of "Strawberry Fields Forever."

# ⬥⟫⟫⟫ 11 ⟪⟪⟪⬥

# Active Listening

"**H**ow's it going to look when the people at *Good Housekeeping* find out about this?" Natalie asked, unlocking the double-keyed dead bolt and coming through the office door to Matt's apartment.

It was close to ten o'clock the following morning, and Matt had restored some order to the place, but the contents of the footlocker were still strewn about—clothes and camping gear—giving the room a kind of post orgiastic look. Matt frowned at her from the edge of the bed, and her smile collapsed. She came over to him, took his chin in her hand, and gave his head a gentle turn right and left. Spotting the bruise under his right ear, she sucked in her breath and winced.

"A midnight surprise," Matt said by way of explanation.

"But who—"

"I didn't get any names."

"Matt, you don't think—"

"I don't know what to think." He told her about his conversation with Rachel, about the missing heirloom. "The lieutenant's no idiot. Maybe he read what was on her mind when she was looking through Billie's effects and figured I might have stashed something after all. Rescate's more interested in what they were carrying than who killed them. Escobar's feeling the pressure to come

118

up with something.'' No sooner did Matt voice the name than he spotted a blue-gray police cap bobbing into view outside the veranda windows. With little in the way of forewarning, he reached up and pulled Natalie down beside him on the mattress.

''Matt!'' she protested, shocked but laughing.

''We've been here all night,'' he told her in a whispered rush. ''We've been having a wild time.''

The confusion left her face as the police announced themselves with three official-sounding raps against the door. ''Well, as long as this is business, I don't think Kit will mind.''

They rolled over on the bed, laughing it up, then looked up in feigned indignation at the sound of Escobar's voice. A uniformed cop accompanied the lieutenant and the two Rescate agents.

Matt said, ''Can't you guys give a man a break?'' while Natalie tugged at her skirt and pushed her hair into shape.

Escobar glanced around at the mess and uttered a short laugh. *''Huevon!* You should try keeping your clothes in a closet like everyone else.''

''Yeah, well, we got a little carried away.''

Natalie eased off the bed and sauntered past the men in the direction of the office. ''See you later, lover,'' she said from the door.

*''Cabrón,''* Agent Ortiz muttered, throwing Matt an appreciative look.

Matt stood up, casually draping a towel around his neck, and offered beer. Everyone declined. Escobar dismissed the cop and straddled the chair Matt had used to defend himself the night before. Ortiz and Suentes remained standing, giving the room the once-over.

''So what brings you by, Lieutenant?''

Suentes produced a folded printout sheet from the pocket of his jacket and handed it to Matt. ''Read it.''

Matt perused what was meant to be a one-page encapsulation of the past fifteen years of his life. He flipped the page over and shrugged, disappointed to find that the computer hadn't gone on to cover future milestones as well. The compilers had done a reasonable job, although several important moments had been over-looked.

Suentes said, "Why didn't you mention any of this?"

Matt set the paper aside, broke an egg into his beer, and downed the mixture. "I was saving it for my obituary."

"It may yet be that," Escobar growled, snatching up the sheet. "Peace Corps," the lieutenant mumbled, running a forefinger down the page. "Here. In 1975 you joined an insurgent group operating in Colombia."

"Joined?!" Matt said, trying to read over Escobar's shoulders. "Is that what it says?"

The lieutenant peered at the print.

" 'Life gives you surprises,' " Matt quoted in Spanish, " 'surprises give you life.' I was kidnapped, guys. As in taken against my will. It was in Cauca department. Check with the U.S. embassy down there, they'll give it to you straight."

"The M-19 released you two years later—unharmed."

Matt thought about arguing the point but simply said, "They thought they'd snatched someone important because of my ties to the Peace Corps. There was some haggling over the terms, and of course we were on the go a lot. They lowered their expectations, and someone finally came through with the ransom money. The M-19 had no more use for me."

Ortiz said, "And they simply let you go."

Matt motioned to himself. "I'm here—at least I think I am. I'm telling you, check with Bogotá. The DEA debriefed me for over a week."

Suentes glowered at him. "What do you know of Raphael Aguilar's group?" He pointed to a black power poster on the wall that had been there when Matt moved in. "Are you a sympathizer—a member of the Marxist Front?"

"What was your involvement with DeLuca and Riordan?" Ortiz demanded. "Were they CIA agents?"

"How are the arms entering the Petén?"

Matt said, "Whoa, slow down. Someone must have

put something in your coffee, Lieutenant. You're not serious about this."

The lieutenant cleared his throat. "Why did you have to kill the North Americans? What did they know?"

Suentes said, "Who ordered you to kill them?"

Matt's grin vanished. "What the hell is this?"

"Alejandro Volan has been picked up," said Ortiz, "the rebel's liaison man. But he is receiving protection from unknown sources in President-elect Guevara's command."

Matt looked from Ortiz to Escobar. "What's this have to do with Billie and Neil?"

"We are asking ourselves the same question," Suentes said.

"Arrested and deported from Panama in 1979 on charges of drug trafficking," Escobar read on. Matt tried to explain, but Ortiz motioned for him to keep silent.

"Frequent visits to Peru, Bolivia, and Guatemala these past three years."

"That's business," Matt protested.

"Always 'business,' " Escobar said. "Perhaps it's Puma's business we should be investigating, no?"

"Do you have meetings with the Shining Path in Peru?" Ortiz wanted to know. "The Tupac Amaru? If we continue to dig, will we find that you have visited El Salvador and Nicaragua as well?"

"Was it antiquities, or was it something else?"

Matt went mute. None of the facts fit together, but Escobar was determined to make them work. Suddenly this was conspiracy on such a grand scale that Matt felt sorely tempted to confess to the charges. It was bigger then Billie and Neil, bigger than Billie and Rachel, capturing all of them in a web of some unimaginable size.

"The girl's sister's in town. Did you know this?"

Matt tried to read Escobar's eyes. He made an offhand gesture to the mess on the floor. "I know. And you know that I know."

The lieutenant grinned. "We think she knows something about this affair. You can help yourself by helping us. Find out what she is hiding. Then come and talk to me."

"I'll sleep on it," Matt said.

"You should do more than sleep on it," Escobar suggested from the door. "Next time, your visitors might not be as easily persuaded to leave."

Matt showered and changed. He took a moment to inspect the bruise on his jaw before attending to the damaged doorjamb and passing into the front office.

"You got two calls," Natalie told him, angry. "Emilio wants to talk to you, and Jules Kul wants to know if you're going to meet him for lunch."

Matt walked over to her desk and lifted her chin, mimicking the way she had examined his face earlier. Her look was anxious; he made a halfhearted attempt to allay her concerns and asked her to contact Cosmo Bustamonte on Rachel's behalf.

"What did you think of her?" Matt said.

"Gorgeous," Natalie told him.

"No, I don't mean that."

She made a noncommittal gesture. "We only spoke for a minute. I feel bad for her."

"And . . ."

Natalie smirked. "I said I feel bad for her. I'm not saying I trust her. What do you want me to tell Kul?" she said, businesslike again.

"Tell him I'll be there. The trip's going to be a pain in the ass, but I think we can make some real money out of it."

Natalie said, "I am *not* doing the cooking."

Matt leaned over to kiss her, but she pulled back. "You better watch your step, Matt. You're acting like some paperback detective."

"What do you think I should do?"

"Get out of it. Tell Escobar what you know, or what you think you know, and come back to work."

She allowed him to kiss her. "Not till I find them," he said. "Not till I know what happened out there."

He took the Rover. The movie crew had cordoned off an area near the Mayabel campground, where they were staging a scene. Matt recognized Natalie's Kit on horseback among the extras.

At the ruins he found Emilio and some of the guides

in the restaurant. A thick smell of sulfur hung in the air, and El Chichón was foremost on everyone's mind. Matt ordered an empanada and a coffee and sat down to read through the lecture notes Emilio Cortes had prepared for Jake's group. He was halfway through the pages when Humberto Obregone made an excited entrance and joined the table.

The head of the murdered man had been found.

Everyone was shocked to learn that the victim was a Lacandon Indian by the name of T'sup Kin, an albino, no less, who had left the Lacanjá *caribal* several years before and moved his family to the Pasión River. Matt knew Lacandons were living near Sayaxche but had never met them. No one could figure what the fair-haired Indian had been doing in Palenque. Humberto speculated that he had come into town to sell handicrafts.

"It's possible that his sudden reappearance rekindled an old blood feud," Emilio ventured.

"Perhaps the very one that took him from Lacanjá to begin with," Obregone said.

Matt waited for the mutterings to simmer down, then pushed his chair back and went over to greet Obregone. While they were shaking hands, Humberto motioned Matt to an empty table where they could talk in private.

"Did Señor Kul come in to see you?"

"He sure did," Matt said, thanking the guide for putting in the pitch. "I saw the two of you in Villahermosa, at the airport."

Obregone laughed. "He thinks he is a Mayan, Matt. Did he offer you chocolates?"

"And Chiclets. He travels with servants, huh?"

"Yes. The one boy, Kim, is Vietnamese, I think. The other one's name is Huatcho. He's from Chamula."

"There was someone else, kind of loose-limbed, blond hair. . . ."

"Dr. Chalker," Humberto said. "Niles Chalker. You know of his work?"

Matt repeated the name and shook his head. "Don't think so."

"An archeologist. He was working at Cuello and Naj Tunich."

"Oh, yeah, right. I've heard of him. So what about this Kul?"

"A Mayan in his past life," Humberto continued. "A ruler, like Pacal, *cierto*? Maybe Kul made his leg like that on purpose, just to be deformed." He chuckled, then wagged a finger at Matt. "But he is wealthy, Matt. Very, very rich and very, very influential. An architect of fine homes and skyscrapers. He designed the place President Portillo uses when he stays in Villahermosa."

"I've seen it." Matt was impressed.

"And his money has financed dozens of archeological digs in Mexico and Guatemala."

"That's good to hear."

"Yes and no." Obregone spoke as though weighing his words. "You see, he has a kind of *possessiveness* when it comes to the Maya."

Matt snorted, guessing what would come next. "A collector."

"Not just a collector. Some say he has the finest private collection in the world. You remember that *maricón* from United Fruit Company and all the things he had?"

"The one from Guatemala City?"

"That's the one. Well, Señor Kul bought out the man's entire collection in one transaction."

Matt exhaled a staccato sound. He recalled hearing that one piece of that collection—a hinged clamshell of jade and gold—was valued at close to $150,000 U.S. Matt explained about the trip Kul had requested.

Humberto said, "I took him on a similar one fifteen years ago. We rode mules from Nahá up to San Cristóbal. I had to sleep on my stomach for the next six months."

"And how'd Kul do?"

"Fine. But it wasn't sight-seeing that interested him. He was after antiquities." Humberto stroked his jaw. "I suppose that is the last thing you need right now."

"You heard?" Matt said after a moment.

"A terrible business." He gestured behind him. "And now a murder in the ruins."

"Why, you think there's some connection?"

The guide shrugged. "Maybe not. But I fear for what El Chicón may be stirring up."

"I know, 'the gods that rule the day,' " Matt said, repeating Emilio's words. "Well, suppose I just sell Kul one of Ángel's pieces. One million pesos, what d'ya think, Humberto?"

The guide laughed, then said, "Ángel is an artist like his father, but Señor Kul is not so easily fooled."

Matt glanced at Humberto's wristwatch and remembered the luncheon invitation. He excused himself, ran through a litany of good-byes with Emilio and the other guides, and hurried off to the Rover.

The El Templo swimming pool was still empty, but Hano Olivar reassured Matt once more that it would be filled in time for the arrival of Jake's group. The hotel manager was surprised to learn that Puma numbered the likes of Jules Kul among its clientele and quickly summoned an attendant to show Matt to the American's suite. A mariachi band with trumpets and violins was set up in the courtyard, running through standards for the guests, movie company production people for the most part.

Kul's party occupied El Templo's finest rooms, the only suite with a private rear patio and garden. Jake had stayed there once as a reward for having booked all the hotel's other rooms. Kim answered the door, standing stiffly aside as Matt entered the air-conditioned colonial elegance of the front room. The boy was wearing loose-fitting white cotton pants—from a martial arts gi, Matt supposed—and black Chinese slippers. He barely topped five-six, but there was a kind of habitual wariness about him that magnified his stature, a defensive tension, amplified by the tightly bunched muscles of his abdomen, chest, and shoulders. The motion of his left hand when Matt asked for Jules Kul seemed less a servant's gesture than a paralyzing move lifted from a Korean kata.

Matt found Kul on the patio, sans jewelry, his long hair loosed and hanging well below his shoulders. He was sitting cross-legged atop an embroidered cushion at a low mahogany table covered end to end with platters of meat and vegetables and baskets filled with native fruits. At a glance, Matt's eye took in corn, beans, pumpkin, chilies, tomatoes, avocados, breadfruit, turkey, venison, honey, and guanabana. The patio itself was fully enclosed by trellis work, surrounded by huge potted plants and dense shrubs with scarlet blossoms. Two songbirds were caged in one corner.

Kul smiled and waved Matt forward. "You'll forgive me if I don't get up."

"No, no, stay put."

Kul, too, was shirtless, the folds of skin around his ribs the same orange-brown hue as his face. He indicated a place at the opposite side of the table and bade Matt sit down. A parrot squawked from the overhead lattice as Matt lowered himself to the cushion, painfully aware all at once of the punishment his body had taken the previous night. Huatcho, Kul's Mexican houseboy, appeared with a calabash gourd bowl, which he set on the table.

"*Balche,*" Kul explained, watching Matt eye the bowl's thick brown grog. "A little ritual of mine, just to have us begin on the right foot."

Matt swirled the drink; it was a bark extract, sweetened with honey and most likely spittle-fermented. "I know what it is."

"That's a very good sign." Kul lifted a gourdful to his thick lips and drank. "Only the finest of natural foods," he said, opening his arms as if to embrace the table. "Mayan foods." He threw a small piece of avocado to a spider monkey that suddenly poked its head out from beneath the table. "You have tasted iguana, of course. And brocket, *mico*, armadillo. What about *tespescuintle*?"

"Love that rodent," Matt said, trying to sound agreeable.

Kul placed his hands on his round belly and laughed. "Fortunate is the man who has dined on *tespescuintle* in the wilds of the Mesoamerican forest."

Matt took a cautious sip, suppressing a grimace. "As one amateur archeologist to another, I would've figured you for a shard-onay man."

Kul beetled his brows, then made an amused sound. "Shardonay, yes, quite so."

Matt grinned stupidly. It was a familiar pun, like "Chac full of nuts," the punch line to the old joke about the Chichen Itza.

Kul was looking at him appraisingly. "You know, the Maya appreciated a man who could pun. It was a mark of intelligence and nobility." He sipped at his gourd, wiping a few droplets of *balche* from his goatee. "So what have you been able to put together for me?"

Matt apologized for not having had time to offer him anything in the way of a written proposal and began to outline the itinerary he had formulated. They discussed costs and logistics while they ate, fingertipping samples of this and that from the table, always under the attentive presence of Huatcho and the vigilant gaze of Kim. After forty-five minutes, Kul leaned back from the table and issued a loud belch. Huatcho placed towels and bowls of water on the tiled floor.

"I'm very satisfied," Kul began, drying his hands. "It has the proper sound of adventure to it. I must tell you, however, that I've taken many such trips through Central America, and while photographs and memories are fine for ordinary travelers, I am a traveler who is only content when he can return with something tangible."

Matt leaned back and waited.

"You see, Matt, I'm a hunter. But I seek neither jaguar nor sajino." He put his hands flat on the table. "I'm going to be honest with you, Matt, because I believe you're a man who appreciates honesty. I'm in the habit of acquiring antiquities, and I'm hoping you and I will be able to agree on a kind of methodology."

Matt returned the stock answer. "Puma will not in any way aid or abet the procurement of cultural artifacts, Mr. Kul."

"Yes, yes," Kul said dismissively, "I realize that. But I'm interested in knowing Matt Terry's personal policy."

"I've just told you."

"And why is that?"

Matt rearranged himself on the cushion, hurting all

over. "First, because the removal of artifacts represents the theft of cultural heritage. Second, because the illicit trade in antiquities has undermined the work of linguists and archeologists. And third, because it's illegal."

Kul grinned. "Laudable, Mr. Terry. A veritable textbook denunciation of the black market. But naive, unfortunately. Now hear me out: I am certainly not in favor of some of the current methods being employed—the theft of stelae and such—but the fact remains that looters are at work and precious objects *are* being stolen and put up for sale. So what is to become of these things? They are mishandled, mistreated, oftentimes damaged, and sometimes completely lost to us. And this is where the private collector can do his or her part. Someone with suitable funds and expertise—one who can penetrate certain realms that are denied to museums—can effect a rescue of these treasures. Or would you rather see them lost to the world?"

"Look," Matt said, hoping to sound lighthearted, "I'm a wilderness guide, not a policeman. I barely know a Mayan polychrome from a Kodak Ektachrome, but I know what goes on. All I'm saying is that I don't involve myself in the trade."

"By that I assume you mean *willingly* involve yourself."

Matt stiffened. "Maybe you should explain yourself, Kul."

Kul fixed him with a gimlet stare. "I told you I know a little bit about you, Matt. For example, I know that you are well respected in Palenque, and despite your . . . shall we say, low-key approach, I would venture to say that in some instances your contacts are more far-reaching than my own."

"Get to the point," Matt said angrily, wondering who had tipped Kul to his recent trouble.

"This time out I'm the hunter who knows his prey. But I don't know where to find it. So what I'd like to propose is that I hire you to do what you do best: locate it for me."

A sudden knot had formed itself in the hollow of Matt's

chest. "What about the itinerary? All this?" he added, gesturing to the table.

"Call it a get-acquainted period."

"And just what is this 'prey'?"

Kul leaned forward to whisper. "A codex, Matt. A Mayan book."

# 12

## Death by Misadventure

Along with the dozens of cities the ancient Maya had bequeathed to the New World, the countless standing stones, and the hieratic glyph panels were the books— the codices—totaling perhaps hundreds and hundreds of volumes, almost all of which had been burned by the Spanish bishop Diego de Landa one infamous sixteenth-century afternoon in the Yucatán. Three volumes, however, had somehow survived the priest's auto-da-fé, the ravages of time, and the whims of fate and succeeded in reaching the safe storage cellars of European museums, where they remained undiscovered for close to three hundred years. The three—the so-called Madrid, Paris, and Dresden codices—were believed to be postclassic copies of texts that had been written centuries earlier. New World papyrus was the pounded inner bark of the Mesoamerican fig tree, gessoed with lime and natural resins, and folded in a screenlike or accordion fashion. Each codex was roughly the size of a trade paperback book sandwiched between hardwood covers; fully opened, the longest of the three, the Madrid, measured over twenty feet.

The extant codices were divinatory almanacs, eclipse tables, and Venus cycles, but experts thought that classical books might have contained tables of genealogies and noble lineages and historical records of tributes and trade exchanges between cities. Spanish friars reported seeing records kept in heiroglyphic writing at Tayasal—near Flores in the Petén—as late as 1697.

The eleven-page fragment of a fourth codex had surfaced at the Grolier Club in New York in 1971. A late postclassic Venus calendar much more sophisticated than the Dresden, it had added little to the amassed knowledge of the Maya, but at the same time it had rekindled the hope that other texts existed and would someday come to light.

Ángel had told Matt about a painstakingly detailed forgery painted on ancient paper found in a cave in Guerrero that had been foisted upon an unsuspecting collector years ago, but nothing had turned up since the Grolier that had passed muster. Even so, it wasn't uncommon to hear collectors mention how much they would be willing to pay for a codex—a fragment, a page. Price was no object if the thing could be authenticated.

Kul maintained that rumors of a new find had reached him in Los Angeles through friends at Sotheby's in New York. Toward the end of the discussion on the patio, he had gone on to explain how the codex had apparently been discovered in Guatemala and smuggled into Mexico. He didn't mention Billie or Neil, but his offhand comments seemed to implicate them in the affair. Matt wondered if Humberto Obregone had said something to Kul, or whether it was Kul's high-placed friends in Villahermosa perhaps the same institute officials who themselves were doing a brisk side business in antiquities.

Matt, in any case, hadn't promised Kul anything, except that he would keep his ears open.

His first promise to himself, however, was to determine whether Jules Kul's codex and Lauren Riordan's heirloom were one and the same thing.

Back at the office late that afternoon, he called the Hotel La Cañada and left word for Rachel to contact him. She phoned back an hour later, explaining that everything had gone smoothly with Bustamonte: the lawyer had agreed to handle the cremation arrangements and see to it that Michael's body was shipped to the States.

Matt asked her to come by the apartment around seven,

hinting that he had something important to discuss. So what if Escobar was watching, he decided. The lieutenant had told him to snoop out what he could.

He spent the next hour straightening up what was left of the previous night's mess. There were dents in the wall, scuff marks across a good part of the floor, and constellations of dried blood. He scrubbed at the marks, stuffed his clothes back into the footlocker, then stood under the shower for twenty minutes, hoping the solar-heated water would pummel some of the soreness out of his back and shoulders. With an hour left to kill, he walked to the market and wolfed down a quick meal at one of the stalls.

Rachel was prompt. She was dressed in a lightweight skirt and a silk blouse, offset by a strand of Venetian glass beads. A smell of gardenias accompanied her in. She dropped her bag on the couch and began to move about the room as though cataloging its contents, pausing here to examine an Otavalo weaving, there a carved gourd from Peru, Matt's albums and cassettes.

She said, "I haven't seen any of these in a while," gesturing to a shelf of eight-track tapes.

"They still play." Matt shrugged. "The music's the same."

"I suppose so," she said without conviction. "So this is where you stay when you're down here?"

Matt sniffed. "This is where I live."

She regarded him with a surprised look. "How does someone get through almost four decades without accumulating anything? I mean, where's your Sony Trinitron, Matt? Where's your phone-answering machine and VCR?"

"I guess I've just got some catching up to do," he told her, going for a beer.

"You've been away too long," she said to his back. "Haven't you heard that the one with the most toys wins?"

He popped the top of a Tecate and poured two mugs, running a wedge of lime around the rims of both glasses. "There's a movie theater next door and a TV in the cantina down the block. Here."

She took the glass and sat down on the cushions, arranging her skirt to cover her knees. "What did you want to talk about?" she asked, maintaining her smile.

Matt drained half the glass. "I've been thinking about our little chat at Xibalba."

"And?"

"And I guess I understand why you came up with that 'heirloom' story—because maybe Lieutenant Escobar's been filling your head with a lot of rot—but just how long are we going to have to keep this up? Just so I can schedule things."

"I don't know what you're talking about."

Matt took another swallow. "Okay. Then maybe you really do believe the boatmen found something. But I'd like to hear the truth. See, I thought if I was square with you about the money, you'd read it as a sign you could trust me. I don't give a shit what Billie was carrying, you understand? The only thing that interests me right now is finding out who killed her."

"You don't even run an import shop," he said, watching her fidget. "Were you and Billie doing business together?"

Rachel looked away from him. "It wasn't like that."

Matt sat on the floor opposite her. "What, then?"

"I knew I couldn't do this," she said in a dispirited voice. "I'm not Laurie. I just don't have it."

Matt waited for her to continue.

She said, "I knew about the smuggling. It started about a year and a half ago. They were importing handicrafts from Guatemala. But the business was a front. Michael had a partner who imported tropical birds. Apparently it wasn't very difficult to bring artifacts in with all the rest of it." She looked up, calculating something. "But you're right. I don't run an imports shop. I . . . work for a museum. I'm an assistant curator at the Museum of Primitive Art in New York."

"So it wasn't any buying trip that brought you to Palenque. What were you doing down here?"

"My areas of expertise are linguistics and epigraphy," she said softly. "Inscriptions. I attended some of the early Mesa Redondas."

"Are you published?"

Rachel nodded. "I was working as a translator at the

UN. A friend got me interested in Mayan glyphs. It started as a hobby and ended up a career. Before the museum, I put together catalogs for private collectors, did some authenticating, whatever I could to gain access to uncataloged pieces.''

"Who raised you and your sister—the goddamn Man from UNCLE?" Matt said angrily, getting up. He paced to the loft ladder and back, wondering whether she was feeding him another lie. "Let me get this straight. Billie and Neil are running antiquities. They hook up with some Honduran with a line on choice objects, and they start importing these pieces to the States. And you—you what? You procure them for the museum? You place them with galleries or private collectors?"

Rachel wore a shocked expression. "Who told you about . . . Did Billie—"

"Alejandro Volan," he interrupted her. "The insurgents' front man. The money went to him, and the guerrillas got arms in return. So is this some SDS leftover? The Riordan sisters' way of helping the cause?"

"No! I swear to you, Matt. This is the first time I've ever gotten involved in this kind of thing." Rachel tapped a cigarette from her pack. "Laurie tried to enlist my support," she said, striking a match. "She and Michael were bringing in vases and figurines, things I dreamed of buying. But the museum won't accept unprovenanced pieces even though the UNESCO accord hasn't been ratified. Besides, I was against what they were doing, but there was no way I could talk them out of it. And believe me, I tried. Every time I saw her. But she was convinced she was doing everyone a favor—more so after she met the Honduran. The art world, the guerrillas . . . they had the money they needed for armaments, and the collectors had what they wanted.

"There's a nice irony built into it, don't you think? Wealthy right-wing Americans financing Central American Marxist revolutionaries? But Michael claimed that the pieces would just end up lost or destroyed if someone wasn't out there buying them up. And in some ways he was right.''

Matt said, "Yeah, I've already heard that argument once today."

"But for all Michael's political rationalizing, it was a business with him."

Matt sipped from his glass. "So what's your stake in this now if you were against what they were doing?"

"I was, Matt. This was the first time. . . . It wasn't only ethics. I was afraid for Laurie, for both of them. They were getting in too deep, and I didn't trust the people they were involved with." She shook her head, tight-lipped. "Then they found something extraordinary."

"They turned up a codex."

Rachel's eyes widened. "You *do* know something—"

"—No." He shook his head. "Billie didn't tell me anything about it. But word must have gotten out. Did they ever mention a man named Kul? Were they into him for this one?"

"Jules Kul?"

Matt nodded. "He's here."

"In Palenque?"

"He came in here and fed me some trumped-up tale about wanting to visit the Lacandons and Yaxchilan. The next thing I know he wants to hire me to track down a codex. I figured all of us might be talking about the same thing. It wasn't exactly two and two, but I'm a long way past believing in coincidence. That's why I want you to be straight with me."

"But why did he come to you?"

"I'm not sure yet. He knows I was with Billie and Neil when they were killed. Maybe that's enough for him to go on. But he's not the only one who's been nosing around. Somebody paid me a visit last night after I left you at La Cañada. They were searching for something when I showed up. Now, maybe it was Kul and maybe it was the police. Or maybe you hired them, Rachel. How about that?"

She glared at him. "You don't mean that!"

"Well, why not? You thought I knew something. You made me an offer for Billie's 'heirloom.' If you didn't have anything to do with last night, then tell me how Kul learned about what they were carrying. What do you know about him?"

Rachel stubbed out the cigarette and laughed shortly. "They say he has a place in California that's designed after Palenque, surrounded by lily ponds and hothouses full of tropical plants. He's obsessed with the Maya, Matt. He keeps bees and imports chocolate. I even heard that he had reconstructive surgery on his face."

"Was Billie working for him or not? Did she ever mention him?"

"Only in passing. He's a fanatic. The heir to a fortune—tobbacco, I think it was—even without his architectural firm. He just might have the finest pre-Columbian collection in the world, Matt. Most of it off limits."

"Come on, Rachel. Billie's dead because of this thing! Tell me how the hell Kul could have found out about it."

She shook her head. "I don't know! Maybe someone in New York told him."

Matt made an impatient gesture. "Who else knew about the codex?"

Rachel stood up and walked away from the couch, one hand to the nape of her neck. "Six months ago, Laurie came to New York with a single leaf from the book. She told me she'd seen the rest of the codex and said that it was in almost perfect condition. I knew as soon as I touched it . . ."

"You had to have it," Matt finished.

She nodded. "I couldn't let it fall into some collector's hands. But I needed to be sure. So I took the leaf to three experts in New York. They work with runners—strictly illicit trade. I thought I could trust them. Then I helped Laurie come up with the money they were going to need for the deal. I knew I could get the museum to acquire it somehow."

"How much money?"

"Two hundred and fifty thousand dollars," Rachel said without expression.

"Two hundred and . . . Where the hell did you get that kind of cash? Is it family money?"

Rachel bit her lip. "It was a private source."

"Meaning?"

"A private source," she said, raising her voice. "I can't say any more."

"I'm impressed," Matt said, regarding her. "That'll buy a fair-sized shipment of weapons. But you're telling me that all this was just for science? Billie brings it in, then you sell it to the museum. I thought you said the museums won't accept unprovenanced finds.''

''The only thing I had to do was prove that the codex had been in the States before 1970. It was arranged that the museum would receive the codex from a collector, who could use the donation as a tax write-off.''

Matt took a deep breath. ''Jesus Christ, I *have* been away too long.''

Rachel said, ''I don't expect you to understand. I've made the Maya my life's work, and I *am* doing this for 'science,' as you say.'' She waved at the air. ''Sure, I want credit for the find, but why shouldn't I? This is my field, and I certainly don't plan to spend the rest of my life as an assistant curator. I'm no different from anyone else. I want people to know my name and respect what I have to say, and this is my shot at making that happen. But all that's beside the point. This find is invaluable.''

There was no hint of apology in Rachel's voice, and Matt decided to back away from the issue of her complicity. ''So your guess is that one of these three 'consultants' passed the word to Kul.'' He forced a disgruntled tone into his voice. ''It still doesn't add up, Rachel. How would Kul get Billie's name out of this? She and Neil must have been dealing with someone else. Either that, or the Honduran gave the same sell to some other runner.''

''I don't know, Matt. She didn't mention Kul or any other competition, and I didn't mention her name to anyone.''

''Then Volan double-crossed them. He must've been testing out the market. For all you know there could be half a dozen pages floating around.''

Rachel was shaking her head. ''They had an exclusive with this man. The guerrilla leader knew Laurie. He trusted her completely.''

Matt tried to imagine the two of them together, Billie and Raphael Aguilar. ''Where were they were supposed to make the buy?''

''Somewhere in the Petén, that's all I know.''

''Then what?''

''They planned to fly to Guatemala City.''

"And you were going to meet them there," Matt said, recalling a sentence from the letter.

Rachel threw him a questioning look and nodded.

"How were they planning to get it out of the country?"

"I don't know that, either. Probably through Michael's partner."

"The bird man." Matt exhaled wearily. "All this blood over a rotting piece of astrology."

"But that's just it," Rachel said, brightening somewhat. "It isn't just some almanac or astronomical text, at least not from what I could decipher from the page they gave me. It's a historical document, Matt. There were names and dates and places. Matt, it's the find of the century. It could answer so many questions."

He gave her a dubious look. The whole business reeked of a scam. By the Honduran, perhaps by Billie and Neil themselves.

"Do you think I would have let myself get involved in this for anything less? That's why I told you she was carrying an heirloom. I didn't know how much I should say to you or even what Laurie might have mentioned. For all I knew, the police were on the right track, and you and the boatmen found something among her things or had something to do with—"

Matt shot her a look before she could finish. "What made you think the killers didn't just make off with the thing? Why did Billie—Laurie—end up coming to the lodge? What aren't you telling me?" he demanded, feeling like Escobar all of a sudden.

Rachel reached for her cigarettes. "I heard from her just before they left Tikal," she said, exhaling smoke. "She said there had been a change in their plans. Instead of flying to Guatemala City, they were going into Mexico by river. I was waiting to hear from them when you called."

"Why the change in plans?"

"She didn't say."

"And they had the codex with them?"

"Yes, yes, they had it with them." Rachel was crying. "But they weren't planning to carry it into Mexico. Laurie said she was going to use someone to mule it across the border, someone they'd used before.''

''Did she give you a name?''

Rachel leaned against the ladder to the loft, wiping her eyes with the backs of her hands. ''Kin. T'sup Kin.''

Matt stared at her, his voice caught in his throat. Rachel had put such an odd spin on the words, it took him a moment to realize that she had named the albino Lacandon who had been found beheaded in the ruins.

# 13

## Smoke and Mirrors

First thing in the morning he phoned Denver. Jake, half-asleep and annoyed, explained that he hadn't been able to turn up any information on Rachel Riordan's imports boutique. He had asked a friend in Manhattan to pay a visit to her address, but the only thing Jake's agent had been able to pry from the building's doorman was that Rachel was away and expected to be gone for a week or so. Matt gave Jake a rundown of the previous night and asked him to use Puma's contacts to verify Rachel's position at the museum.

"She says she's been published," Matt said. "You could check the Mesa Redonda proceedings. Go back about five years."

Jake said that he would.

Talk of the existence of the codex seemed to spark a cooperativeness in Jake that Matt grew uncomfortable with as their conversation progressed. He realized that in some indirect way he had been counting on Jake to act as a kind of tether, and all of a sudden Jake was as hooked into things as he was.

Matt had been awake for most of the night, running it over again and again, from a new angle each time. He was convinced everyone had been scammed—right up until Rachel brought up the Indian's name. But even that didn't guarantee the book was on the level. The guerrillas could have come across a single page, a leaf, and slapped it on top of some fake that had been kicking around for ten years. But T'sup Kin's murder lent a credibility to everything.

Rachel was another concern. Shortly before midnight he had walked her back to the La Cañada, but it had been on his mind to ask her to spend the night, a kind of transference-in-progress that put her where Billie stood in Matt's thoughts. Rachel was seductive, her own brand of dangerous, and he still didn't trust her. But he figured he could learn as much from her lies as from anything else. As long as he stayed there, he told himself.

He got on the shortwave to the lodge next. It took thirty minutes of call signs to bring Silvio to the transceiver, and when he picked up he sounded as though he had been sampling a bit of that potent *mota* from his garden. Matt told him to get into Sayaxche and see if he could learn where T'sup Kin's family was living. Matt instructed him to take Paolo and Emil along. They were to find out if anyone had stopped by the Lacandons' home during the past two weeks and radio in a reply as soon as they could.

Then Matt called Kul and arranged to meet with him later that morning at El Templo.

Sometime just before dawn he had decided to rule out circumstantiality across the board. Billie, the murders, the Lacandon, the break-in, Kul . . . everything fit together somehow, and the piece to concentrate on was the one that linked or separated Jules Kul from Lauren Riordan.

The morning was clear, even off toward El Chichón, but an oppressive heat remained anchored over the town. Several of the hotel's guests were watching the pool fill, circling it with heat-crazed looks while strolling musicians harmonized on "La Paloma."

Matt knocked twice at the door to Kul's suite. Kim was in his customary place and pose, and the lord himself was on the patio, puffing away at a large hand-rolled cigar. Matt accepted one and lighted it, drawing in a mouthful of pungent smoke. "I've made a few inquiries," he announced.

"Have you now, Matt," Kul said with undisguised skepticism. "And what have you learned?"

"Seems that your people didn't get the full story," Matt continued in the same laconic tone. "The codex made it to Palenque all right, but it changed hands along the way." He tapped an ash from the cigar. "And things are wide open now that the Indian's dead."

"What Indian, Matt?"

"The one killed in the ruins. Maybe you read about it."

"I'd prefer to remain isolated from the details, Matt." Kul set aside the cigar and began to massage the backs of his hands. Matt found the silence reassuring.

"I'm curious," Kul said at last. "Why this abrupt about-face? I have to ask myself: What is Matt Terry getting at? This man who claims to support the UNESCO decision on the illicit transfer of cultural properties. Why, to phrase it in Mayan terms, is Matt Terry suddenly wearing a loincloth that is not his?"

Matt smoothed his mustache. "It's what you said about private collectors, their being able to preserve the past. Guess I'm starting to understand some of the lessons I learned on the Usumacinta."

Kul's nostrils flared. "Yes, the river has much to teach us. And you believe you can locate the codex even though it has 'changed hands,' as you say?"

"I might be able to. But you'd have to give me a little more to go on."

Kul shrugged. "As I mentioned yesterday, I learned about the codex in Los Angeles. It was my understanding then that someone here in Palenque was offering it up for sale. I considered using Humberto Obregone as an intermediary, but he didn't impress me as the man for the job. So I decided to take a chance on you, and now it appears my hunch has paid off. In fact, you seem to know more than I do at this point."

"How many people know about the book?"

"That remains to be seen."

Matt tried to conceal his frustration. "Suppose I do find it. What's there to prevent me from turning the thing over to the authorities?"

Kul grinned and hooked his hair behind his ears.

"Nothing. But I don't see much hope of your procuring it without the necessary funds at your disposal. That is, unless you already have it."

He ridiculed the idea before Matt could answer. "Allow me to save both of us the bother of hashing through this. You see, I'm fully prepared to pay any amount you see fit to charge for your services. If and when you have the codex in hand, we can notify the proper authorities."

Matt studied Kul's face and uttered a perplexed laugh. "Now I'm the one wondering."

"It's the quest, after all, Matt. Not the object itself. What would you say to our involving an impartial third party?"

"Who, for instance?"

Kul relighted his cigar. "Dr. Niles Chalker," he said, fanning away his own smoke. "He's an authority on Mayan codices. And I happen to know he is currently researching some matters in Villahermosa."

Matt smiled to himself. Humberto Obregone had identified Chalker as the archeologist who had met Kul at the airport. Matt said, "I don't know. I think we'd be better off surrendering it to the Mexican authorities. We could turn it over to the Institute of Anthropology in Villahermosa."

"That won't do," Kul said too quickly. "You must understand that there are problems of provenance here. After all, the codex was discovered in Guatemala."

"Right, you did mention that. But who's to say it wasn't found in Mexico? Like the Grolier. Midnight trips to darkened airstrips and all that. You could ask your sources in L.A. just so we could be sure."

Kul was stone-faced. "You're complicating matters. As an American, Dr. Chalker is the obvious choice. An impartial third party."

Matt left the suite feeling confused by the exchange. Kul could have learned about the codex from the people Rachel had contacted in New York or in any of a dozen ways. The Honduran—the arms dealer the Rescate agents were so centered on—must have mentioned Billie and Neil to a group of competitors. Kul had read about the murders and was tipped off to Matt's involvement. . . . It was clear enough why he would want to slip Chalker into the scene, just to make it seem that purchasing the book was a praiseworthy move. Matt had hoped to tie it up in one neat knot. But how could Kul have ended up empty-handed if he had been involved with the murders?

There were still too many missing pieces. And until some of those surfaced, Matt told himself, he could do little more than continue to bait everyone, promising things he didn't have.

At the front gate to the El Templo courtyard, he pulled the Rover aside to make way for a black Jeep he had noticed earlier that morning in the pueblo. The Jeep bore tags from a rental company in Mérida, and something made him give it a second look now.

Slowing the Rover to a crawl, he reangled the rearview mirror to watch two burly-looking men emerge from the vehicle. They were Americans, Matt decided, dressed alike in tight-fitting faded jeans and cowboy boots. They could have been *petroleros* from Villahermosa or stunt-men with the film crew. The shorter of the two had a thatch of blond hair and a rectangle of white adhesive tape across the bridge of his nose. Kul's houseboy, Hu-atcho, ran out to meet them.

Matt spent the afternoon in the office glued to the radio. Silvio's call finally came in at six o'clock, just as he and Ángel were finishing the last of the tamales Natalie had brought in from one of the food carts parked across the street from the Cine Twilite.

The news from Sayaxche wasn't good: someone had torched the Lacandons' hut on the Pasión, and T'sup Kin's family was nowhere to be found. Paolo got on the radio to say that five gringos had reportedly rented a boat in Sayaxche two days after they had started off downriver with Billie and Neil. The Peténero who had piloted the gringos downriver was in Cobán, and Paolo had yet to talk to him, but he was familiar with the boat and claimed that it was easily capable of over overtaking them on the Usumacinta. Matt told him to stick with it and contact the office as soon as he had anything in the way of descriptions. He already had the two cowboys in mind.

"We know they had the codex with them when they left Tikal," Matt said afterward, thinking aloud at Natalie's prompting. "So someone either knew they planned to pass it off to the Lacandon or got as much out of them before they were killed."

"But why burn the house down?" Ángel thought to ask.

Matt made a hopeless gesture. "To find out from whoever was there where the codex had been taken. To get rid of witnesses, maybe. I don't know. I'm new at this."

Natalie said, "So the killers track T'sup Kin to Palenque, kill him, and take the codex. I guess that puts Jules Kul in the clear, even if he did send his goons around to search your place."

Matt wiped his hands down his face and stood up. "What d' you say we close up and get out of here. My treat at Xibalba."

Natalie offered her arm as if to say *twist it*.

Ángel was already heading for the front grate. He was all set to lower it when Rachel made a vexed entry into the office, one hand pressed to the top of her straw sun hat. Ángel turned to close the door behind her, but just then a small disheveled-looking Mayan woman hurried in on Rachel's heels. Matt saw the faces of two children appear at the window.

Rachel threw Matt an imploring look. "Could somebody *please* try to explain to her that I don't want anything. I've tried everything. She followed me all the way from the *zóalco*, but I can't seem to make her understand. All day long it's been nothing but lewd remarks. Now this."

The Indian wore her hair in a long braid that fell almost to the bundle of belongings she had tied around her narrow shoulders. She was barefoot and dressed in a stained skirt and several layers of blouses.

Natalie laughed sympathetically, mimicking the street boys' favorite pun: *buenas nachas*, which translated as "nice cheeks."

Matt gave the woman a gentle smile and asked what he could do for her.

The woman ignored him and said something to Rachel.

"She's speaking Yucatec," Ángel said, surprised. "No, no, wait . . . it's Lacandon."

"Well, whatever it is, tell her I don't want any," Rachel barked, sitting down.

"Señora, señora," the woman repeated, closing on Rachel.

Matt and Natalie exchanged bewildered looks. Ángel was listening intently to the woman's rushed words.

"She says she knows you," he told Rachel. "She saw you in town two days ago and has been looking for you ever since. She's been waiting all night and all day in the plaza, and she wants to knows why you didn't appear. Her children are hungry, and she's frightened."

Matt looked at the children, then back at the Indian woman. All at once it dawned on him. "She thinks you're Billie!"

"*Sí, sí,*" the woman enthused, reaching for Rachel's arm. "Señora Billie, Señora Billie."

Natalie started to say something, then gasped. The woman had pulled a bulky object wrapped in banana leaves from the folds of her clothing. She was holding it out to Rachel in her shaking hands.

"Matt! Do you think . . ."

Rachel looked around uncertainly. "What is it?"

Matt stood paralyzed for a moment. "Ángel, get those kids in here," he said suddenly. "Natalie, get the shades."

Matt took the package from the woman's hands and placed it gingerly on his desk, as though handling Pandora's box. When the grate came down and the front door had been locked, he switched on the lights and began to work on the leaf wrapping. Natalie, Rachel, and Ángel crowded around him, eyes fixed on his fingers. The Lacandon woman huddled fearfully in a corner with her two children.

"Be careful, Matt," Rachel cautioned him.

The innermost leaf was unfolded, revealing a flat, ten-by ten-inch rectanglular case of burnished aluminum. Matt lifted the box from its shiny green bed and used his thumbs to flip open the two spring clips that secured the case's gasketed lid. But before he could raise the lid, Rachel pushed his hands aside. Her eyes were feverish when he looked over at her.

Matt said, "Go ahead," stepping back.

Rachel placed her fingertips around the edge of the lid and lifted it off with a rocking motion. The interior of the case was lined with a thin layer of packing foam folded envelope-fashion and crowned with two small pillows of desiccant. Rachel peeled back the foam, draping each fold over the edge of the case.

Matt caught a glimpse of bright colors; then, when Rachel had removed the final piece, his eye took in the whole of the top page: column after column of black hieroglyphs, interspersed with bar and dot numerical notations and three color renderings of Mayan lords and deities.

"Is it real?" Natalie gasped.

Ángel let out an excited giggle.

Rachel carefully grasped the pages between the laquered fingernails of her thumb and forefinger; as her hand came up, the codex scissored open like an Oriental screen. Each page was crowded with circular glyphs—animal faces, abstracts, and symmetrical designs—along with crude illustrations that seemed to leap from their white plaster background.

Rachel folded the codex back into the case and collapsed into a chair, removing her hat. Matt could hear the rush of her breath. The Lacandon woman was motioning to her, chattering away in her native tongue.

"She wants to know why the señora cut her hair," Ángel translated. The woman continued to talk.

Matt said, "Ask her how she got the case."

Ángel interrupted her, then listened closely for a moment. "Her husband sometimes carried things to Puerto Barrios for the señora, but this time the señora wanted him to take it to Palenque. The señora was afraid that someone might come . . . uh, looking for the thing. So her husband hid it behind their *choza* and left for Palenque without it. She had pleaded with him to refuse. She was dreaming of *xtabay*—uh, consorts of gods—and *achiote*. Omens of blood." Angel listened a moment longer. "Three *ts'ul* . . . three white men, big men came and threatened her. But they didn't find the thing. Her husband had made her promise to tell them that he had gone to Palenque, so she did it. She always does as she promises."

Matt watched as the woman walked the fingers of her left hand down her right forearm until the heels of her palms met.

Matt said, "Ask her why her husband didn't have the thing with him."

Ángel translated, nodding while the woman answered. "He knew it was something of special value. He planned to leave it buried in the earth, ask the señora for more money before he delivered it. The men were angry and threatened to kill her children. They set fire to the house and went on their way. She wanted no part of the thing. She dug up the box and came to Palenque."

Matt turned to Rachel. "She saw you on the street and mistook you for Billie."

"The señora came to the *zócalo* today, but she wouldn't stop," Ángel was saying. "So she decided to follow. She wants to know if the señora has already seen her husband." Ángel looked to Matt.

"Oh, Christ," Matt muttered, regarding the woman's dark-eyed children. He clenched his teeth. "Ask her if Billie promised her anything to deliver the thing."

Ángel translated and said, "She says her husband has already received some of it. The señora always gave them things first, before her husband would leave."

"Matt," Natalie said suddenly, "we can't keep her here."

"I know, I know," he told her, throwing open the top drawer to his desk. He unlocked the cash box inside and took out several thousand pesos. Then he dug into his pants pocket for the key to the Range Rover and tossed it to Ángel. "I want you to take them to San Cristóbal."

Ángel threw up his hands. "Matt, that will take all night!"

"See that they get to Trudi Blom at Na Bolom." Blom was something of a stepmother to all the Lacandon and usually had more than one family staying with her at the museum and guest house she owned in the highlands. "Tell her about the woman's husband. She's probably already heard about the murder, anyway. Say that the wife showed up in Palenque looking for him." Matt glanced at the woman. "Try and make her understand what you're going to tell Trudi. I don't think she'll say anything about the codex, but we'll worry about that later. I just don't want Kul or whoever killed T'sup Kin to find her.''

Ángel was frowning. Matt caught up with himself and put a hand on the boy's shoulder.

"I'm sorry, Ángel. Forget it. I'll do it myself.''

Ángel considered it, then shook his head. "No, I'll go.''

Matt gave Ángel's shoulder an affectionate squeeze. ''Take out what you need for the trip and give her the rest of it," he added, handing over the pesos. "If she refuses, then make sure Trudi holds on to it for her.''

"Matt, I've got all that money,'' Rachel said softly. "I want her to have something.''

Matt nodded. "All right. We'll see that she gets it. Now you better get going," he said, turning back to Ángel. "And watch out for yourself on that goddamn road. There's no rush, understand?''

Ángel said a few words to the woman; she stood up, relucantly at first, then followed him out the door to Matt's apartment, the two children hand in hand behind her.

A moment later Matt heard the door to the veranda slam shut and swung around to look at the aluminum case where it sat on the desk. It seemed an evil presence in the room.

# 14

## Borrowed Time

Matt felt Rachel stir beside him; she made a small troubled sound and rolled over on her side, tugging the sheet over her head. Forcing his eyes open, he reached for the clock and turned its luminous face toward the bed. The hands read 6:15. The roosters had been at it since five, when Rachel had slipped under the covers, pressing her length against his back, her bare legs and soft breasts. Earlier on he had offered her the couch.

Even so, she was partially clothed beneath the sheet, wearing black bikini panties and the short-sleeved shirt she had had on when she walked into the office the previous evening, T'sup Kin's widow and children in tow.

An eternity ago, it seemed.

Matt eased away from her back and raised himself up against the headboard, hands behind his head. Her skirt and bra were draped across the chair, and her sandals were alongside it on the floor. The moment seemed poignant somehow; he thought how odd it was to see her clothes there. How odd to have this near-stranger beside him in a bed he hadn't shared for six months, not since Natalie at the end of their time together.

The three of them—Rachel, Matt, and Natalie—had shared a couple of drinks after Ángel left with the Indian woman. For a moment there was something akin to excitement in the office, but it vanished with Natalie's good

150

night. Rachel had wept, talking about Billie and Neil, T'sup Kin and his family. Matt held her, recalling the first time they had spoken on the phone, and that, he would decide later, was what had started it all. His holding her, her face to his chest, and the smell of gardenias. He had tried to cut a path to grief through the tangle of his own thoughts and feelings but could not.

Rachel had rushed off for the hotel to fetch the notes and texts she had brought down from New York and returned with her luggage. It was easier to bring the whole thing, she had told him, and Matt found that he was neither surprised nor against the idea, something celebratory still ruling him, overriding his concerns about having the codex there, the papyrus screen three people had already died for.

They had unfolded the book then—all five feet of its precious bark fabric—across a sheet Matt had spread on the floor of the apartment. He could see where the first page or pages had been torn free. Rachel marveled at the book's state of preservation. She pointed to examples of Mayan wordplay and linguistic design, and gradually, as Matt watched, she seemed to retreat into a kind of rapturous silent dialogue with the text.

Rachel had photographed each leaf of the codex, first with a compact 35-mm, then with a Polaroid. The instant prints were less than perfect, but Rachel seemed in too much of a rush to let that concern her.

She labored over the codex for the rest of the night, examining individual glyphs with a self-illuminated magnifier, computing dates on a calculator. She consulted her books and jotted down notes while Matt paced and tried to keep himself awake. He caught himself dozing off once or twice but was alert enough at five A.M. to see her slip out of her skirt in the dim light of the room.

He was already hard when she climbed into bed, and there was an urgency to the first few moments of their lovemaking, a passion that had less to do with the newness of each other than with the thrill of having found the codex. But something had changed then, and Matt was thankful they had both recognized it. Maybe it was the codex again, or perhaps it was that they had both been thinking about Billie. Matt was suddenly on guard, promising himself he'd keep Rachel safe, return her to New York safe and sound.

"Did you love her?" she asked, without moving, reading his mind perhaps. She had her back to him still, her long legs drawn up under the sheet.

He told her he hadn't. It had never been for love from the start. It was just that he'd failed Billie; and then the thing had taken on its own crazy momentum.

"But you could have?"

"It doesn't matter now."

Rachel sighed a knowing sound. "She had that effect on people. Never telling anyone more than they had to know. Always maintaining an air of mystery, even when there was no call for it. It drew people to her. Everyone seemed to assume she had all the answers." She scratched at her shoulder. "Sometimes I think she did."

Matt thought to argue the point but kept quiet. "Were they married?" he said after a moment.

Rachel rolled over to show him a crooked smile. "He was gay, Matt."

Matt fell silent. Then he said, "I read about some disease, a virus or something?"

"Yeah. They don't know what it is." Rachel shook her head. "Laurie would fly off with him to Bangkok or some other place just so he could be himself for a while. Marriage was their little charade. It gave both of them a kind of freedom. They used it."

Rachel slipped into the crook of his arm, one hand on his shoulder, then caught sight of the purple bruises over his ribs. "Jesus, Matt, what happened?"

"Souvenirs from the other night," he told her, feeling the soreness return.

She forced her breath out and stared at the raftered ceiling. "Have you ever been to New York?"

"It's been awhile—three years at least."

"Did you like it?"

"I wasn't there long enough to make up my mind."

"You should give it another try. You wouldn't even have to change your life-style. I know plenty of people who are still living on cushions and crates."

Matt smirked. "A year ago I wouldn't have considered

it. But things are getting strained down here, from El Paso on down.''

"I think you'd like New York."

"Is that right?''

Rachel moved against him. "I guess I just want you to know that I have a spare room if you ever decide to give it a try—it wouldn't have to mean anything, but we could see what happens.'' When Matt didn't say anything, she sat up and studied her nails. Sunlight was streaming into the room, and children's voices were rising up from the barranca paths. "So what now, Matt? Do you call Rescate, the rescue police?''

Matt twisted his head to look at her. "That's for you to decide. You paid for it. Billie and Neil paid for it.''

Rachel tightened her lips. "But it's over now, isn't it? You could just let me take it back to New York. It's not as if I'm planning to hide it away somewhere like Kul. You could live with that, couldn't you?''

Matt shook his head. "Nothing's over. You've got the codex, but your sister's dead and I still don't know who killed her. I can't let that go, Rachel.''

"But isn't that the point, that Laurie died for this? You can't let anything happen now. You owe her that much.''

Matt cursed softly and turned away from her. "Do yourself a favor and turn it in. Nobody can take away the fact that you saved it, no matter what anyone claims.''

"But what good would it do?'' she asked in a panicked way. "It would only complicate everything. Mexico, Guatemala, and Honduras would all claim it. We have no proof of its origin. It'll end up rotting away in the Bodega in Mexico City.''

Matt laughed derisively. "You're already in this thing over your head and you're worried about complications? If you surrender it here, it might count for something. If you don't, you're walking in Billie's footsteps, and I don't know if I can help you.''

"Would you stop me if I got up and left right now? I could be in Villahermosa in two hours, New York by tonight.''

"You'd just waltz through customs, huh?''

"I think I'd be willing to try.''

Matt said, "Then I guess I'd have to stop you. For your own good."

Rachel propped herself up on an elbow and gazed at him. "Will you just hear me out before you make up your mind? It's incredible, Matt. Absolutely incredible."

Rachel had returned the codex facedown to its airtight case, so it was the back page she showed Matt after they had dressed and downed a cup of strong coffee.

"The introductory portion is missing," Rachel explained as she unfolded the final few pages from the case. "But what we appear to have is twenty pages of history dating back to the late classic." She used the eraser end of a pencil to point to several columns of glyphs at the top of a page.

Matt recognized them as numerical glyphs, although they differed somewhat from the stelae and bas-relief panel blocks with which he was familiar.

"These dates refer to the period between A.D. 810 and 850. And all of it centers on this man." Rachel indicated an animal-profiled glyph that reappeared throughout the text, then a drawing of a Mayan ruler seated cross-legged on a throne, flanked by what looked to be maidservants and attendants. "His name was Serpent Skull. I got that much from the page Laurie gave me, along with this name." She carefully folded the codex back into the case and ran her fingers down a column of hieroglyphs on one of the final pages, blockish, composite symbols nothing at all like Egyptian. "Here. I call him 'He-Stops-the-Sun.' A northern warlord, a great conqueror. His army was laying siege to Serpent Skull's city when these final pages were written."

Matt gave Rachel an incredulous look. She had on a pair of oversized glasses that magnified the size of her eyes. "Are you telling me you've got a last will and testament here?"

"No, not quite. But I think we do have Serpent Skull's final recorded words."

She pointed to a series of colorless drawings and the text beneath them. The final pages of the codex had a hurried and unfinished look, as though the scribe had inserted material that was never planned to be included.

"Look at how hasty this is compared to the earlier sections. And everywhere you look there are glyphs for warfare, blood, and death." One page portrayed a woman running a thorned rope through her tongue; on another stood a man with a fanged snake poised in front of his face. " 'She let blood and died,' " Rachel read. " 'He fought and died.' They must have been trying everything they could to appease the gods and forestall the end."

"Did it work?"

"Apparently not. But look at this." She showed Matt a small detail glyph that was carefully woven into one of the illustrations. "This is the scribe's individual mark— his signature. Now, here it is again." Matt peered at a drawing of a loinclothed man in a spangled turban, his breast adorned with a stylized water lily. "He's identified himself for us," Rachel said.

Boar-bristle brush in hand, the scribe was seated at the foot of Serpent Skull's throne and was surrounded by ceramic paint pots. "He's recording these final events, Serpent Skull's words, the warfare going on outside the temple, all this self-mutilation taking place in the throne room."

Rachel caught Matt's look and said, "Don't say anything, just listen. This scribe must have had a thing about signing his work." She turned a page. "He managed to work his signature onto every leaf of this codex. And I've seen it other places as well."

"Other places," Matt repeated evenly.

"Yes. On three codex vases Laurie brought up to New York during the past six months. I know the collector who purchased the pieces, and when I saw the scribe's sigil on the sample leaf, I double-checked it against the vases." Rachel took out two roll-out photographs of a type Matt had seen in *National Geographic*. Black glyphs and multicolored polymorphs adorned the vases. The magnifier brought the scribe's mark to light.

Matt shook his head. "I still don't get it."

"Don't you see? Laurie got all three pieces from the guerrillas. *In addition to the codex.* The point is, they all came from the same site—some site in the Petén the guerrillas have been systematically plundering."

"Okay," Matt returned, uncertain where Rachel was leading.

"We even have the name—sort of." She flipped forward two leaves in the codex. "Do you know what an emblem glyph is?"

"It's a place-name, isn't it?"

Rachel nodded, pointing out a somewhat rectangularly shaped glyph she had drawn in her notebook. "This is Serpent Skull's city. 'Rock River.' " She showed Matt the same glyph on the funerary vase photos and on several pages in the codex. "God knows what site this is, but I'd be willing to guess that it's somewhere near Yaxchilan."

Matt rubbed his jaw. "But . . . this place could be anywhere. There are, what—twenty-five hundred cataloged sites? Sometimes every other hill in the Petén looks like a Mayan pyramid. Did Billie tell you anything about where they were making the buys?"

Rachel shook her head. "She was very careful about that. But maybe it doesn't matter," she added on a more cheerful note. "All we have to do is figure it out. I can't find any correlation between Rock River and any known site or present settlement in the Petén or Chiapas, but it could be a site we know by another name, or even a *place*-name—a land formation or something."

"Río Piedra, Río Roca . . ." Matt tried. "Doesn't ring a bell."

"It could be a Mayan word."

"I'll talk to Ángel."

"Then you'll think about it?"

Matt heard Kul's voice in his thoughts. He paced away from the table, smoothing out his anger, then whirled on her. "A while ago you were ready to fly off to New York. Now all of a sudden you're not content with getting the codex. You want the goddamn city it came from." Matt muttered a curse. "How much did you know about this before last night?"

Rachel looked hurt, then merely tolerant. "I had no idea I'd find the city's emblem glyph in the codex. I knew the vases were all from the same site, but I didn't see any connection between them and the codex until today. At exactly four ten, if you want the specifics."

Matt said, "I'm surprised you could sleep."

"Sleep was the last thing on my mind, Matt."

They looked at each other through the silence. "But what do you expect to find?" Matt said at last. "If the guerrillas have been working the site for six months, there probably isn't an unopened tomb left."

Rachel tapped the final page of the codex, where some of the glyphs and drawings were incomplete. "I want you to see something."

At the bottom of the page was a crudely drawn Palenque-like temple supported by five emblem glyphs stood on end. At the base of the pyramid, or perhaps inside it, was a rectangle containing a single abstract glyph. And jutting out from the rectangle on all four sides were smaller equally placed squares, sixteen in all, each bearing the same animal-profiled glyph.

Rachel ran a finger over the text above. "What does this look like to you? What do you see?"

Matt studied the drawing a moment. "I'm not sure. A fringed rug or mat." He inclined his head. "A monster in a box. A kind of flag."

"How about a crenellated sun symbol?" Rachel suggested.

"How about a table with sixteen chairs. I don't know, a Mayan IQ test."

"Why would the scribe decide to show it? That's what I keep asking myself. It's like Serpent Skull is directing him to bring the codex here." Rachel leaned over the drawing. "Maybe it is an IQ test. But I also think it's a tomb. And a very special one at that."

Later Matt was at his desk in the office, doodling notes to himself on a pad of Puma stationery. He had swiveled his chair around to face the wall relief map when Escobar and the two Rescate agents walked in. The top sheet on the notepad represented a stream-of-consciousness time line detailing the hour or so he had spent ruminating over Rachel's theories and the present state of affairs— abbreviated phrases and questions; exclamation marks, dollar signs, and arcane symbols; a coded chronology of events; and dozens of possible Spanish and Mayan translations of the emblem glyph, Rock River. By the time

Matt was aware of Escobar's presence, and before he could safely place the jottings out of sight, the police lieutenant had perched himself on the edge of the desk directly over the notepad.

Matt shook hands all around, motioning everyone to chairs and insisting that they take some coffee. Natalie threw him a nervous look from the coffee maker, where she was preparing four sweetened cups. Ortiz gazed intently at the room's maps and colorful posters; he gave Natalie an appraising look and whispered something to his partner. Suentes turned around to regard her, and the two agents leaned back in their chairs as Natalie eased between them to set two steaming mugs on the desk.

Matt could hear Rachel moving around in the apartment, getting ready to go out. An American couple living in Palenque owned an extensive collection of books on Mayan studies, and Rachel thought she might be able to research some of the questions that had arisen. Matt had persuaded her to leave the codex behind and showed her a place in the loft where she could conceal it for the day.

But she had taken the Polaroid prints with her and planned to mail off the roll of 35-mm first thing. Matt had nixed the idea of getting the slides developed in Palenque.

Peripherally he could see that Escobar was glancing down at the notepad. "Is this a social call, Lieutenant?"

Escobar studied the pad for a moment. "You should have such luck," he said, lifting his head.

Matt made a toasting gesture with his cup.

Escobar turned to watch Natalie for a moment, coming to some decision about her presence. "The body found in the ruins," he began. "The man has been identified as T'sup Kin, a Lacandon who was living in Guatemala."

"Near Sayaxche," Ortiz added, sipping at his coffee.

"I've heard," Matt told them.

"Our first guess was that the Indian had been murdered because of some vendetta," Escobar continued, "but we have reason to question that now. It's been some time since he was last seen in Palenque, and his old friends were surprised to see him. But they were even more surprised by the money he was waving around.

Buying everyone drinks, looking for *chamacas* . . .'' The lieutenant made an obscene gesture with his fingers. ''He told everyone that he was working for a couple of rich gringos and making lots of Yankee dollars. That, if fact, was what had brought him to Palenque. Big business.''

Matt heard water running in the apartment. Escobar turned briefly to the sound, then swung back to Matt with a menacing look. ''Did your clients mention the Indian?''

Matt assumed a thoughtful pose. ''No. But I see what you're getting at. You figure the murders are related.''

''We think the Indian was working for them,'' Suentes said. ''Carrying their contraband across the border.''

''When did you last see Rachel Riordan?'' Escobar cut in.

Matt fought to keep his face blank. ''Yesterday. I asked her to stop by.'' From the apartment came the sound of steps on the loft ladder.

''You had a long talk.''

''Ms. Riordan was upset. We talked about Lauren, not much else. I'm trying to take things slowly. You know, see what she knows.''

Suentes made a disgruntled sound.

At the same time, Escobar reached down to give the notepad a quarter turn toward him. Most of it was initials and questions Matt had written to himself in English, but the list of Rock River possibilities would be clear enough to the lieutenant's eye. Then all at once Escobar was on his feet.

''Villahermosa wants me to bring this investigation to a conclusion,'' he told Matt angrily. ''This is no longer a simple case of murder or smuggling. Green and gold credentials are showing up. Do I need to explain what that signifies? Portillo,'' he whispered in harsh tones, rubbing his fingertips together. ''Portillo.''

Matt tried to conceal his amazement. The colors meant Gobernación, a select intelligence group that answered to the president himself.

''A person of some influence seems to have taken an interest in the case of the North American runners and has been spreading his theories around Villahermosa.

Now everyone is asking questions about Rachel Riordan.''

Kul, Matt thought.

Ortiz said, "Did she say what type of work she did?''

Matt heard Rachel on the ladder. "Imports,'' he heard himself say.

The two Rescate agents traded looks. "She works for a New York museum in the department of acquisitions.'' Ortiz waited for a reaction. "She is a Mayan scholar.''

Matt said, "Who would have figured it?''

"She told us that a friend who lives in Mexico City informed her of the deaths.'' This came from Suentes. "But it appears that she arrived in Mexico the very same morning the articles appeared in the newspapers, *before* the consulate tried to contact her. How could she know to come to Palenque?''

Ortiz stabbed the air with his finger. "Unless she was planning to come here all along. We checked with the airlines. She cancelled a flight to Guatemala City to come to Mexico instead—two days early.''

Matt uttered a silent prayer of thanks that Rachel hadn't booked the flight through Puma.

"What have you two been talking about?'' Escobar said, leaning over the desk.

"I was helping her make arrangements for the bodies. You can ask Bustamonte.''

"We already have.''

"So what do you want from me?''

"Where is she now?''

Matt heard the door to the veranda open and slam shut. "Well, she's not here. Look around if you don't believe me.''

"Her hotel room is empty,'' Suentes said. "She didn't even inform the desk clerk that she was checking out.''

Matt made a note to thank the La Cañada desk boy for his discretion. He was about to tell Escobar that Rachel had mentioned something about a flight home from Mérida, when the shortwave radio suddenly erupted into life. It was Silvio calling from the lodge.

Matt and Natalie sat dumbfounded, regarding each other across the room.

"Don't you think you should answer it?" Escobar suggested.

Matt said, "Sure, I just didn't know if we were finished here."

"We can wait," the lieutenant said, thrusting his chin out.

Matt turned to Natalie. "Take that, will you, Nat?"

She threw him a brief but angry look and got up from her typewriter to adjust the radio's tuning knobs. "This is Palenque," she affirmed, keying the mike. "Go ahead, Posada Paraíso."

"It's a beautiful lagoon," Ortiz mused.

Matt said, "Yeah, one of my favorite places," on the edge of panic.

Suentes nodded. "Good fishing. Snook, peacock bass . . ." He held his hands apart, approximating the size of a fish he had once caught.

Matt urged him on, wanting nothing more than to swap tall tales. He could hear Silvio's voice coming through the speaker. "We ave us a profile on doze clients ya ben askin bout," the Belizian was telling Natalie. "De ones gon downriver."

Natalie said, "Go ahead," a pencil poised.

"You heard about the skirmish?" Ortiz was saying.

Matt turned to him, perplexed.

"Between the insurgents and the troops stationed at Pipiles. The rangers have been chasing them ever since the American archeologist was released."

". . . Americans. Dis mon say dey look like rodeo guys, or Tabasco cowboys. Snakeskin boots and such . . ."

"Near the site where they are holding the scientist."

"One wit a tattoo of a dancin' girl on his left arm . . ."

Escobar was listening to Natalie, a grim look on his face.

"A battle?" Matt enthused, loudly.

"Colonel Reyes caught up with them near San Diego. You know it?"

". . . nothing else for the moment, Paraíso. We'll be in touch. Over."

"Yeah, I've been to the *petroleros'* camp," Matt said to Ortiz.

Suentes said, "Aguilar escaped with his life and a lot fewer men."

"Colonel Reyes thinks that Aguilar might be moving toward the Usumacinta, perhaps hoping to get to one of his jungle camps or cross the border into Mexico."

Matt pressed his hands together, then fingertipped his mustache back from his lip. Natalie had returned to her typing and Escobar was pacing back and forth in front of the desk. He looked at Natalie again and said, "Tell him about the Honduran."

Ortiz threw a look at his partner. "Volan has been released." Quietly now. "We believe the American Central Intelligence Agency is involved."

Matt looked from face to face, baffled. "But Volan was working for the guerrillas, wasn't he?"

"You tell us," Ortiz said. "You tell us what your two clients were doing holding hands with a double agent."

"Villahermosa has ordered me to arrest all the principals," the lieutenant said without turning to look at Matt. "I told them to give me another day or so." He swung around to face the desk and squared his shoulders. "Tell the Riordan woman to surrender herself."

Matt returned a tight-lipped nod.

"I want you to bring her in personally. You have until tomorrow afternoon."

"Shit, Matt!" Natalie said as soon as Escobar and the agents had left.

He echoed the curse and shot to his feet, tearing the top sheet from the pad and balling it up. Natalie handed him what she had written down at the radio.

"Does it sound like those guys?"

"I'll lay you odds," he said, reading over the descriptions.

"But Paolo said there were five of them."

"Kul could have a small army working for him."

"You really think it was him?"

Matt nodded. "And I'll bet he knows about Rachel. She's at the Gradys' library. You willing to go down there?"

Natalie folded her arms across her chest. "Is this for love, or are you planning to give me a raise?"

Matt stared at her and grinned. "You name it. Any ideas where we can stash her?"

"How about my place?"

Matt cracked a smile. "Thanks, Nat, but—"

"What else can we do? And let me take care of her things." She took two steps toward the back door, then turned.

"You think I'm being a bit foolhardy here."

"No," she told him. "Just suicidal."

Matt glanced again at the descriptions. It was time for him to pay an unannounced call on Jules Kul and company.

# ⧫⧫⧫15⧫⧫⧫

# The Long Count

**A**ngel wasn't expected to return from San Cristóbal for several more hours, so Matt caught a taxi out to El Templo. The driver recited a list of complaints. Too much heat, he told Matt. Too much tourists, too much bad news. The worst of it he reserved for El Chichón, blaming the volcano for everything from the haze to inflation and unemployment. *Too much El Chichón!* In the back seat, Matt undid his shirt and let the hot breeze assault him.

The rented Jeep was parked in the hotel courtyard between two pop-top vans bearing California tags. Matt walked directly to Kul's suite and knocked. Kim opened the door as far as the security chain would allow, gave Matt a brief once-over, and pushed the door closed. Matt heard a short muffled exchange from inside the room, then Kul's laugh before Kim undid the lock and let him in.

"Well, Mr. Terry," Kul said, amused, "to what do we owe the honor of this surprise visit?"

Matt took a look around. Kul's two cowboys were present. The dark-haired one was standing by the patio door as though he had been prepared to bolt. The blond was sitting on the couch, leaning slightly forward, forearms atop his knees. The bridge of his nose wore a smaller version of the bandage Matt had noticed the day

164

before. Matt could see that his eyes were underscored by twin yellowish-purple crescents. His arms were clean, but Matt wasn't sure about the dark-haired hombre; he had on a white cotton shirt of a type that was popular in the Yucatán, with an open neck and three-quarter-length sleeves. Not that confirmations of this sort were necessary.

A third man, with long limbs and bony hands, sat at a wicker table near the doorway to the suite's kitchenette. He was gaunt and sandy-haired, dressed in ill-fitting pants, a striped shirt, and desert boots. Niles Chalker, Matt guessed. Huatcho was serving him lunch.

"That rare book we were talking about," Matt said to Kul. "Something you should know about it before we start off on our little walkabout."

Kul said, "Indeed." He was barefoot, gnomishly hunched over the walking stick, his topknot braided. "Something you couldn't tell me over the phone, I trust."

Matt looked at him evenly. "You know how phones are. I wanted to be sure we understood each other."

"Of course, of course. My associates," he said, motioning behind him.

Matt nodded to the man at the door. To the blond he said, "Been using your face for demolition work?" The cowboy tensed and made a move to get up, but Kul was quick to wave him down, laughing.

"No, no, Mr. Terry. Josh was involved in a little accident on the drive down here, isn't that right, Josh?"

The man glared at Matt from the couch. From the look of it, Josh's nose had been broken before. His eyes were close-set under a pronounced brow ridge.

"Isn't that right, Josh?" Kul repeated.

The cowboy swallowed hard and forced a thin smile. "Yeah, that's right, Mr. Kul, I ran into somethin'. But I got the guy's number, and I'm plannin' to look him up."

Matt said, "Lawsuit, huh?"

"We'll see," Josh told him.

Kul coughed meaningfully. "Well, Stormy and Josh were just on their way out." Kim already had the door open, and the two men exited, muttering curt good-byes.

"A drink," Kul said.

Matt said, "Coffee," moving to the table.

"Niles Chalker," the gaunt man said, getting up and extending his hand. "I've heard good things about your company."

Matt shook hands and sat down. Kul hobbled over and joined them, wearing a sober expression. "Now, Matt, what do you have for us?" He saw Matt glance at Chalker and added: "It's all right. I've explained everything to Niles."

"I didn't say I had anything for you. I just said I wanted to talk about the codex."

Chalker said, "Then you do have it?"

Matt thought he detected a Midwestern accent. "I'm close to having it. But I want to know if our deal still stands."

Kul and Chalker eyed each other. "Of course it still stands. That's why Niles is here. To . . . verify the co-dex. He will take possession of it."

"In the name of the academic community."

"Naturally, Matt," Chalker said, sounding sincere. "I have no intention of letting a find of this magnitude end up in a private collection."

"It's great to see all this concern," Matt said to the table.

Chalker turned to Kul. "Mr. Kul will be credited with the discovery and the donation."

"For my efforts."

Matt said, "Let's talk about those efforts for a minute. You know, this thing isn't going to come cheap."

Kul smiled tolerantly. "I don't want to quibble, Matt. Price is dictated by effort. And we all know how much effort has already attended this piece. Simply name your price."

"Three hundred thousand," he said. "That's adding some on top for *my* efforts."

Kul said, "Done. How and when?"

"Dollars. Two hundred no later than tomorrow eve-ning; the rest on delivery."

"And you'll have something to show us by then?"

"A page, a leaf, whatever you call it. It's yours when I see the money."

Kul's thinned eyebrows went up. "Matt, you surprise

me. One would almost think you've been involved in this sort of transaction before.''

Matt grinned. ''I took a correspondence course.''

Chalker said, ''When will you have the rest of it?''

''Within two days.''

''And you've seen it? The fragment is intact?''

Matt leaned back and folded his arms, studying Kul as Kul regarded Chalker. The archeologist's face went red. ''Mr. Kul, I'm—''

''Nonsense, Niles. Let's be honest, shall we? Matt seems to have a weakness for it.'' There was something confessional in his tone. ''We know that the codex is . . . incomplete.''

Matt said, ''I don't know anything about that. You'll get whatever I get.''

Kul shrugged his shoulders and grimaced. ''Well, then it really doesn't matter, does it? A fragment, a half, it makes no difference.''

''No difference to me.''

''Then it's settled,'' Kul said, pushing himself upright. ''Contact me tomorrow and we'll make arrangements for the first part of the payment. Oh, and Matt,'' he added when they had reached the door, ''let's try to keep everything as simple as possible. Remember the river and those lessons you mentioned. You might remind your client of this when you see her.''

Matt turned and walked out, feeling as though he'd stepped into a blast furnace. There were two dozen hotel guests sprawled in the shade near the swimming pool. He spied Hano Olivar among them and went over to congratulate him on finally getting the pool filled. They stood together on the tiled apron watching a shapely Mexican teenager backstroke her way through the cool, spring water. Matt assured Olivar that Jake would be thrilled to hear the news. He was happy about it himself and offered Matt a ride back to town.

Olivar got himself entangled in a conversation with a travel rep from New York before they could set off, so Matt took a seat in the shade and closed his eyes for the first time in what seemed like days. When he opened them a few minutes later, he saw Kul's *pistolas* approaching the pool in swimsuits. They had hotel towels draped around their necks. Matt eased himself out of sight but was close enough to poolside to catch a glimpse of the hula girl tattoo before the one called Stormy hit the water.

Matt had Olivar drop him off at the main highway intersection, figuring it would be quicker to walk the few remaining blocks to Puma rather than fight the traffic. Palenque was supposed to be an Andean village for the day's film shoot, and all sorts of locals were walking around in the heat sporting striped ponchos and Colombian fedoras. The scene, as false as it was, brought back memories Matt was in no mood to confront, memories of the corps, of Susan and their too-brief time together.

He stopped in front of the Cine Twilite, pretending to read the coming attractions posters when what he was actually doing was studying the reflection of the beat-up Ford parked across the street. Two of Escobar's plainclothesmen were in the front seat eating tacos and keeping an eye on the office entrance.

"Did you see them?" Natalie asked as he came through the door. She was at her desk, fanning herself with the morning paper.

"We might as well invite them in," Matt said, dropping into a chair and plucking his sweat-soaked shirt from his shoulders. "Everything go okay?"

"Yeah, finally. I practically had to drag her out of the Gradys' library. She doesn't want to believe she's in trouble. I sent her out to the *finca*. Kit's there with her."

"You didn't tell her anything about Kul's men?"

Natalie shook her head. "Are you kidding? That's your department, Matt. I just told her about Escobar."

"Anything else come up?"

"La Cañada called."

"And?"

"They want to talk to you."

"Probably to tell me about the police. One of us should stop by there later and square Rachel's bill."

Natalie said, "I'll take care of it," penciling a note to herself.

Matt closed up the office for siesta and got the long-distance operator to put through a line to the States. He poured himself a beer while the call was being placed, and brought his chair over to the wall map of the Petén. His finger found the town of Paso Caballos at the headwaters of the Río San Pedro. Raphael Aguilar's rebel band had been looting a ruin complex somewhere close by when the archeologist and his police escort had wandered in unannounced. Then Reyes's Kaibil rangers had caught up with them, a battle had ensued, and the guerrillas had apparently fled southwest in the direction of San Diego, which was some forty miles due east of Yaxchilan. It seemed a risky move given the fact that Aguilar was placing his forces within easy striking distance of La Libertad on the Flores-Sayaxche road, but not if the rebels were attempting to make a run for the border, as Reyes suspected.

Matt was scanning place-names on the map when the operator rang back, and Jake Welles came on the line a moment later. Matt caught him up on everything, including his plan to hand Jules Kul's head to Escobar. He asked if Jake had been able to learn anything about Rachel.

"I located a few of her articles. They're brilliant."

Matt said, "What about the museum?"

"Kurt Stevenson's the head of Mesoamerican acquisitions. When I brought up Rachel's name, he wanted to know where I'd met her. I told him I hadn't actually met her, but an associate of mine in Palenque had. I thought that was the end of it. Then I get a call this morning from somebody named Sol Nagel, who turns out to be one of the museum's directors. And this guy is practically frantic. He wants to know where Rachel is, how he can reach her."

"What'd you tell him?"

"I said she was still in Palenque as far as I knew. Told him I'd contact him if I found out where she was staying."

"Nagel, you said?"

"He's a heavyweight from what I gather. I vaguely remember meeting him on that last promotional swing through New York."

Matt made note of the name.

"About this codex, Matt," Jake asked. "Do you think it's authentic?"

"What the hell do I know? She seems to think so. And Kul's convinced."

"So what happens now?"

"I have a talk with Escobar."

"Does Rachel know yet?"

"Not yet. But she doesn't have a choice."

"At least she'll get most of the investment back."

"Except Billie," Matt said. "But you're right. And Kul won't be able to say anything. It's as good as drug money."

Jake grew quiet. "I think you better take some time off, amigo," he said after about twenty seconds of long-distance static.

"Am I reading you right, Jake?"

Jake let out a slow exhale. "We've got the company to think of, *compadre*. Look, I want you to do what you have to do, but we've gotta try not to track mud all over the place. Panama's already off limits for you, and I don't want to see Mexico added to the list. Maybe a week or two at the lodge until everything blows over. Natalie can mind the store while you're gone."

Matt thought a moment and said, "I was thinking along the same lines, Jake."

Jake went on to say that he would be leaving for Guatemala City in about ten days to meet the group for the next Classic Maya tour, but that he was figuring in a quick stopover in Palenque on his way down.

Ángel returned from his grueling trip to the highlands just as Matt was reopening the office. T'sup Kin's wife and children were safely tucked away in San Cristóbal for the time being. Ángel had informed the people who would be watching over the family of the murder in Palenque, and they had agreed to break the tragic news to the Lacandon's widow. He had had to talk the woman into accepting the money, but she seemed to comprehend that it was in her best interests to remain silent about her husband's involvement with the Americans.

Matt sent Ángel home early for some much-needed rest. An hour later Natalie left in the Range Rover, the codex secreted in her day pack. Matt hung around for another fifteen minutes; then, with Escobar's men continuing their watch, he exited through the veranda door, plunged into the barranca's maze of trails, and hurried off to the rendezvous point he and his partner had established.

The *finca* Natalie rented was five kilometers down an unpaved track that ran south off the ruins road and ended in a cow pasture bordered by an undisturbed stand of bamboo forest. It was a small whitewashed place surrounded by shade trees and jacaranda, with a tiled roof and an ancient-looking door. They had lived there together during their rough stretch, before Kit had entered the picture. He was a short and compactly built New Englander with a beard of tight brown curls and the pale eyes of a visionary, a former Outward Bound instructor who had done extensive caving in the Yucatán and central Belize. Natalie had met him in Isla de Mujeres, where she had gone to think things through. "My caveman," she had called him. Matt hadn't liked him much at the start, but they had gradually grown to be friends. Kit was quiet and compassionate; he read books on metaphysics and got by selling bags of psychedelic mushrooms to the campground freaks.

He was standing in the garden when they drove up. The large mutt he and Natalie had adopted struggled to its feet, yapping excitedly, and walked over to the Rover, putting its front paws up on the driver's side door. Matt patted the dog's rump and shook hands with Kit. The caver wore a beatific smile, the sunny side of a mushroom high.

He said, "Rachel's a trip. She put the whole Mayan thing in perspective for me in like two hours. I'm fucking dazzled."

Natalie rolled her eyes. "Let's go for a walk, babe," she said, taking Kit's hand.

Matt saw them off with a nod and continued up the path to the house. He found Rachel in the spare room, glasses perched on the tip of her nose, bent over a book she had weighted open with four volcanic pestles from Kit's hand-dug pre-Columbian collection. She stood up and almost came over to him, but restrained herself at the last moment, reading some of the distance he was projecting. He laid the aluminum case on the bed beside her bag and sat down in a wicker throne chair, resting his elbows on the armrests.

"Matt, about the police," she started to say.

"We'll get to that," he said, cutting her off, holding her gaze for a moment. "I know who killed them. They work for Jules Kul."

Rachel made a pained sound. "Kul?! But Matt, why—"

"This is why," Matt snapped, gesturing to the codex. "They tracked Billie to Sayaxche. They asked around, found out we were going downriver, and followed us. They must have thought she had it with her. I don't know what went on in camp . . . maybe they got the Indian's name, or maybe they already knew about him. But when they couldn't find the codex, they either went back to Sayaxche to pay a visit on T'sup Kin or they came here, knowing they'd find him in Palenque.

"But he didn't have it, either, and I don't think they managed to get him to talk before they killed him. So Kul began to think that I had it, or at least that I knew where to look for it. He even had my place searched, but nothing turned up. That's when he decided he was going to have to negotiate with me. In the meantime, he learned that you were down here, and I'm sure he knows you work for the museum. He put a bug in some politico's ear, and whoever that was set the Villahermosa authorities straight. Kul was probably figuring that Escobar would pick you up before you could cut a deal with me. Leave himself an open field. But there's a bunch of high-level shit going down that I can't make heads or tails of. Something about your sister's involvement with the Honduran."

"Cut a deal with you?" Rachel asked, confused.

"I let him believe I knew something, even before T'sup Kin's wife showed up."

"But how could he have known about it, Matt? I was the only one who knew, I swear it."

Matt put up his hands. "I don't know how he found out. At first I thought Billie was dealing with both of you."

"She wouldn't do that!"

"All right, so it could have been Michael. The only other thing that makes any sense is that Volan or one of the guerrillas let it slip. I still think there was more than one sample page floating around, despite what they promised Billie." Matt looked hard at Rachel. "Kul knows it's a fragment. How could he know that? Did your sister tell you it was only a partial codex?"

Rachel looked away. "No. I mean, she told me it was *intact*, but now I don't know whether she meant complete or in good condition."

Mat rubbed his hands on his pants. "I told Kul I'd turn it over to him on the condition it went directly to the authorities."

Rachel made a panicked gesture. "Matt, no!"

"You know what he did? He brought in an archeologist—a guy named Chalker—to convince me that it's all on the up and up."

Rachel stared at him aghast. "Niles Chalker?"

Matt nodded, wondering about her reaction.

She said, "They're practically partners. Kul writes out the checks for Chalker's fieldwork, and in exchange the good professor supplies him with some of his most priceless finds." She flashed Matt a bitter look. "You can't do it, Matt. He'll lock it away somewhere. I can prove what I'm telling you."

Matt shook his head. "Save it. I found out about Kul and Chalker."

"Then you're not serious about turning it over to them?"

"We're going to hand the whole works over to Rescate," he said after a moment.

Rachel started shaking her head back and forth. "No you're not, no you're not."

Matt got up and took her by the shoulders. "Do you think we have any *choice* in this? Kul's already had three people killed. He's not going to stop now. You're thinking you can just bring it to New York, aren't you?" Matt forced her to look at him. "He'll find you, Rachel. He'll get it, one way or another."

"He won't find me," she said, breaking out of Matt's hold. "I'll turn it over to the museum. It'll be too late for him to do anything about it."

Matt turned and stormed away from her. "You've got
your head up your ass. This whole thing is blown wide
open. You show up in New York with the codex, and
Interpol's going to be all over you. They've got this thing
down, Rachel. You'd have to sit on that codex for ten
years."

"You're trying to save your own neck," she seethed,
crying out of anger and frustration.

Matt's lips tightened. "I won't deny it. But we're in
this together. And we've gotta give them something if we
want to walk. If we don't, Escobar's going to pull the
roof down on us for conspiracy and anything else he can
come up with."

Rachel's eyes were narrowed when she looked up. "Do
you know what you're throwing away?"

"Why don't you tell me," Matt said, sitting down.

"It isn't the money or any of that. It's the icing, Matt,
the news it would make. You start people talking about
you, and doors begin to open." She gestured broadly to
the room. "Aren't you sick of living like this? You've
got to think of Puma, Matt. Or think of *yourself*. Do you
know what this could mean for you?" She waited for him
to absorb it. "We'll split the find—everything, right down
the middle."

Matt looked out the window. "Our pictures on the
cover of *People* magazine."

She glared at him. "It wouldn't be the strangest
thing."

"Oh, yes, it would." Matt laughed. "And what do we
do for an encore?"

"You know how many clients you'd have at your
door?"

"That's just what I need," he muttered. "They'll be
interviewing us in prison, Rachel. It's finished. We're out
of it."

She cursed him. "Would you do it if it was Laurie
asking you?"

"No," he said evenly.

Rachel regarded the aluminum case with a wry expression. "How are you going to do it?"

"I want all the signs to point to Kul. But you let me
worry about that part of it. Right now, we've gotta figure

some way to get you out of the country." She kept her eyes on the case, looking up absently when Matt said her name. "D' you hear me?"

She gave her head a toss and offered him a weak smile. "All right, Matt. Whatever you say."

"Good," he said without meaning it, her easy response throwing him off track. "I can drive you to Mérida and get you on a plane to Dallas or Miami."

"When?"

"I wish it could be right now, but we're going to have to wait until I arrange the buy. Escobar's giving us a bit of lead time, and I don't want to rile him just yet—not until I have Kul wrapped up."

Rachel nodded. "I understand."

He glanced over at the case. "What's going to happen to it?"

She shrugged. "Some Guatemalan or Mexican epigrapher will get first crack at it. It'll be a mad scramble."

Matt thought about the strange journey the codex had taken since leaving the hands of Serpent Skull's scribe. "I'm going to need a page to show Kul. He's willing to pay two hundred thousand up front. You'll have to write the rest off as a loss."

Rachel bristled. "I told you the money doesn't mean anything."

Matt was glad to hear her say it but refrained from speaking Billie's name. He stood where she had to look at him. "Where did it come from, Rachel? You said it was private funds."

She shook her head. "I'm sorry, Matt."

"Sol Nagel, maybe?"

The color drained from her face. "Please, Matt, you have to promise me you won't bring his name into this."

"Wouldn't look good for the museum to have one of its directors financing a smuggling operation, huh? Nice of him to let you and your sister take the heat."

"I can't talk about this now," Rachel said, turning away from him.

He reached for the case, and her hand came down on it at the same time. "I'll give you your damned page."

Matt stepped back, trying to read things from her side, Billie's death and all. Maybe it was all twisted around, he thought. What he should do was let her walk away with the book, a compensation. But it felt wrong, and impossible on top of that. Later, as Rachel was slipping the bark leaf into a plastic folder, he told her that he'd been giving some thought to Rock River.

"I was just fooling around with different interpretations, like 'hard water' or 'underground river.' And I remembered hearing about a spring in the Petén, not far from Piedras Negras. A place the *xateros* call—"

"*Xateros?*" She shook her head in a puzzled way.

"*Xate* gatherers," he told her. "A small palm that looks like a fern. It grows all over the Petén and Chiapas."

Rachel nodded. "I know what you're talking about. *Chamaedorea*, the 'hotel lobby palm.' I thought it was called *chib*."

"Well, *xate*'s what they call it on the Usumacinta. Anyway, this spring I'm talking about is called *Aguaculto*. It could mean 'water cult,' or even 'cultivated water,' but I thought it might be a corruption of *agua oculto*—'hidden waters.' Like Rock River."

Matt saw a look of recognition begin to surface on her face. She rushed over to the table and opened one of her ring binders to a sheaf of printout sheets. "Aguaculto," she said to herself.

Matt looked on from behind the chair, watching her fingernail trace a path through columns of alphabetized site names. Ultimately, she pushed the book away and let out an exasperated sigh. "It's not here. But I know I've heard that name." She looked over her shoulder at him. "I'm going to have to go back to the library."

Matt straightened up. "I don't want you leaving here."

Rachel regarded him a moment, then laughed. "Are you thinking of adopting me, or what? Look, Matt, I appreciate your concern, but I can handle myself. Now, I need to get back to the library. I might also have to call New York to check out another source. We're on to something, I can feel it."

Matt picked up the page and walked to the door, a fuck-you lodged in his gut, even though he knew it was his own goddamn fault. "Just make sure you stick with

Natalie. And you ride with your head down, understand?''

"That's ridiculous," Rachel said, then agreed to it.

"I'll call Bustamonte and tell him that you'll be by to use the phone. But make it quick and try and get back here before siesta." Matt put his hand on the door latch.

"You're not going to stay?"

He shook his head, beyond trying to figure her out. "Escobar's got his men watching the office, probably hoping you'll show up. It'll be better if I'm back there to keep up appearances."

Rachel looked around uncomfortably.

Matt said, "You'll be all right."

She bit her lower lip and offered him a tight-lipped nod.

# 16

## Bread and Chocolate

"Señor Jules Kul?" Escobar said, a mixture of anger and disbelief in his voice.

"That's the name," Matt told him. "You can check it out for yourself. He's staying at El Templo."

Ortiz and Suentes traded worried looks, as if to say, *it's too early in the day for this*, when actually it was almost noon. Matt had allowed Escobar's plainclothesmen to tail him right into police headquarters, where his unannounced arrival had taken the lieutenant completely by surprise. He was leaning forward across his desk, shoulders bunched up. "Do you know what you are saying, man? Do you know who you're talking about?"

"The influential person who's been ringing all the bells in Villahermosa."

"Then how can you expect me to believe this story?"

"Because it's true," Matt said, holding Escobar's gaze. "The North Americans had an antiquity Kul wanted, one they'd purchased from Raphael Aguilar's insurgents. Only they didn't have the thing on them when they were killed because they'd given it to the Lacandon to carry into Mexico. Thing was, it was T'sup Kin's wife who had the piece. She showed up with it in Palenque and mistook Rachel for Lauren Riordan. Except for the haircut, they look alike."

Escobar made a sour expression. "Rachel Riordan was part of the plan all along. She came down here before she learned of her sister's death, and she lied to us about her work."

Matt said, "Rachel did come down here to meet Lauren. But it had nothing to do with the antiquity. She was joining them for a few days of travel. Lauren phoned New York from Tikal and told Rachel that her plans had changed. That's why Rachel canceled the flight to Guati. When she arrived in Mexico City, a friend met her at the airport and showed her the newspaper articles."

"Bullshit," Escobar said. "Why did she lie?"

Matt shrugged. "She was scared."

"Then she has this antiquity?" Ortiz asked after a moment.

"We know where it is."

Escobar said, "What's to stop me from arresting you right now? You've withheld evidence. That makes you an accomplice to murder and theft."

"You could do that. But you're the one who told me to stick with her and learn whatever I could. Hear me out and you'll have everything you need to tie this up. Earn some points with the green and gold in Villahermosa."

Escobar snorted. "Big balls . . . But you're going to have to show more than that. What proof do you have?"

Matt looked over at Ortiz. "If you check with Pipiles, you're going to find the names of Kul's *pistolas* written down in Colonel Reyes's ledger under whatever identities they were using at the time. At least two of them are in Palenque now." He looked back at Escobar. "I know where T'sup Kin's wife is hiding. She'll identify the men as the ones who burned down her house after they came looking for her husband. If that's not enough, I can arrange it so you can catch Kul in the middle of the buy and pull everyone in at the same time."

The room fell silent for a few moments. Matt tipped his face up to bask in the gentle currents of the overhead fan.

"What exactly are you asking for in return?" Escobar said at last.

"Twenty-four hours to set everything up," Matt told him, renewed.

"That's it?"

"Plus immunity for myself and the Riordan woman when this thing goes down."

"Big balls," Escobar said.

Suentes asked about the antiquity, and Matt pictured the codex. He said, "Something worth dying for."

Escobar's eyes bored into him. "I want to hear it, all of it. From day one."

Stormy Skye, Kul's dark-haired *pistola*, was making anxious movements on one of the trails below the veranda. Matt approached him from behind and tapped him on the shoulder, sidestepping as the man swung around. Skye was momentarily confused, then enraged when he saw Matt standing off to the side of the trail.

"Take it easy," Matt said with a grin. "At least I didn't keep you waiting here all day."

"Fuckin' asshole," Skye spit.

"Sure thing," Matt said, waiting for the man to step in. But Skye's conflict was all too obvious. "Tell your boss I want to see him this afternoon, two o'clock in the office. Make sure he brings the paperwork." He started for the stairs and turned around. "Oh, and I'll be sure to mention how well behaved you were."

Once upstairs, Matt got on the radio to the lodge, telling Silvio to have Paolo call the office. Matt hoped he could persuade the boatman to take the fast launch downriver to Echeverría and meet him after the buy. His plan was to get himself across the border and into the lodge while Escobar was busy sorting out the details of the murders, assuming for the moment that the lieutenant could be trusted to honor their deal. Matt had no illusions about being able to walk away from everything clean, but he reasoned that he would be safer on Guatemalan than Mexican soil. Rachel would be safe back in New York.

Jules Kul, accompanied by Kim and Niles Chalker, showed up just before two. They left Stormy outside at the wheel of the Jeep. Matt showed them into the office, glancing at Escobar's Ford before securing the front gate. He pulled two chairs up to his desk and told Kim to feel free to sit on the floor. The boy threw him a sharp look from the door but kept silent.

"Really, Matt," Kul laughed. "You could use a refresher course in hospitality."

"Yeah, I'll be sure to use your money to enroll in one. Did you bring it?"

Kul waved his hand in the air. "What's the use," he said to Chalker, indicating Matt. "Give it to him." Chalker snapped open a briefcase and placed several individually banded stacks of U.S. currency on the desk. "Two hundred thousand, as per your request."

Matt felt his palms begin to tingle, his stomach contort, more than when he'd unwrapped the codex. Money did this to people, he supposed, especially when it was enough to fill an attaché case. A friend of Bustamonte's had agreed to give the cash the once-over. But Matt didn't imagine that Kul would waste their time with funny money. As he reached for one of the stacks, Kul rapped his walking stick against the floor, bringing Kim to full alert. Matt looked from Kim to Kul, his hand theatrically poised.

"You said you would have something for me in the way of proof."

Matt leaned away from the desk. "I did mention something about that, didn't I?" He opened the top drawer and showed them the plastic-wrapped page. Chalker's eyes lit up.

"May I?" the archeologist rasped, extending a hand.

Matt held back a moment, then slid it across the desk, grinning. The two men bent over the page, making gasping sounds while Matt counted the money. "You satisfied?" he asked minutes later.

Kul swallowed and found his voice. "And you can obtain the rest of it?"

Matt held up one of the stacks. "This'll help things along."

"I'll hold on to this," Chalker said, carefully placing the page into his briefcase.

Kul said, "When can you have it?"

"Tomorrow. Noon."

"Where?"

Matt shrugged. "You call it."

Kul looked to the archeologist. "Then why don't we make it at El Templo," he said, relaxed now. "Since I've already taken the liberty of telling Señor Olivar that you and I are planning a tour."

"Swell," Matt said, not really meaning it. Puma had a good thing going with Hano Olivar, and Matt's involvement with the police and Kul could end up jeopardizing that. At the same time, he didn't want to plant any suspicions in Kul's mind by suggesting an alternative meet. He thought that being in the hotel might even keep Escobar's men under control in the event things got nasty.

Kul got to his feet. "Until tomorrow, then."

Matt unlocked the door and grate and showed them out. The black Ford followed the Jeep down the road.

Paolo radioed later that afternoon and agreed to meet Matt in Echeverría. He promised to be there no later than Monday afternoon, leaving Matt a little less than two days to carry through with the meeting at the hotel, get Rachel to Mérida, and get himself across the border. He discussed some of this with Ángel, who agreed to keep Sunday open to drive Matt to the river, even though it was something of a feast day, marking the last sabbath before Palm Sunday and the Semana Santa. Matt instructed him to make certain that the Rover was filled with petrol and ready to leave at a moment's notice. Ángel insisted that Matt consider spending Sunday night at his cousin's *choza*, which was just south of Chancala on the Echeverría road. That way they could at least avoid an all-night drive to the Usumacinta. An early start from Chancala on Monday would give them ample time to reach the settlement before Paolo arrived.

Matt phoned Escobar and explained that everything was in motion. The lieutenant gave him the go-ahead, saying simply that his men would be there when it mattered.

An hour later he rode a cab out to the corner of the *finca* road, the money stuffed inside a Puma travel bag. The mutt met him along the road and kept him company until just short of the gate, when he took off to rout a group of cattle egrets that had alighted in the pasture.

The Rover was parked out front, and Natalie's horse was grazing in the yard.

"Come on in," Natalie called out before he could knock.

She was in the kitchen, dressed in a long tie-dyed skirt and blouse, a leather headband in her blond hair. Matt said, "Are the Dead in town or what?"

"My big scene's tomorrow," Natalie said over her shoulder as she stirred the contents of an iron pot. "Figured I'd do some method acting, really get into the role."

"What're you supposed to be?"

"The person I was ten years ago," she told him.

Matt sniffed at the pot. "Let's hear it."

"Did you really tell her to ride with her head down?"

"Yeah, I did."

She shook her head in a disapproving way and held out a shaky hand for his inspection. "Look at this, I'm a goddamn basket case."

"Where'd you go?"

She shrugged. "To the library, to Bustamonte's, to market."

"Any problems?"

"No."

"Where is she?"

Rachel gestured to the spare room. "Studying for the finals."

Matt indicated the pot with his chin. "Smells great."

"You're invited."

He asked where Kit was.

"*Hongo* hunting."

"A little dry for that, isn't it?"

"He'll come up with something."

"Just don't put them in the chili, okay?"

Natalie promised not to, and Matt went off to find Rachel. He knocked twice against the jamb, then let himself in when he got no response. She was asleep on the bed, dressed in jeans, a T-shirt, and running shoes, one arm tossed across her face. Matt had a fleeting image of Billie, dead on the jungle floor. An icy mixture of fear and misgiving depleted him of the confidence he'd been running on all day. Rachel stirred and gave a start when she saw him standing at the foot of the bed.

"I didn't mean to frighten you."

She opened her arms to him.

Matt set the travel bag down and slipped into her embrace, uncomfortable with it, wanting her out of Mexico, away from Kul before it was too late.

"I found three references to it," she whispered into his ear. Then all at once she was on her feet, a notebook in hand when Matt turned around.

"Teobart Mahler mentions an 'Agua Culta'—two words—not far from Lake Flores. But listen to this—it's from one of Désiré Charnay's letters. I had my friend in New York dictate every word. Quote: 'There are the remains of buildings there'—at Aguaculto—'but with the rains pressing us to move forward into the Petén we could effect no more than a cursory exploration of the place, that will undoubtedly prove of some future interest, situated as it is in close proximity to Yaxchilan to the west, Altar to the north, and Tikal to the east; thus acting as a conduit for trade between the cities of the Petén and the Chiapatecan highlands.' "

"A love letter," Matt said from the bed.

Rachel frowned at him and flipped over the page of her stenographer's pad. "Are you familiar with Carlos Frey?"

Matt nodded.

Frey was something of a legend in Chiapas. He had come down to Mexico at the end of World War II, gone native, and ended up living with the Lacandon Indians, who were still at that time burning copal incense to the ancient Mayan deities in Yaxchilan and other sites. According to some writers, Frey was intrigued by the fact that the tribe would periodically disappear to carry out its rituals, and subsequently learned—through a bit of alcoholic chicanery—of the existence of Bonampak. Those same writers maintained that Carlos Frey, not Giles Healy, was the first outsider to discover the site, renowned for the murals decorating the walls of one of its temples. Frey drowned in the Río Lacanjá just as news of the find was reaching the United States.

"Frey mentions the place twice in his journal," Rachel was saying. "He even claims to have accompanied Chan Bor there on a hunting expedition." She glanced at her notes. "He goes on to say that there were 'half a dozen small mounds, each one crying out to be opened. But my Lacandon friends were extremely fearful of the place and urged me to leave after they had set their small god pots ablaze on the steps of the largest of them.' "

Rachel put the notepad aside. "What do you think?"

Matt stroked his chin. "You're a born detective. But we still can't be sure that Aguaculto and Rock River are one and the same place."

"There's more," she told him. "I found a copy of a survey undertaken in 1961 by a Guatemalan archeologist. He named the site El Fuente, 'the spring,' but he mentions that the *chicleros* knew the place as Aguaculto." Rachel gestured to her notes. "Under El Fuente I found a report by a British epigrapher who visited the site in 1968." She showed Matt a drawing she had copied from a book in the Gradys' library. "These are glyphs he copied from a stela."

Matt recognized one of them as the emblem glyph for Rock River.

"His initial report lists more than half a dozen stelae at El Fuente. But all of these were gone by the time he made his second trip to the site in 1971."

"So looters have been hitting the place for over ten years," Matt said.

Rachel stared at him, deliberating, then said, "I don't want to go back to New York just yet, Matt."

Matt uttered a short, surprised laugh, but he could see that she was dead serious.

"I think we should try and get into Aguaculto."

"You really think we can just drop all this and take off on a treasure hunt?" He was more incredulous than angry.

Rachel took a step toward him. "What's stopping us?" We'll be rid of the codex. Kul will have his share of problems."

"What's stopping us," Matt repeated, laughing again. "You mean aside from the fact that we don't know where it is?"

Rachel said, "But we do know. You said yourself that

you've heard people mention the place. We know its near Piedras Negras, north of Altar.''

Matt went over to the table and picked up a *National Geographic* map of Guatemala. "Look at this," he said, pointing to a blank area east of the Usumacinta.

Rachel took the map out of his hands and studied it. "We just have to find someone to take us there." She looked at Matt. "You must know some of the people who live around there. What about in . . . Bethel," she said, chosing a name from the map.

Matt shook his head. "I don't have time for this craziness. In case you've forgotten, we've got other plans. Tomorrow afternoon I'm turning the codex over to Kul, and by tomorrow night you'll be in New York.''

"Will you cut out this protector routine! I'm not leaving. Or are you planning to wrestle me onto a plane?''

Matt encouraged her to sit down and listen. "Escobar's willing to cut us a deal, but we're not going to hang around here and wait for him to change his mind. Which he will, as soon as Kul gives his version of this thing. He has a lot more pull than we do down here. I doubt they'll keep him overnight. But Rescate will have the codex, and Escobar will have Billie's killers.''

"And we're both just going to take off?'' Rachel said, as though the idea were incomprehensible.

"You're going to New York. I'm heading into the lodge.''

"Then let me go with you.''

"Rachel—''

"I'm going to do it one way or another, Matt. There's something important at Aguaculto, I'm convinced of it. More important than the vases Laurie was running, maybe more important than the codex. I told you, I plan to come out of this with with *something*.''

Matt picked up the bag and dropped it on the bed. "There's two hundred thousand.''

"Good," she said without bothering to look inside. "Now, who do I see about hiring a guide?''

Matt put a hand to the back of his neck. "How about we at least get out of Palenque first.''

On Sunday morning Matt stuffed his rucksack with the things he would need for the trip into the lodge and left it with Ángel, who had come to the office straight from mass. They went over the details of the reworked plan once more, then Matt set out in a taxi he had had Ángel secure from the *zócalo*. The black Ford followed for a while but overtook the windowless cab on the ruins road well before the turnoff to the *finca*.

The day was hot and hazy, with a strong dose of sulfur in the air, the sky toward El Chichón ominously overcast. The movie company was filming along the road, a chase scene involving horses and jeeps.

"Stop at the corner," Matt told the driver as they were nearing the *finca* road.

From the car Matt could see Kit and the dust cloud his horse was kicking up. He instructed the driver to wait, climbed out of the backseat, and scrambled down to the pastureland below the tarmac. Kit, too, had left the road, and in a minute he had dismounted and was hurrying over to Matt with the codex case in hand.

"Just sign on the dotted line," the caver said, presenting the case in a ceremonious fashion.

Matt squatted down with it, snapping open the spring clips. Rachel had returned the codex to its original packaging, complete with foam padding and dessicants. "It's in there, man," Kit said as Matt began to unfold the foam. "I watched her pack it."

When the top page was in view, Matt nodded and put things back in order, replacing the case's gasketed lid. "I just don't want any surprises, Kit." He stood up.

"I could argue the point," Kit said.

"Don't," Matt said, glancing back at the cab. "Tell Nat to leave right away. Ángel's waiting in the office. If I'm not back there by four o'clock, she should leave for Mérida. And tell her not to let Rachel talk her out of it. If there's any arguments, cut her loose."

"Meaning?"

"Just read her her rights. If things turn bad, I'm not going to be in a position to help her."

"It's your show," Kit said dubiously. "Good luck."

Matt walked back to the cab and got into the front seat. "Ready," he said to the driver.

There was a lot of activity in the hotel courtyard; guests were milling around the pool and the buffet tables that had been set up for Sunday brunch. A marimba was in the middle of "Guadalajara." Matt scanned the crowd for some sign of the *federales*. Closing on Kul's suite, he spied two of Escobar's men posing as grounds keepers. A grim-looking Hano Olivar was pacing in the grass by the pool.

The arrangement in the suite was much as Matt remembered it from his last visit. Chalker and Kul's *pistolas* were on alert, with Kim vigilant at the door. Kul was on the couch, his good foot tucked under him, the other resting on the floor somewhat curled over on itself.

"Mr. Terry," he said with a half smile, "punctual as always."

"Timing is everything," Matt said. He returned the grin.

That seemed to please Kul immensely, and he offered a drink. Huatcho peeked out from behind the kitchenette's louver doors and disappeared back inside.

Matt noticed that Kul was wearing makeup for the occasion. Josh and Stormy had on jeans and khaki safari jackets. "You two always dress alike?" he asked the blond cowboy.

"Why don't you have a drink like the man says," Josh said, making it sound like an order.

Matt looked him over; the bandage on his nose was a mere Band-Aid now. "How about if we just get on with this?"

Kul made a hopeless gesture. "Perhaps it's just as well."

Matt tapped the case under his arm. This time it was Josh who handled the money. Matt passed the case to Chalker, who quickly conveyed it to the couch, where Kul could watch him open it. At the same time, Matt checked the cash and fixed Josh with a curious look. "Bet he doesn't pay you half this much for your machete work," he said just loud enough to be heard. "But then, you're something of an amateur, aren't you?"

"You scumbag," the gunman snarled, dropping the

case. "I've had about enough of you." He was reaching out for Matt's shirtfront when Kul's rebuke cut through the air.

Kul banged his stick against the floor and regarded Matt disapprovingly. Huatcho moved in to pick up the money.

"Really, Mr. Terry, you continue to disappoint me. I've tried my best to conduct business with you in an honorable fashion. You stipulated that you wanted the codex to reach the proper authorities, so I brought in Dr. Chalker. You asked for more than half the amount in advance, and I gave it to you. Now you have three hundred thousand dollars and we're at the end of our transaction. What more do you want?"

Matt grimaced. "What d' you take me for, Kul? You think I wouldn't do some checking up on our guest of honor here?"

Chalker looked up from the codex, his lips in a thin line.

"Why do you do it?" Matt asked him. "Because his money backs your digs? You go into the field full of noble purpose and end up turning over your best finds to his private collection. You pay your *obreros* a little extra to sneak things off site. Maybe you have college kids running the things back to the States for you."

"What is it, Mr. Terry?" Kul asked wearily.

"Did he tell you there's more than Mayan blood on that thing? That at least three people have already died for it?"

Kul watched Chalker for a moment, then heaved a weary sigh. "It's obvious that you've been talking to the wrong people, Mr. Terry."

Matt saw him nod once and took a backward step as Josh and Stormy drew sound-suppressed automatics from their jackets. Behind him he heard Kim grunt, "Stay!"

With some effort, Kul pushed himself upright on his stick. "I was afraid it might come to this, and now you've left me no choice." Another nod and Josh came in, catching Matt behind the knees and dropping him to the floor. He put the automatic to Matt's head and forced him up to a kneeling position.

The second gunman said, "Put your hands where I can see them, asshole."

Matt slowly raised his hands and clasped them on top of his head.

Kul tugged at his scant beard. "You see, I simply couldn't allow the museum to have it, Matt. There is far too much at stake here, much more than you realize." He was standing over Matt now, leaning forward on the stick. *"Ornamenti dei barbari.* That's how the Italians used to refer to pre-Columbian artifacts. But some of us know the Maya as they really were. Do you understand the significance of this?" he asked, indicating the Masonic ring on his middle finger.

"International order of blockheads, isn't it?" Matt tensed for the blow, but Kul motioned his man back.

"I could easily have you punished, but I would rather have you understand." Reverently, Kul took the codex from Chalker's hands. "This is a key to the understanding of our world, Matt. Not some simple calendar or almanac, but a mystical tract."

Matt said, "Yeah, the Maya were displaced Lemurians. They harnessed the cosmic forces, vanished into some space-time dimension. . . . Save your breath. I've heard it all before, and none of it's going to keep you from going down for murder."

"Murder?" Kul laughed. "Try to think of it as sacrifice, a necessary bloodletting to ensure good fortune. Blood, Matt, is the stuff of the world. Ritual murder brings the gods into the human domain. You're a man of some learning; you know that the ancients collected blood on bits of bark paper, which they burned to the heavens. Think of the codex in those terms. Your clients' blood helped to sanctify the book."

Matt glowered at him. "It was self-mutilation, Kul, only you don't realize it. You cut your own throat."

The blond cowboy slammed him hard between the shoulder blades, then dragged him up by the hair, slipping a knotted rope around his neck. Matt tried to wedge his fingers beneath the noose, but Josh pulled it taut, choking off his breath. He felt his throat instantly dry up, his eyes bulge.

Kul was offering him a thin smile. A minute of this

and he waved for Josh to ease the pressure somewhat. Matt nearly blacked out as he fell forward, gasping and coughing, his hands flat on the floor. Josh pulled him upright by the loop.

"Do I have your attention now?" Kul said.

Matt nodded, his lungs bellowing.

"As I was about to say, the Maya were unlike any other civilization. They were captivated by the concepts of energy and entropy, just as our own culture is. But out of their fear of empty space and their obsessions with time came wisdom that is nothing short of transcendental. And this is what they strived to incorporate into their writings, their art, and the very architecture of their cities."

Again, Kul showed Matt the ring. "The Masonic symbol of the great architect. Through no coincidence it is also the sign of Hunab Ku, one of the Maya's chief deities.

"Robert B. Stacy-Judd, Matt . . . He wrote that 'architecture consists of frozen symbols which can be thawed into a palatable language.' And it was the Maya he looked to for inspiration, the corbeled arch—similar to that of Palenque's own Temple of the Foliated Cross—which he chose to use as a gateway to the Masonic temple he designed for Los Angeles. Are you aware that Pythagoreans place Palenque precisely at the geographical center of the area embraced by the continental American landmass? Even Wright looked to the Maya after coming across Désiré Charnay's *Ancient Cities of the New World*. John C. Astin, Ernest Batchelder, Morgan, Wells, and Clements, Wright's own son . . . they all understood. 'Measures and motifs are words and sentences,' and I, too, have incorporated these mystical utterances into my buildings, confident that they are working a peculiar magic on all those who enter and dwell there, priming and preparing select minds for the greater glories to come.''

"We're all looking for the black bird, Kul," Matt said. "But that's not it. It's a chronicle. You killed three people to get a goddamn autobiography." Matt tried to swallow, hoping to coat his throat. "No mystical messages, no Mayan mumbo-jumbo . . ."

"None that you can read, none that can be read by the eyes alone, Matt. But believe me, these 'mystical messages,' as you call them, are there." Kul handed the codex back to Chalker.

"Bishop Landa burned all the books he could find because he learned that children were being sacrificed, and he knew he had to strike where it counted most. I, on the other hand, am *preserving* works, but for similar reasons. Humankind continues to be its own worst enemy, a victim of its own barbaric urges. Knowledge of the supernal realms must therefore be carefully controlled and distributed by the enlightened few. Le Plongeon knew this, Churchward knew it.

"What the Maya termed the Fifth World Age is almost upon us, Matt, the culmination of a forty-five-hundred year cycle of planetary configurations. But these secrets must remain concealed until that time. 'Timing,' as you yourself said a moment ago, 'is everything.' December 23, 2012. I hope to be alive on that day." Kul touched Matt's shoulder. "You, on the other hand, have no such hope."

Matt rasped, "Isn't this where I'm supposed to say you'll never get away with it?"

Kul's face clouded over with disapproval. "Oh, but I will get away with it. As I told you, Señor Olivar believes that you and I have been planning some sort of exotic adventure. And that's precisely what we'll have." Kul looked over at Stormy. "We're going to have to arrange an accident for Mr. Terry."

"We shoulda killed him with the other ones, Mr. Kul."

"Now, now," Kul told him. "How would we have procured the codex?" He swung around to face Matt. "No. Mr Terry has been most useful to us. We should reward him with a swift and uncomplicated demise. A fall, perhaps. Or drowning. Do either of those strike your fancy, Matt?"

Josh tightened his hold on the rope and put his mouth close to Matt's ear. "I'd like to off you like I killed the girl," he sneered. "Just a little pressure . . ." As Matt's hands came up, the rope bit into his neck, strangling him. "You shoulda seen her squirm. But her husband just wouldn't talk. So we started sticking it to him, and then he told us what we wanted to know. Thing was, I got a little carried away. That happens sometimes, you know?''

Kul rapped his stick against the floor. "Josh, I don't think it's wise to discuss these matters.''

"What's the difference? This guy's history, isn't he?''

"Then you murdered the Indian,'' Matt bit out.

Josh tightened up on his grip. "Well, no, not exactly. That was Stormy's gig. The fucker had already left Sayaxche by the time we got there. But we didn't have much trouble finding him.'' The cowboy laughed. "His wife kept screaming, 'Palenque, Palenque!' I think it was the only Spanish word she knew.''

Matt moistened his lips with his tongue. "Bet it pissed you off he didn't have it.''

"It pissed Stormy off, you bet. Didn't it, Stormy?''

"Josh, shut the fuck up,'' Skye told him.

"*Phwhoosh!* Took that freak's head clean off. I couldn't fucking believe it.''

"You figured I had it. You had your *pistolas* here search my rooms.''

Kul said, "I really didn't expect them to find anything. I was simply hoping to draw you out in the event you did have it. Which brings us to an interesting juncture. Just how is it that the codex ended up in your hands, Matt? Josh and Stormy assure me that they searched your camp. Did they overlook something? Or did your clients take you into their confidence?''

Matt looked up at him. "I'll explain if you tell me how you got wind of the thing to begin with.''

Kul's arched an eyebrow. "That seems a reasonable enough request.''

He was about to say more when someone knocked softly at the door. Kul motioned with his stick for Kim to answer it. Skye moved in to back him up. Josh pressed his gun into Matt's temple and warned him to keep his mouth shut.

Kim opened the door the length of the chain and leaned toward the opening. Matt heard someone say, "*Policía.* ''

"Wait a moment," Kim said in accented Spanish,

closing the door and turning a determined face to the
room. Kul started gesturing with his head and hand.
"Quickly, quickly," he said in a throaty whisper.

The gunman slipped the noose from Matt's head and
yanked him up by the arm. He shoved Matt into one of
the chairs, holding the gun to Matt's face and pressing
a hand against his chest. "You play it smart, understand?"

Kul shot Matt a worried look, but the police were
banging away by then. Josh and Stormy reholstered their
guns and positioned themselves on either side of Matt's
chair. Chalker had tucked the aluminum case beneath a
cushion on the couch.

Kim undid the latch at Kul's nod.

Escobar was standing in the doorway.

"*Policía,*" he announced, flashing an ID. He was
flanked by Ortiz and Suentes.

Kul shuffled forward, smiling. "Well, Lieutenant . . .
Escobar, isn't it? We met some years ago if I'm not mistaken."

"At the Masonic lodge, Señor Kul."

"Of course, of course. And how is our local master
of the universe?"

"He is very good, señor." Escobar indicated the Rescate agents. "These men are with Interpol, Señor Kul.
May we come in?"

Kul motioned to the room. "As you see, I have guests
just now."

"This is official business, señor," Escobar said more
firmly.

"In that case, come right in," Kul responded gra-
ciously.

Escobar glanced around the room, then pointed in an
off hand way to Matt. "We have reason to believe that
this man is in possession of a stolen artifact."

Kul put on a surprised face. "Mr. Terry? There must
be some mistake, Lieutenant. Mr. Terry is well known
to me, and I'm certain he wouldn't involve himself."

"Then you'll have no objections if we search this
room," Ortiz said.

"Now wait one moment. There are laws—"

"This is Mexico, Señor Kul," Escobar interrupted.

Kul grinned. "So it is, Lieutenant, so it is."

Matt glimpsed the slight shift in Kul's eyes and knew enough to dive for the floor. At the same time he heard a splintering sound from out back and saw a man crash through the pergola onto the tiled terrace. Skye swung to the sound with his gun drawn and put a muffled shot through the screen and into the man's chest as he struggled to get to his feet. The front door meanwhile had been kicked open by two of Escobar's men, catching Kim unaware and hurling him against the wall with enough force to drop him to the floor. Josh's first shot found the first man through the door, but his follow-up rounds missed and tore into a glass-fronted cabinet in the corner of the room.

Ortiz drew his gun while Skye was firing on the terrace; he pivoted through a half turn and triggered three rounds at Kul's man, clipping Skye in the wrist and neck. Escobar and Suentes ducked as Skye staggered back against the table, emptying the rest of his magazine. Kul was already headed for the floor by that time, and his eyes locked on Matt's as he came down hard on his face, Skye's barrage tearing through the space Kul had abandoned and impacting against the couch and the wall above Chalker's petrified face.

Josh was still loosing fire at Escobar's man, who had tripped over his companion and was trying to roll for cover behind a colonial-style trunk near the couch. Escobar came up armed and put one round into Josh's thigh. The blond cowboy screamed and fired wild but succeeded in keeping everyone pinned down. Matt saw Josh glance in his direction and started to belly-crawl toward the table, but there were too many bodies in the way.

Two shots cracked against the floor tiles and went zinging off across the room at oblique angles. Josh screamed again as someone nailed him in the shoulder. Matt scrambled forward and was somersaulting for the dining area when three ear-splitting noises exploded from the terrace. By the time Matt turned around, Josh was down for the long count with half his head blown away. Someone crashed through the patio screen door yelling in Spanish.

Escobar answered him.

Matt looked up and saw Stormy Skye not three feet in front of him, slumped against one of the dining room chairs with a perplexed look on his face, bleeding from his wrist, upper arm, and neck. The nickel-plated 9mm was on the floor within easy reach, and Skye seemed to be regarding it stupidly. Matt felt a foot on his back and flattened himself.

"Don't move! Don't move!" someone warned him.

Matt was amazed to find that his pants were dry, but his body was shaking uncontrollably. Peripherally he could see Kul being hauled to his feet, Escobar supporting him while Suentes picked up the man's stick. Chalker, too, was on his feet, being frisked from behind by Agent Ortiz. The owner of the foot nudged Matt in the ribs and ordered him to get up and assume the position. One of Escobar's ersatz gardeners had a frightened Huatcho against the wall. Kim, it seemed, had been knocked unconscious.

Ortiz ordered Matt, Kul, and Chalker to sit down while a second plainclothesman checked Skye's wounds. Suentes was out on the patio seeing to one of the downed cops. Escobar said a few words into his radio and glared at Matt from across the room.

"There's been a terrible mistake," Kul was saying. "I don't know why those men began shooting. There's been a mistake."

Escobar told him to keep quiet. Ortiz and Suentes were tearing the room apart; Matt caught Ortiz's gaze after a moment and indicated the couch with his eyes. The agent flipped up cushion after cushion.

"Lieutenant," he said at last, proudly displaying the case.

"Jesus Christ!" Suentes muttered a moment later. "It's a Mayan book—a codex!"

Escobar had turned to watch them; now the lieutenant looked hard at Matt.

"Lieutenant Escobar," Kul said. "*Jefe*, there are things we should discuss before you do anything with that book. This is Dr. Niles Chalker, who is well known to the Institute of Anthropology and History. I enlisted his aid in this simply—"

"Keep silent!" Escobar told him harshly. "You are all under arrest."

"On what charges?" Kul demanded. "I had nothing to do with those men!"

A plainclothesman stepped in to address him. "You were attempting to receive stolen property in violation of Mexico's laws governing the transfer of cultural property and antiquities."

Kul continued to protest, so Escobar ordered him removed to the bedroom. Forty-five minutes later Matt and Chalker were led out of the suite just as the medical team was arriving.

A small crowd had gathered in the courtyard, braving the afternoon heat for a glimpse of the action. Matt could see Hano Olivar in the background, engaged in a furious argument with two detectives.

Chalker was shoved into the backseat of the black Ford, where he was joined by two *federales*. Matt was driven off in Escobar's Dodge, along with Ortiz, Suentes, and Captain Segundo of the DFS. They were halfway to town before anyone spoke, the movie chase still in progress north of the road.

"Is it genuine?" Escobar asked from the driver's seat, glancing down at the codex.

Matt told him it was, his voice raspy and full of fear-induced tremolo. He could barely hear his own words above the ringing in his ears.

"Aguilar's group must have opened up a sealed tomb or something. The Honduran realized how valuable it was and got the North Americans interested in a major deal. Somehow Kul learned about it and decided to shortstop it." He repeated the gunman's confession, gently messaging his neck while he spoke. "Then they went after T'sup Kin. His wife and kids are up in San Cristóbal if you need them. Were you able to get through to Pipiles?" he asked Ortiz.

"Not yet. Colonel Reyes and most of his cadre are still tracking the insurgents. But we're going to send a man out to the *garita* to check the records."

Escobar pulled the car to an abrupt stop across the street from the movie theater. He twisted around from the wheel to fix Matt with a threatening look.

"I know," Matt said before Escobar could speak. "Don't leave town."

"You or the Riordan woman," Escobar added coldly.

Matt realized that the lieutenant wanted to make sure the DFS man had heard it. But, in fact, he wanted Rachel and Matt as far from Palenque as possible.

Matt climbed out and slammed the door, his eyes on the Range Rover as he hurried up the street to the office.

# 17

## Outward Bound

"**I** think there are fleas in this bed," Rachel announced a moment after Matt opened his eyes. Her right hand was cupped over her naked left breast, while her other hand scratched at three small welts on her rib cage. "Do these look like flea bites to you?"

Matt rubbed his eyes and leaned in for a closer look. "Maybe bedbugs," he said, tenting the sheet to gaze down his length. His throat felt like liquid fire. Rachel uttered a dismayed sound and twisted around to one side, craning her neck to inspect her back and rump.

Dim gray light filtered into the room from a pair of casement windows high up on one wall. The bed was handmade by Ángel's cousin, narrow and hard as a rock; Matt's feet had overhung the end all night, and his back and neck were stiff. A rickety night table stood on his side of the bed, with a stub of candle driven into a Pepsi bottle. The room had been painted recently, and the perimeter of the wood floor was still speckled with a scabrous overspray.

They had arrived shortly before eight P.M., after an uneventful drive from Palenque. Natalie and Rachel had embraced like best friends. Matt made her promise to tell Escobar that she had put the two of them on the train for Mérida on Sunday night. The money was in Bustamonte's care until Matt could figure a way to move it into the States. Now there was only the river crossing to contend with, and Matt was confident that Paolo would be in Echeverría waiting for them.

Ángel's cousin, Obsim, and his wife, Xochil, had welcomed them with freshly butchered chicken, rice, and refried beans. Obsim worked in the nearby Chancala lumber mill; he was proud of his Mayan heritage, his job, and the small house he had built. It was set among banana plants and palms, well away from the Echeverría road, seven miles from Chancala. Obsim bicycled to and from the lumber mill seven days a week.

Matt thought he might be able to catch Obsim before he left for work to thank him again for the hospitality. The quality of the light in the room suggested that sunrise was still half an hour away, but when Matt checked his watch, it read eight-thirty.

"Something's weird," he said, getting out of bed and going to the window.

The air was cool and thick with a kind of incandescent haze that brought him back to September mornings in Montana.

"Maybe it's an eclipse," Rachel said.

Matt looked over his shoulder at her. She wore a playful smile that left the tip of one front tooth caught on her lower lip. Her short hair was mussed and standing straight up from the crown of her head like a kid's cowlick.

She hugged him as he climbed back into bed. In the middle of the night, spooned against each other on the narrow bed, she had reached over to fondle him, then made love to him with a gentleness that drew all the tension of the past weeks out of his body. In a floating state of half sleep, he had stroked her head and neck while she drank him in, gyrating beside him, her own hand between her thighs.

"Matt, your neck," she said suddenly, holding her hands near his face in a helpless gesture. "God, every time I wake up you, you're covered with bruises."

He touched himself gingerly. "How's it look?"

"Like somebody tried to strangle you. How else would it look?" She pulled his hands away and placed her own around his throat in a kind of healing gesture. Matt saw a tear in her eye and said, "Don't think about it."

She collapsed against his chest and sobbed. "I can't help it. I keep picturing her—"

"Don't think of her there, Rachel. Just remember her the way she was the last time you saw her." He lifted her face and said, "We got them, didn't we?"

She returned a wan smile. "You got them, Matt. I haven't done anything except complicate things. When I think about the things I said . . ." She looked away from him. "I mean, you were right, we had to give them the codex. Otherwise Escobar would have arrested us. Or Kul would have sent his men out looking for us." She shrugged. "I guess all sorts of things could have gone wrong. In the end I would have made the museum look bad. But at least I got to look at it, and who knows, maybe something interesting will come out of my notes. Something the lucky son of a bitch who gets it won't notice."

Matt watched her go from sadness to rationalization to anger in less than a minute. He thought he knew what was on her mind and wasn't much surprised when she added, "But we've still got a shot at something."

Rachel stopped him before he could restate any of his arguments. "I know what you're going to say, but will you just let me show you something?"

"We've been through all this."

"Just one more thing, okay?"

Animated, she hopped out of bed and hurried over to her luggage, returning with a black and white map and what looked like photographs. She switched on the low-wattage bulb that dangled from the ceiling and knelt on the bed, at ease with her nakedness. "You see this line right here?"

Matt had to pry his eyes away from her. He looked uncertainly at the photograph; it was an aerial shot of dense forest, bisected by a discernible straight line, a causeway or a road. "Where'd you get these?" he asked, leafing through half a dozen similar shots.

"I borrowed them from the Gradys' library," Rachel said, impatient to move on.

"You borrowed them?"

She looked at him, beetling her brows. "I'm going to return them, Matt." She held his gaze for a moment, then repositioned the map so he could study it with her. "They correspond to this region right here. The lines are vestiges of Mayan roads. Now look at this. This one runs straight out of La Florida—a known site—directly into the area where both DeSilvio and McGowan locate El Fuente—our Aguaculto."

Intrigued, Matt oriented the map. "Yeah, it sure looks that way. But what's interesting is what the map doesn't show."

"What's that?"

"A group of impenetrably forested tumbled-down mounds that have probably been picked clean by every *huachero* and hunter in the area. Not to mention mosquitoes carrying quinine-resistant malaria." Matt threw up his hands. "There's dozens of places like this! There's an unexcavated site ten miles from the lodge, but I sure as hell doubt it's a Bonampak."

"But you can't tell by just looking at a mound," Rachel persisted. "We don't know that they got *everything*. They could have overlooked a tomb or the entrance to a temple. People knew about the mounds at Bonampak before anyone thought about taking a look inside. Frey missed the murals; so did Franz Blom. Now we *know* what treasures we can expect to find. I just want to be sure about Aguaculto."

Matt said, "Look, let me tell you about the lodge. It's on a hill above the lagoon. Fruit trees, flowers, great sunsets. There's a—"

"I don't care about the lodge, Matt!" Rachel jabbed her finger at the map. "We're practically on top of the site right now! Once we cross the river at Echeverría, it can't be more than thirty miles in."

"Have you done any fieldwork," he asked after a moment, "or has all your research been armchair stuff?"

"An astronomer doesn't have to visit Mars to understand what the conditions there are like," she told him. "Anyway, I've visited plenty of sites, Matt."

"Palenque, Tikal, Copan," Matt ticked them off on his fingers. "Quirigua, Chichen, Uxmal, Tulum . . ."

"I did my graduate work in Belize," Rachel said angrily. "I've also worked at Yaxha. You don't have to tell me what the *selva*'s like if that's what you're getting at.

And for your information, I'm in excellent shape. I jog five miles a day.''

Matt frowned. "I read where that's dangerous—dropped uterus or something.''

''Who said so?''

''Experts, I don't know. Besides, I'm not saying you couldn't cut it. I'm just trying to tell you what to expect. We used to advertise the lodge as a 'rustic retreat.' And everybody would come down from the States with all these Hollywood images in mind and flip out when we told them there were bats in the latrines and bushmasters in the forest. Now we tell them up front, and it makes for a much easier time.''

''Who do you think you're talking to, Matt?'' Rachel laughed. ''I've been studying this area for fifteen years.''

Matt gave the map a half turn in Rachel's direction. ''You see this area? This is *bajo*—swamp. Even now it would be an unholy mess. And I'm not talking about jogging, Rachel. This is . . . slogging. Plus we'd have to provision ourselves or live off what we could dig up—literally. We'd be lucky to have tortillas and rice for one or two meals.''

''I live on fruit and vegetables.''

Matt looked beseechingly at the ceiling. ''How's this sound? You go back to New York. You tell the museum directors the whole story, or however much you think they'll sit still for. You tell them about Aguaculto and the codex. You get funded. You mount a proper expedition, with mules, *obreros*, a resupply chopper, a bunch of volunteers from the University of Chicago or somewhere. You do it right.''

Rachel was still shaking her head when he finished. ''Of course I plan to get some funding. That's exactly why I need to get in there! I have to have something to demonstrate that the site is a worthwhile find, not just another hopelessly plundered ruin. The guerrillas have already been there, so how long can it be before word leaks out? Some nobody with a master's degree in anthropology is going to bump into the right *chiclero*, and that's that.''

''Then just go back and *predict* the find. Let somebody

else do the legwork. Didn't some astronomer do that with Neptune or Uranus?''

"Herschel," Rachel said absently.

"Well?''

She looked at him. "It wouldn't be the same.''

Just then someone knocked at the door. Matt slipped into his jeans to answer it.

"El Chichón," Ángel said excitedly, making a bursting motion with his hands.

"The volcano!" Rachel said from the bed, the sheet pulled up to her chin.

Ángel had just returned from Chancala, where everyone in town was talking about the mountain's midnight eruption and the morning's ash and haze.

Rachel was already dressing when Matt turned around.

"I can't believe it," she said breathlessly.

Matt said, "The gods must be pissed about something.''

Hours later on the Echeverría road, the Rover was continually flagged down by homesteaders desperate for information about the catastrophe. Over and over Ángel explained that they had only come from as far as Chancala and had no news about how Palenque, Villahermosa, or any of a score of sierra pueblos had fared.

Given its distance from El Chichón, Matt doubted that Palenque had received more than a dusting of ash and was beginning to think of the eruption as something of a personal godsend, whereas a like event fifteen years before had seemed the devil's work. Chichón would seem that for the Zoque Indians whose farms and ranches dotted the mountain's slopes, but it was unlikely now that Escobar or anyone on the Villahermosa force was going to mount a search for two missing gringos. On the other hand, Kul and his bunch could be realizing something positive out of the catastrophe as well. What with families fleeing the highlands for the safety of the plains, the chaos soon to overtake Palenque was easy to imagine.

The air began to clear as they neared the Usumacinta, and blue skies prevailed by the time the Rover had reached the Echeverría cutoff. Matt had Ángel drop them off well outside of town, figuring that he and Rachel would be safer going the rest of the way on foot. Numerous red clay trails led to the riverbank, most of which bypassed the center of town. Anxious to return to Palenque and check on his family, Ángel was nothing if not agreeable to the idea. He exchanged an *abrazo* with Matt and a warm handshake with Rachel; then the Rover was gone, leaving the two of them standing in the heat amid insects and the distant sound of the river.

"You going to be all right with that?" Matt asked, gesturing to Rachel's shoulder bag while he slipped into his rucksack.

"I'll be fine," she said harshly, setting off ahead of him on the trail.

The discussion concerning Aguaculto had continued intermittently through most of the ride from Chancala. Matt had a weakness for little-used trails and blank areas on the map, but he was trying his best not to give in to it. He knew that as rational as his concerns and objections might have sounded in terms of logistics, terrain, and a host of unknowns, there was really nothing to prevent them from making a few inquiries. When it got right down to it, there was no reason why they couldn't attempt the trek. The site—the Aguaculto the *xate* gatherers talked about, at any rate—had to lie within twenty-five miles of the river. *Xateros* wouldn't hump any farther than that for the sought-after palm.

But when Matt asked himself the real reason for his ambivalence, he recognized that it had little to do with maps or trails of a geographical sort. He was all right with the choices he had made in Palenque but as Rachel had pointed out, they were as much for his own benefit as for anyone else's. And the truth was that she really couldn't be blamed for what had gone down, not directly, anyway. So he continued to feel that he owed her something for letting the codex get away. And something for Billie, for letting her die.

Twenty minutes' walking brought them to a white sand path that paralleled the steep western bank of the Usumacinta. Rachel had been silent and unresponsive, and Matt was in a sour mood. He couldn't help but feel differently toward the river's swift flow and tricky currents. But the dark thoughts lifted as he caught sight of Paolo's motorized dugout tied up below them on a narrow band of beach. Matt shouted a greeting, and they began to pick their way down the bank through a tenacious growth of high grass and barbed vegetation.

Paolo was limping up the beach in their direction, his fused leg describing a small outboard arc with each powerful step. He waved his Caterpillar cap, and Matt waved back. Then all at once Matt saw the boatman freeze and cross himself. Matt's smile collapsed, and he swung around expecting to find Escobar or someone equally malignant on the trail. But there was only Rachel, in her jeans, tank top, and sun hat, struggling with the bag.

"Take your hat off," he told her. "Just take it off for a minute." When she had complied, Matt said to Paolo, "This is Billie's sister."

The boatman lowered his head and muttered something. *"Son gemelas, cierto?"* The fearful look was still there when he raised his eyes. "Twins, no?"

"No, not twins," Matt said, shrugging the pack off his shoulders. He glanced back at Rachel. "She looks like Billie from a distance."

"Yes," Paolo said, unconvinced. Then he smiled and embraced Matt. "It's good to see you again, *mano*."

Rachel introduced herself. She was short of breath but self-satisfied. Paolo hesitantly took her hand. He touched his Vandyke and gazed at her as if she were a superstition incarnate.

Matt motioned Rachel to follow Paolo into the *canoa* and began handing her the bags. "Pile them in the center."

He took off his boots and socks and tossed them into the dugout. Paolo brought the outboard to life and threw him an "okay" sign from the stern. Matt let the gurgling sounds of the river overtake him. Macaws overhead were making for a sandbar islet midstream. Beyond that rose the densely forested fringe of the Petén. He shoved the boat into the current and threw himself aboard.

"To the south?" Paolo yelled, pointing upstream.

Matt watched Rachel on the plank seat amidships. She flashed him a hopeful look and turned away to contemplate a smear of dark clouds to the northwest.

Matt directed Paolo to the opposite shore. "There!"

he shouted back, standing up in the bow. "We have a stop to make."

Bethel, on the Guatemalan side of the Usumacinta, was even less of a town than Frontera Echeverría, three small stores and a linear arrangement of thatched homes spread out for almost a mile along the bank. Sharing beers outside one of the *tiendas*, Matt gave Paolo a quick rundown of the events in Palenque and explained why they had been in such a rush to leave Mexico. The boatman was overjoyed to learn that at least some of their assailants had been captured, and kept slapping Matt on the shoulders, congratulating him. But when the talk turned to Aguaculto, Paolo grew sober and attentive, eager to know the clues that had led them to suspect the existence of ruins there.

Rachel pressed herself against Matt's back while he spoke, his hand tight between her own.

"You remember that *xatero* we met last year, the one with the mules?"

"Plácido Godoy," Paolo said. "He lives up near El Arbolito."

"You know where?"

Paolo shook his head. "But I can ask." He downed the last of his beer, pushed himself up, and disappeared into the *tienda*.

Rachel said, "I like him."

Matt nodded. "He's a good man."

"Is he uncomfortable with me?"

Matt scratched at the dirt with the toe of his boot. "Paolo and his brother knew Billie longer than I did. They brought her to the lodge. They blamed themselves for what happened."

"Will you make sure he understands that I don't hold him responsible for anything?"

"I think he knows that," Matt said, looking at her. "Or else he wouldn't be here."

Paolo returned a few minutes later with three more beers. "I know the place. But Godoy doesn't own the beasts. They belong to his *patrón*, who lives here in Bethel."

Matt took a swallow of Gallo and wiped his mouth.

"Let's go talk to Godoy first. I'm not wild about hanging around here for too long."

"*Vamos,*" Paolo said, taking hold of all three bottles.

The trailhead to Godoy's *choza* was just north of the abandoned settlement of El Arbolito. There was nothing to mark the house as such, but on the bit of compacted beach below the trailhead were two *cayucos* loaded down with bundles of fernlike *xate*.

"*Buenas,*" Paolo called out as he led them slowly up the canopied trail. One hundred feet in and the sound of the river was lost to them.

In return, a mutt with a lot of German shepherd in it came bounding out to meet them, barking his best but keeping a safe distance. The dog had a long jagged scar across its muzzle from a jaguar or a machete. "*Perro, perro,*" Paolo barked back playfully as a small man came into view ahead, regarding them warily from the edge of a clearing. "We're looking for Plácido Godoy," the boatman told him.

The man said, "Follow. Pass in." He was dressed in pants that had once been white, a straw hat, and tall rubber boots.

The dog had his tail up, but when Rachel reached out to pet him, he bolted as though pushed and commenced barking again.

In addition to the one who had greeted them, four men were in the clearing, all dressed somewhat alike, although one was barefoot. They were in the process of off-loading *xate* from five mules tethered to a hitching rail at the head of a forest trail. Two small thatched dwellings and a dilapidated open-sided shelter sat in dazzling sunlight, where an Indian woman and a young girl were busy spreading corn to dry atop a woven mat. The girl stopped her work and shyly approached Rachel to ask for a pen. Rachel found one in her purse, and the girl smiled, reaching out to caress Rachel's arm.

Paolo meanwhile was trading hellos with the men, most of whom appeared to know him. Godoy was really the *arriero*, the mule skinner among them. Everyone had already put aside bundles and machetes and squatted down to exchange news. Matt told them about El Chichón, and that led to stories about the earthquake one of the men had survived as a child in the highlands near Quetzaltenango.

Plácido Godoy brought out coffee and sugarcane, aiming an accurate kick at a scrawny hen that ambled in front of him from the brush. Matt was about to suggest that Rachel offer her cigarettes around, when he turned and found her doing just that. The little girl had seated herself close by, and when Rachel removed her hat, she let out a surprised sound, calling to her mother and gesturing to Rachel's hair. The men laughed, and Matt thought he saw Rachel blush.

The courtesies and gossip continued for some time before everyone fell silent, drawing deeply on Rachel's Marlboros and waiting for Matt to explain himself.

"My friends and I would like to go up to Aguaculto," he told them. A few of them repeated the word, murmuring to one another; then two of the men laughed.

*"Si púes, hay cerritos allí."*

"They want to see the ruins," the bearded one said knowingly to his companions. Matt and Rachel exchanged looks. "Yes, yes, there are mounds there," the man continued, trying to convince the skeptics in the group. He left the circle and walked off in the direction of the mules.

"We don't go up there anymore," Godoy offered. "There is only *xate macho* up there." The *macho* wood made for good walking sticks, but the plant's stems were of no value to Stateside florists. "Besides, it is dangerous."

Matt asked him why.

"Guerrillas. And there are *huecheros*, too."

"What are *'huecheros'*?" Rachel asked quietly while some discussion began about the recent battle between the insurgents and the rangers from the Pipiles *garita*. Matt kept one ear on the *xateros'* conversation and answered, "Tunnelers. Looters."

The bearded man had returned and was unwrapping a bowling ball–size object for Matt and Rachel's inspection. "Look," he said, a glint in his good eye.

It was a maculated ceramic figure of a Mayan lord, with traces of color in his shoulder-length hair and thin-lipped mouth. He had a small, straight nose and a pro-

nounced chin and was relatively unornamented. A trophy
head dangled from a thong around his neck. *"Un san-
tito,"* the man explained. "An idol. Very old, very valuable." Matt caught a whiff of must and dampness.

"It's Altar style," Rachel ventured. "Fine Orange-
ware. Classic, I'd be willing to bet."

"Do you want to buy it?" the man asked hungrily.

"Tell him no thanks," Matt said. "Otherwise we're
going to have every campesino in the area looking for
us."

Rachel mulled it over, then shook her head and handed
the antiquity back, offering the man an apologetic smile.
Confused, he looked back and forth between Matt and
Rachel, muttered a short curse, and began to rewrap the
figurine.

"We'll pay someone to take us to Aguaculto," Matt
said, getting back to Godoy. "But we need to leave
soon."

Godoy raised his eyes. "It's very far. Two days walking. And the trail is very bad. There are swamps and
many *barbas amarillas*."

"We understand. That's why we can pay you well for
the trip."

In low tones, Godoy discussed the financial prospects
of such a venture with his friends. "How many beasts
would you need?"

Matt looked to Paolo. "Three would do it."

"You are going to accompany us?" Godoy asked the
boatman.

Paolo nodded.

"First I would like to discuss everything with my *patrón* in Bethel."

Matt told him that wouldn't present a problem.

"Then, all right," Godoy said, neither here nor there
about it. "But what about food?"

We can buy everything we need in Echeverría," Paolo
assured him.

"Very well, then."

Matt shook hands with Godoy, who went back to un-
loading the last of the pack animals. "Matt," Rachel
said, full of excitement.

"This is going to be Petén-style trekking, Rachel. I'm

talking about scorpions, sleeping on the ground, checking each other for ticks, and eating fruits you've probably never seen before."

"Don't worry about me."

"I'm going to try not to," he said uneasily.

It took until noon of the following day to strike a deal with the *arriero*'s *patrón*, purchase supplies, and get the mules harnessed, packed, and readied for the trail.

Matt had put himself in charge of the business end of things and left the shopping to Paolo, but Don Julio Morón, Godoy's *patrón*, had left Bethel by the time Matt arrived, which necessitated a second trip downriver early the next morning. Paolo, however, fared well in Echeverría and managed to scrape up everything on the list he and Matt had compiled: tinned goods, rice, beans, chili peppers, salt, sugar, coffee, miner's headlamps, rubber boots, hammocks, enamel cookware and utensils, plastic water bottles, batteries, rope, candles, matches, machetes, shovel, pickax, blankets, and mosquito netting. He had also located a boatman who was headed upriver and was willing to carry a message into Silvio at the lodge, saying in effect that everything was under control but that their arrival there would be delayed five or six days. Unsolicited, Godoy's wife and young daughters saw to it that the hastily formed expedition had enough *pozole* and double-toasted tortillas to last a week.

Matt and Rachel, wrapped in the thin Mexican blankets Paolo had procured, spent the night on straw mats in the damp *palapa* Godoy used as a storage place for feed and *xate*. In the morning, while Matt and Manuel were in Bethel, Paolo packed the supplies and had everything ready to load when the two of them returned.

Leaving most of Rachel's luggage behind, they set out at two P.M. along a trail only Godoy could discern and made just over seven miles by sunset. It was easy walking through burned milpas and relatively flat open forest for the first couple of miles—howler monkeys, toucans, and macaws overhead—but as the afternoon wore on, the trail became a roller coaster course over undulating terrain thick with thorn palms, strangler figs, creepers, and lianas. The forest was so impenetrable in parts that scarcely any sunlight filtered in. Matt took frequent compass readings and jotted down a few notes on Rachel's map; their heading was north-northeast toward the small lake and *petrolero* camp at San Diego. A final mile through ankle-deep black mud took more than an hour to cover, and twice the supply loads had to be relashed to the animals' wooden back frames. While they stopped to attend to that, the mosquitoes picnicked greedily on everyone.

Godoy held the point for most of the trip—a machete in one hand, the lead beast's rope in the other—with Paolo a distant second, toting a shotgun over one shoulder. Next in line was Rachel, which put Matt at rear guard, passing the better part of the afternoon staring at Rachel's long thighs and shapely blue-jeaned derriere. She spoke about her parents and the philosophical differences that had separated her and Billie for several years, Rachel working for the UN then while Billie was off galavanting with hippies and vagabonds. Things had gotten back on course as Rachel found her way into Mayan studies, although in part it was that that had turned Billie to antiquities smuggling—trying to outdo her older sister again. But mostly Rachel talked about the Maya and the codex and was as full of questions about the forest as Neil had been.

"Tamarind," Matt was telling her as Paolo passed the word that they would be stopping for the night. "It's usually used for support posts."

"Like the *tinto* we saw," Rachel said without turning around.

"You're catching on."

She pointed to another tree off to the left of the trail. "What about that?"

"I think that's *jobillo*," Matt said, stopping to gaze at it. "It's a furniture-grade hardwood."

"Better than . . . what was it? *Chacahuante*?"

"Different. That's a redwood. Check out Godoy's axhandle later on. That's *chacahuante*."

Rachel pivoted through a quick one-eighty to face him. "You really do love it out here, don't you?"

Matt stabbed his machete into the spongy ground and wiped sweat from his forehead with the back of his hand. "I like it all right."

"You're not a survivalist or anything, are you?" she asked worriedly. "One of those people who thinks he can escape Armageddon by holing up in the wilderness somewhere. Because I don't think Central America is exactly the safest place to be right now for someone who's into surviving."

Matt took a drink from the water bottle and offered it to her. "No argument."

Rachel spilled some water into her cupped hand and conveyed it to the back of her neck. "The building I live in is going to last a lot longer than this forest."

Matt thought back to the devastated fields they had crossed earlier and said, "I don't doubt it. But I'd wager the Maya said the same thing about their pyramids, and look where it got them."

Rachel shrugged and began to talk about New York, about after-hours clubs and Soho lofts, the museum crowd, and city life.

"Do you have a water bed?" Matt asked her when they had resumed walking.

She leered at him over her shoulder. "Why, do you like them?"

"They make a damn good water supply in case of emergencies."

"I'll be sure to remember that," she said without conviction, hurrying to catch up with Paolo.

They made camp in a clearing where the trees had been cut back by hunters and overeager *xateros*, next to a stream at the foot of a ridge of low hills. Plácido explained that there wasn't much game left in the region, and what little remained was moving steadily north toward inaccessible areas across the Río San Pedro.

Rachel and Matt shared a rope hammock. They slept fitfully and woke an hour before sunrise, chilled to the bone. Paolo got the fire going, and Matt made coffee while Rachel inspected a rash of chigger bites on her waist and ankles. Vampire bats had tapped two of the mules during the night.

They ate cold tortillas in the eye-smarting smoke, the only mosquito-free zone available.

The second morning was rough going, and by midday some of Rachel's good humor and strength had left her.

Still, she trudged on, uncomplaining and refusing to allow them to stop on her account. She was like Billie in that regard. She took a couple of bad spills on slick tree roots, but Matt maintained his distance, letting her deal with the hurt in her own fashion.

They picked their way over the hills and down into an ancient, misty forest of enormous mushroom-canopied ceibas, oaks, and cedars, then lower yet into alternating areas of swamp and parched compacted high ground as brutal on the feet as concrete. The mules were growing more obstreperous with each step, but Godoy managed to keep them in line. Twice, with benevolent obstinacy, the lead beast alerted him to the presence of a fer-de-lance on what passed for the trail.

To take his mind off Rachel's plight, Matt occupied himself with thoughts about Serpent Skull and He-Stops-the-Sun, the theories Rachel had developed from her study of the codex. Matt thought he had a pretty clear picture of the final events depicted in the book: of Serpent Skull and his retinue sequestered at the top of a pyramid while the invader's hordes fell upon the city, setting fires, murdering warriors and noblemen alike; of the last-minute bloodletting rites in the temple while court attendants dressed Serpent Skull in his most fearsome raiments; of the scribe, cross-legged on the floor, driven to record each of his lord's utterances; of the suicide of Serpent Skull's wife and family, the death of his faithful protectors, his slow and stately descent down the pyramid's stairway, eyes peering out from an open-mouthed jaguar mask, manikin scepter and ceremonial shield held high; and finally of the grisly scene of his death at the hands of He-Stop-the-Sun's warrior priests: the laying open of his chest by an obsidian blade, the adept extraction of his still beating heart, blood spilled on the plaza stones, spattered on the face of a carved stela. Blood left to dry all those centuries and fade like the paints and pigments themselves while the jungle sought to reclaim what had been cleared from its midst.

Young shoots the color of virgin jade would have sprung up from crevices and rifts in the limestone plazas, seeds blown in on the winds and nourished by seasonal rains. Parasitic plants dropping thirsty tendrils from for-

est boughs, creepers climbing the steep sides of temples
obscuring the hieroglyphic inscriptions on stairway risers
and door lintels, attacking the brilliant colors that had
been so compulsively applied—the reds, yellows, and
blues that once separated Rock River from its verdant
surroundings.

The young shoots would have become stalks, compet-
ing with one another for moisture and sunlight, yielding
to the demands of the forest's true citizens—the mahog-
anies and oaks, the cedars and ceibas. And so it would
have gone for a thousand years—the tropical sun bleach-
ing the stones of color, and the jungle burying and res-
urrecting itself as many times, dismantling bits of the
city with each season. The massive buttressed trunks of
forest giants would have overturned the plazas' hewn
stones and wreaked havoc with stairways and platforms.
Unsupported, temple roof-combs would have collapsed,
corbeled arches given way, standing stones displaced or
tipped to the ground, rain and wind lashing away at their
meticulously rendered personages, pitting their soft sur-
faces, all but erasing the details of their dynastic glyphs.
Rotting vegetation would conceal what remained, encas-
ing dwellings and ceremonial structures alike, a once-
grand city now little more than earthen mounds rising
from a limitless expanse of luxuriant forest.

Rachel had a theory about He-Stops-the-Sun as well.
Imagine, she had said, with the light of inspiration in her
eyes, that he was not some warrior chieftain out of central Mexico, but a kind of messianic Mayan thinker whose
beliefs about the growing division between the lords and
the common people had become the focal point for a
populist movement—a millennial movement—at the
height of the classic era, the end of the Fourth Sun, when
the demands of the lords and the priesthood who backed
their arcane theocracy had reached an unbearable limit,
when population growth, invasion, and internecine
struggles were already undermining the solidarity of the
city-states.

Rachel pictured He-Stops-the-Sun embarking on what
had amounted to a holy crusade through the heartland of
the Petén, with the disenfranchised rallying behind him
as his warriors took city after city. But his aim would not

have been to destroy the cities the god-kings had raised, but to leave them abandoned, a sign to the gods that their rule was finished, their yoke thrown off. No, it would have been He-Stops-the-Sun's aim to move the entire populace north toward Yucatán, where the older ways of simplicity and communalism might have a second chance. So it was only the nobles who were put to death, and the rest had either fled or become willing captives to the messiah's grand experiment in cultural realignment.

A little like Pol Pot in Cambodia. And a lot, Matt thought, like contemporary Guatemala, with Raphael Aguilar and his insurgents attempting to redress the wrongs of a subversive regime and point the way toward an older belief in communal values.

Those things were on Matt's mind as he sidestepped down into a cathedral-still hollow where Rachel had paused to catch her wind. There was an eeriness to the forest there, a cool bubbling spring overshadowed by ceibas and rough-barked sapodilla trees, their fruits ripening as April approached. To the north and east there was a tight grouping of wooded hills. Matt heard a jaguar cry in the distance.

"Look at this," Rachel was saying, gesturing to the masses of clay that were her running shoes. "I must be carrying ten pounds on each foot." She gave Matt a weak, hopeless look, fixing her eyes on his comparatively clean boots.

Matt brought his hands to his mouth and sounded three shrill whistles. Paolo returned the call a moment later.

Rachel sighed. "I guess I should have taken Paolo's advice. But my feet aren't tough enough. I feel every root and rock through those things."

Matt knelt down and used the flat of his machete to help her scrape the clay from the shoes. "They take some getting used to," he told her. "Anyway, I think we're back on high ground for a while."

Rachel reached out and stroked his shoulder. "Matt," she started to say, then stopped herself. He looked up and followed her gaze toward the trees at the foot of the nearest hill.

"Breadfruit," he said with a smile. *Ramon* was the

Spanish word, and where one found *ramon* trees, one often found the ruins of Mayan temples.

Just then Paolo came limping into sight. *"Por allí,"* he said, pointing up the trail. "On the other side of this hill."

Rachel stood up. "Aguaculto?" she asked, revitalized.

*Sí, sí.* " Paolo nodded. *"Vamos."*

Matt took another compass reading and drew a small circle on the map. Godoy, Paolo, and Rachel were standing together in a pocket formed by three towering mounds when he caught up with them. The mules were munching on breadfruit leaves the *arriero* had cut from nearby trees. Cut blocks that had once formed the base and steps of human-made structures poked at all angles from the face of the tree-covered mounds.

*"Las ruinas,"* Godoy announced proudly. "Aguaculto."

Paolo, Rachel, and Matt spread out to search the immediate vicinity for carving of any sort; eventually Paolo located a badly eroded stela that retained traces of glyph blocks on one side of its three worked faces. Rachel splashed water on the stela's half-dozen legible glyphs and went to work on them with a nylon-bristle paint brush. A smile took shape on Rachel's face when the last of glyphs stood revealed; she had found what she'd been looking for: the emblem glyph for Rock River.

# 18

## Ornamenti Dei Barbari

The circle of blackened stones had once contained a campfire. "Not for several weeks," Godoy said in Spanish, poking at congealed masses of gray ash with the tip of his machete.

Matt bent down to inspect the ground around the fireplaces, his fingertips locating small dollops of metal in the dirt.

"*Soldadura,*" the *arriero* commented.

Unsure, Rachel said, "Solder?"

They were half a kilometer north of what she speculated might have been Rock River's central plaza, where they'd set up camp the previous night. The land was terraced there and sparsely wooded. Ceibas and gumbo-limbos had reduced the quincunx of neighboring temples to rubble. Someone had erected three small *palapas* on the flats, whose age Godoy and Paolo had determined by the freshness of the thatch. Inside were the remains of fires, plastic trash, hammock *sogas*. A hundred feet east of the largest shelter, a five-foot-deep garbage pit contained tin cans, fruit rinds, and strips of plastic sheeting.

Matt wiped his hands on his pants and walked to the adjacent shelter, carefully checking for scorpions under some of the fallen fronds. There was a scrap pile of mostly rusted iron fragments in the far corner: small gears, thumbnail-size pieces of welder's stock, lengths of

218

galvanized pipe, and odds and ends of plumbing hardware. Elsewhere, he saw a short stack of sharpened stakes, none more than eighteen inches in length. A crude cord-bound tripod assembled from the stakes stood off to one side of the stack. Matt was regarding it when Paolo appeared with two cast-iron skillets, which he dropped into the dirt like dead things.

The *arriero* gave a worried look around. *"Los guerrillas."*

"Matt, what—"

"Homemade claymores—mines. You fill them up with black powder and iron fragments, attach some det cord, and you've got an effective killing device." He motioned to the stakes. "They were making stands. Most of the time they stick them in the crotch of a tree." He glanced up at Paolo. "We're going to have to watch our step. We're lucky we made it in in one piece."

Rachel turned a disappointed look to the boatman. "But you said they haven't been here in weeks."

"They must have been using this place as a temporary base," Matt answered for him.

"Were you in Vietnam?" Rachel asked, fixing him with an uncertain look.

Matt shook his head and tossed one of the stakes aside in a disgusted way. "We better complete our little fact-finding tour and get the fuck out of here."

"You think they'd come back?"

"I don't know that much about them," Matt said angrily. "And I don't want to know."

They set out early to survey the site and its environs, leaving Plácido behind to watch the camp. Monkeys threw sticks and urinated on them from the treetops; howlers barked. Everywhere they went they found evidence of the guerrillas' destructive brand of archeological handiwork: narrow clefts, open-air trenches, and tunnels had been pushed into each of the major mounds, and in some cases entire structures appeared to have been dismantled stone by stone. Most of the stelae had been defaced by saw cuts or broken down into transportable fragments. Paolo discovered some intact glyph panels and a fragment of sapodilla lintel with traces of color, but by and large the site had been stripped. Matt and Rachel cautiously explored the open wounds the looters had left behind, musty shafts and bat-ridden tunnels to emptied tombs. One of them bore traces of huge rubicund glyphs, but little else.

All the while Matt regaled her with the stories he'd heard—the rumors of temple cave-ins that had buried men alive, the gun battles over turf, the big money, the government complicity. He knew Rachel didn't need to hear any of it, but that didn't stop him from trying to make his point. He wanted her to come away from it all thinking as he did: that things were better left alone, that no relic was going to change the world, that there wasn't one worth dying for.

He was ready to believe that their several hours of futile probing into the site's plundered past had convinced her, when they chanced upon a mound near a dry moat far removed from the main group, trenched like the rest but in Rachel's eyes instantly recognizable as the temple depicted on the final page of the codex.

"This *has* to be it," she said, leaning back to frame the mound in her boxed fingers as one would a snapshot.

The forest was triple-canopied, the mound covered with brush and young trees, but the guerrillas' enlisted workers had cleared wide swaths of level ground along the front of the temple, an open area of cedar and oak. Rachel cleaned an area on the ground with the toe of her sneaker and bent down to sketch out the drawing with her finger.

"There were five emblem glyphs turned on end, like columns supporting the base of the temple. And a room centrally located inside or under the pyramid, like this, with sixteen small squares radiating out in a kind of crenellated motif."

Matt stooped over to study the drawing, sheathing the machete and moving it to the rear of his belt. Then he shifted his attention to the mound itself. A gaping hole—cavernous compared with the trenches they had been investigating all morning—had been opened up through a slide of rock and faced slabs that had once been a stairway to the summit. Fronting the mound were the pitted

remains of five pedestal bases. Rachel speculated that
they might at one time have held stelae or statuaries.

"And I'll bet we would have found Rock River's emblem glyph on each of them," she said.

Matt felt his chin, running his fingertips over a three-
day growth of stubble. "Well, let's find out if they left
us anything."

As they approached the mound, Matt could see that
the looters had taken precautions to shore up the tunnel
entrance with support posts and cross members of Santa
Maria and *popiste* cut from the forest. Someone had at-
tempted to conceal the entrance with brush and tarps,
which were now scattered about. He slipped a miner's
lamp over his forehead and switched it on; the light was
powered by a six-volt lantern battery in a clear plastic
case hitched to his belt. Three small bats fluttered out
from the entrance.

"Can you see anything?" Rachel asked, coming over
to him from one of the pedestal bases.

Matt manipulated the beam with his hand, lighting the
tunnel's mortarless rubble walls and supported ceiling;
fifteen feet or so in, it narrowed to a crawl space. The
place had become a regular population center for ham-
merhead spiders.

"They must have had highlanders working on this
one," Matt said. "Somebody with mining experience,
anyway. You want the honors?"

Rachel flicked on her own lamp and moved it about.
She had already demonstrated that she wasn't the slightest
bit claustrophobic, but something held her back this time.
"I did the last one," she told him, a hint of timorousness
in her voice.

Matt grimaced. "I thought you said that stalled ele-
vator cured you once and for all."

"It did. But . . . well, I thought I'd give you a
chance."

"Don't do me any favors. I'm not the one itching to
get my face on a magazine cover. Bad enough it's going
to end up hanging in *correos* all over Mexico."

Rachel made an impatient sound. "Then why are you
bothering to help me?"

"That's a good goddamn question," Matt muttered,

ducking his head and starting off. "Just stay put for a minute."

The air was clammy, the tunnel filled with dripping sounds. He went as far as he could at a crouch, then squatted, moving the machete scabbard around to the small of his back, and duck-walked to the entrance of the narrowed portion. He bent over, flooding the passageway with light, and saw that it continued dead straight for perhaps thirty feet. The beam picked up a reflective surface at the end, which Matt guessed might be a painted area of wall—the white stuccoed inner lining of a tomb.

"All right, come on in," he said just loud enough to be heard. "But watch your head and hold up right here." He squinted as the beam from Rachel's lamp found him, then turned around and crawled through the second opening.

Less than ten feet along Matt grew certain that ahead rose a section of painted wall; the looters had managed to punch their tunnel right through the wall of a tomb, just above floor level. He stopped at the hole, directed the light around the arched room, and whistled softly.

"Matt, what is it?" Rachel called out from the darkness behind him.

He twisted around to answer her. "Come and see for yourself."

Matt bellied down onto a kind of wall, a chill running through his body, and swung himself into a ten by ten-foot room; Rachel joined him there a moment later, emerging from the tunnel and gasping at the sights the miner's lamps illuminated.

"I guess I owe you an apology," Matt said, overwhelmed.

The crypt was not like Pascal's tomb in the Temple of Inscriptions, nor did it resemble any of the three rooms of Structure I at Bonampak, with their brilliantly executed scenes of courtly life. It was, rather, three entire walls covered floor to arched ceiling with painted figures and glyphs, each no larger than the cover of a paperback book, running in detached columns and stately rows clear around the room except where interrupted by the ragged hole through which they'd entered and a collapsed section of wall where perhaps some internal stairway had been hastily filled with rubble from above.

"Oh, my God!" Rachel rasped. She took hold of Matt, her fingernails digging into his upper arm.

Their lamps highlighted emblem and dynastic and numeral glyphs, color-coded directional and planetary notations, pantheons of seated deities, panel after panel of history, science, description, exegesis, exposition—who knew what. A chronicle of war, the rise and fall of an American empire.

They pivoted together like dancers across the room's stone floor, the twin beams of the lamps caught up in a dazzling interplay.

There was a knee-high stone bench along all four walls, its front lip a continuous band of bas-relief depictions of a kind of monkey demon; its top, or seat, was adorned with a series of repetitive glyphs the color of dried blood, nine in all.

Save for three ten-inch-deep, foot-square cavities along the room's south wall.

Rachel let go of Matt's arm to inspect the smooth inner surface of the hewn basin nearest them. "These must have been fitted with carved inserts," she said, running her fingertips over a lip three inches below the opening. She contemplated the basin for a moment, then moved slowly toward a far corner of the room, floating her palm along the surface of the plaster seat. Without warning she whirled on Matt, blinding him with the light. "Give me your machete—quickly!"

Matt shielded his eyes, hesitantly unsheathed the tool, and handed it over to her butt first, wondering what she had in mind. She grabbed it in a two-handed grip and began driving the tip of the blade down into an area of painted plaster a few inches back from the front lip. On the fifth or sixth stab, the machete took an outward turn along the convex edge of the blade and arced up and away from the bench, narrowly missing Matt's face and nearly winging the miner's lamp from his head.

"What are you trying to do?" he snapped, snatching the tool away from her.

Rachel's right hand pawed at the spot the blade had

scored. "There has to be some kind of fingerhole, a hand grip of some sort. There *has* to be . . ."

"Get back," Matt warned her. "But keep your light trained on the seat." Holding the machete upright in both hands, he hammered at the plaster with the hardened grip, utterly destroying the main sign of the glyph. A minute of that left exposed a pair of one-inch-diameter plaster-filled holes, aligned along an axis perpendicular to the front lip of the seat. The raised curve of a carved glyph block showed beneath the now-cracked limestone top coat.

"Now here," Rachel said excitedly, indicating an area as far from the wall as the holes were from the lip.

Matt repeated his actions, exposing a second pair identical to the first. Suddenly he grasped what she had in mind and started hammering out the parimeter of an imaginary square approximating the size of the hewn basins. Shortly the plaster was sufficiently deteriorated to allow them to see not only the glyph that adorned the cover of the concealed basin but its outline as well. Matt flipped the machete around and wedged the tip into the space between the lid and the seat, applying a controlled twisting motion to the blade. He succeeded in dislodging some of the trapped plaster and continued this procedure every two inches or so, painstakingly working his way around the perimeter of the cover. Rachel was quivering beside him, shaking so much she could hardly keep the light still.

Twice around the rim and Matt felt the cover begin to loosen, but he couldn't get the blade wedged deeply enough to lever it free. He smashed at the finger holes, managing to loosen the plaster there, then shoved the machete into the gap as deep as he could and left it there sticking straight up out of the bench top.

"I'm going to see if I can lift it up. Slip the blade in if the cover begins to move." Matt wet his fingers with saliva and pushed his right thumb and middle finger into the set of holes nearest the wall and his left middle finger into one of the holes above the lip of the seat. "Whatever you do," he cautioned her, "don't let the blade slip."

Rachel clasped both hands on the black plastic grip and nodded.

"All right. Ready?" Matt said. "Here goes nothing."
He flexed his hands and lifted for all he was worth; the
cover came up an inch, and the blade dropped home.
Rachel gave him a startled look in the light from their
lamps. "Okay," Matt continued, out of breath. "Now
comes the tricky part. Just try to lever it up while I lift.
Easy does it," he hastened to add.

He leaned into it again, straining, jaw clenched. He
could see that the blade was flexing under the weight of
the cover, but the three-inch-thick square was rising, and
all at once it broke free of its precision fit. Matt got his
fingers underneath it and managed to flip the slab upright
in its cradle.

Rachel nearly fainted when she saw the codex.

The book's wooden cover was lacerated where the
blade of the machete had pierced it, but it was otherwise
intact, similar in size and condition to the one Billie and
Neil had died for.

Rachel took a moment to kneel and weep; then she
was back on her feet, maniacal, smashing away at another area of plaster on the adjacent bench. Judiciously,
Matt moved in and managed to wrestle the machete out
of her grip before she did much damage to the bench or
to herself. He threw the tool aside and took her by the
shoulders. "Cut it out!" he yelled, shaking her.

"The s-sixteen," she sobbed, stiff in his arms. "The
sixteen glyphs . . . they're codices. They're here, right
here. . . . That's why the scribe depicted this place . . .
it's a repository, a library."

She went limp in his grip, and he held her for a moment, then eased her down onto the bench, gently slapping her cheeks to bring her around.

"Listen to me, okay," he said quietly and as calmly
as he could. "If they're here, they're not going anywhere. So we'll go outside for a while and think things
through. Then, if we decide to come back in, we can
bring—"

Rachel sat up, a terrified look contorting her features.
"What do you mean, *if* we decide to come back?"

"I'm only saying that we need to think about what
we're doing. Okay?"

She glanced around the room, feverish and wide-eyed, tightened her lips, and gave Matt a palsied nod.

"I'm putting this back for safekeeping," he told her, lowering the carved basin lid back into place.

Ten minutes later they were back in the heat, their eyes narrowed against oblique shafts of afternoon sunlight. Matt lowered Rachel down onto one of the pedestal bases fronting the mound. She sat with her forehead pressed to her knees.

"The camera . . ." Rachel said absently. "Which way is our camp?"

Matt whistled a signal to Paolo, waited a minute, and then repeated the call. He heard Paolo's voice a minute later and answered him. The boatman appeared at the saddle between two mounds east of the repository temple and began to sidestep down the slope toward the clearing, the shotgun over one shoulder. Matt met him halfway, noting the consternation in his dark eyes.

"There's something you have to see," Paolo said evenly.

"Yeah, we've got something to show you, too," Matt told him, looking over his shoulder at Rachel.

"Whatever you have can wait, *hermano*."

Matt gave him a quizzical look. "What is it?"

Paolo motioned over the mounds. "A cache of weapons. Rifles, rockets . . . enough to equip a small army."

"Goddamn it," Matt said, pacing back and forth along the rim of the pit Paolo had quite literally stumbled across. He cursed again, directing his words to no one in particular.

The pit was a common enough find in Mayan sites—a bottle-shaped chamber known as a *chultun*—thought to have served as a kind of cistern. The normally constricted opening had been enlarged to accommodate the cache. Paolo had dragged the hole's wormwood lattice cover and camo tarps aside and pried the lids off two of the weapons crates. One contained recoilless rifles glistening with Cosmoline and Starlight scopes wrapped in plastic. The second contained bazookas and armor-piercing rounds. Matt was shocked to discover that the weapons were U.S.-made.

"Where's Godoy now?" he asked, turning to Paolo.

"Back at the *palapa*. He's getting ready to leave."

"Matt, you can't let him!" Rachel said, clutching him.

He disengaged himself and ran a hand through his hair. "The fuck I can't. Whoever cached this stuff is going to come back. Maybe not today or tomorrow, but soon." He explained what the Rescate agents had told him about the recent battle near Paso Caballos and the speculation that Raphael Aguilar's insurgents were headed for the Usumacinta River.

"Caballos is less than fifty miles northwest of here. I don't blame Godoy for wanting to split."

Rachel said, "Then let him. Tell him to leave us two of the mules. Tell him we'll pay for them."

Matt shook his head firmly. "I can't ask him to do that. No way. The mules belong to his *patrón*."

Rachel stepped in his path as he started off toward the shelters. "You've got to convince him, Matt. You've got to tell him how important this is."

He regarded her a moment, then shouldered past without a word. Godoy was beneath the largest of the *palapas*, hastily securing supplies for the beasts' pack frames. One look at the mule skinner's face and Matt decided not to bother trying to dissuade him.

"You talk to him," he told Rachel as she caught up.

She showed him a scowl and began to lay it out to Godoy, telling him how they had all made an important discovery and how she would see to it that he shared in the notoriety. She offered to reward him if he would stay, explaining that the find had to be protected at all costs until the Guatemalan government sent in troops to guard the site. Godoy continued to adjust the loads while he listened; when he was certain that Rachel was finished, he turned to Matt and Paolo and said, "The gringa is crazy."

"Then just tell him to go!" Rachel seethed. "But make sure he notifies the authorities that we're up here and we need immediate assistance."

Matt and Paolo looked at each other. "You're planning to stay here," Matt said.

"Well, of course I'm going to stay here. What do you

expect me to do, leave this place to the mercy of the guerillas? I've got to get as much of it copied as I can."

"Then what? Pack the codices out of here on your back?"

"Why not? We know the way out. You have the compass bearings. I'm sure we can seal the room up somehow, temporarily at least."

The lead mule gave a sudden start. Paolo brought the shotgun off his shoulder and scanned the forest at the edge of the clearing. It took Godoy a full minute to calm the beast down.

Matt fantasized about dragging Rachel out: moving quickly, gagging and binding her, throwing her over the wooden pack frame . . .

"And if the guerrillas show up?" he asked.

Rachel held his gaze. "I'm willing to take my chances."

He offered her a half smile. "I thought you were going to suggest we make a stand of it."

"I'd do just that if I knew how to use those weapons."

Matt said, "Guns wouldn't solve it." He mulled over the situation. "You wouldn't be content with that one codex, huh? After all, they didn't think to dig into the bench the first time through. Shoot your shots, get it down on film. We could take our chances."

"Absolutely not. I'll stay here alone if I have to."

"I believe you would." He laughed. "What about it?" he asked Paolo. "You willing to hang around here for a few more days?"

The boatman was about to answer when a voice from the rear of the *palapa* said, "So very, very noble." The four of them swung around just in time to see Jules Kul step from a stand of *ramon* trees, cooling his face with a large paper fan. Huatcho and Kim were with him. Paolo raised the shotgun.

"Drop it," someone off to Matt's left said in Spanish. As Paolo turned to the voice, Matt caught sight of Niles Chalker, holding an automatic weapon at high port.

"Better do as he says," Kul intoned. Both Huatcho and Kim were showing handguns.

Matt wanted to believe that he was seeing things, that Kul's sudden appearance was the result of something he'd eaten, some foul spores he'd inhaled in the tunnels. His thoughts returned to the guerrillas' arms cache, and he berated himself for not picking up a weapon when he had had the chance—peaceful solutions something of a joke now. "Put it away, Paolo," he said at last.

The boatman gave him a sorrowful look and laid the weapon down.

"Excellent," Kul said, shuffling toward the *palapa*. He instructed Huatcho to tell their muleteers to bring the animals up. "Matt, how very lovely it is to see you again. And this," he continued, appraising Rachel, "must be the infamous Ms. Riordan."

Rachel took a step forward as if to greet Kul and, with one deft motion of her right foot, swept the walking stick out from under him, dropping Kul, his paper fan, and his imperious grin face first into the dirt.

Matt had been slow to read Rachel's motives, but he was quick to read Kim's; without a thought he side-stepped in front of Rachel, taking the full force of the boy's side kick high in the chest. He was thrown backwards with neck-wrenching force, knocking Rachel off her feet and leaving himself wide open for Kim's follow-up spin kick. When he lifted his head a moment later, he found Rachel kneeling alongside him and Kul back on his feet. Chalker was standing to one side, still holding the rifle on everyone. Matt heard voices behind him and turned to see two of the *xateros* from Bethel leading a pack train into the plaza, the lead beast outfitted with a crude saddle.

"That was extremely foolish," Kul was saying. Kim was poised, awaiting further orders. "Obviously, Ms. Riordan, Matt neglected to inform you that I have a strong aversion to unwarranted violence. I have been known to go to great lengths to see that such acts meet with violent consequences."

"You slimy bastard!" Rachel said under her breath. "You killed her!"

"Technically, no," Kul told her, dusting himself off. "My former employees were to blame for that, but they have both paid for their sins of excess."

Matt shook his head clear. "How did you find us, Kul?" he managed.

"A simple matter, really. You see, once I had a chance to explain my position to Lieutenant Escobar, he was quick to realize that I had in fact been duped and that all that gunplay at the hotel would never have occurred were it not for your hand in this affair. I must credit certain . . . friends in Villahermosa for helping to see to it that the lieutenant drew the proper conclusions.

"And when it was learned that you and Ms. Riordan had, well, skipped town, the case I presented appeared all that more credible. The good lieutenant happened to recall seeing some jottings on one of your notepads, Matt—something about Rock River and Aguaculto, I'm sure you remember. Well, Dr. Chalker and I put our heads together, and I placed a few calls here and there, and what do you suppose I came up with? Aguaculto, again. So I began to ask myself why Ms. Riordan had so willingly surrendered the codex. The meager financial profit couldn't have been enough, and I sincerely doubted she was the type who frightened easily. So was it, perhaps, that she had happened upon some even greater discovery?" Kul laughed. "This was, of course, before Dr. Chalker learned the truth about what you sold us.

"In any case, we decided to see for ourselves just exactly what you were up to. The volcano complicated matters to our advantage, and it proved a simple matter to pick up your trail from Echeverría on. Then, as luck would have it, we met these two fine specimens, who told us where you went and agreed to help us follow you. For considerable remuneration, I might add."

Matt glanced at the *xateros* and gave a derisive snort. "So Villahermosa just let you walk away. For considerable remuneration, I suppose."

Kul grinned. "I told you once about the power of our Masonic fraternity, did I not? Money, however, had its place. But the plain and simple truth of the matter is that the police and those fools from Interpol had nothing but circumstantial evidence to link me to any of the deaths."

"What about the codex?" Matt asked. "Did you buy your way out of that, too?"

Kul traded looks with Chalker and laughed. "You see how he persists? Matt, there is no reason to maintain the charade at this late stage. We all know the codex fragment was a fake.''

Matt looked over his shoulder at Rachel, who averted her eyes.

''It took me only a moment to recognize it,'' Kul explained. ''A brilliant forgery. A masterpiece in some ways. In fact, it had been offered to me in Zurich long before Sol Nagel embarrassed himself by acquiring it. I believe he's your boss, is he not, Ms. Riordan? Although boss is surely too restrictive a term.''

Kul threw Rachel a theatrical look from behind the fan. ''A bat seems to have made off with Ms. Riordan's voice.'' He tittered and looked at Matt. ''You see, Matt, Sol Nagel's presence in this helped to answer some of my other questions as well, chiefly my nagging suspicion about the original source of the funds and the reason behind all these dark rumblings I was hearing in Villahermosa about Ms. Riordan's sister's involvement with Alejandro Volan, the guerrillas' liaison—their arms supplier.''

Matt stared at him uncomprehendingly.

''Mr. Sol Nagel,'' Kul continued, ''in addition to his museum work, has very close ties with Washington. Correct me if I'm wrong, Ms. Riordan, but it was *cryptography* work that brought you and Sol together to begin with, wasn't it? At the United Nations, wasn't it?''

Rachel said nothing, and Kul laughed.

''In any event, it seems that certain men in high places—secret places is perhaps a better way to say it—want to make sure that the guerrillas receive funding for their activities. The codex was paid for with special funds which went right back into the organization by way of the Honduran Volan. Money for *narcomilitares,* money for antiquities, what does it matter as long as it serves its intended purpose?''

''U.S. weapons,'' Matt muttered. ''The motherfuckers are arming the guerrillas, playing both sides.''

''You sound surprised,'' Kul said. ''Think of it as their way of insuring a proper fight, as it were. Guevara's military government will have its hands full dealing with state-of-the-art weaponry, so they'll agree to cut back some on all these so-called human rights violations, make a new appeal to our illustrious president—''

''And Reagan can begin by sending them helicopters and tanks again. Solidifying their allegiance to the democratic way.''

''Bravo, Matt. You see how simple it is? It's close to ritual warfare, is it not? The sort the Maya practiced for the capture of sacrificial victims. No wonder that Presidente Portillo decided to take such an interest in the deaths of two North American runners, eh? Nicaragua, El Salvador, he has to be asking himself just where it will end.''

Matt saw the tightness in Rachel's face and imagined how his own must have looked. ''But the codex . . . all along it was a fake?''

Kul stared at him as if puzzling something out, then threw his head back in knowing laughter. ''You didn't realize it was a fake! She tricked you as well!'' He made a downward motion with the fan, then tapped the point of his stick on the ground in a merry fashion. ''She substituted the fake for the fragment her sister purchased from the guerrillas.''

''Matt,'' Rachel said, reaching out for his shoulder.

He pulled back to regard her. ''You gave me a fake that morning.'' He tried to remember the telex, something about a complicated plan, a deferral to Billie's judgement. ''A fake. Which means that you had to have the thing with you.'' He looked at her, hoping to discern something from her silence. ''You brought it down with you from New York. But why?'' he asked her. ''Why would you bring it down with you?''

''Matt, listen to me—''

''Unless you knew all along that something had gone wrong. That's why you were ready to leave Palenque. You didn't care if Chalker discovered the switch. Either way you were going to win. If they offed me, you beat them to New York. If they didn't . . . we end up here.'' Matt turned to Kul. ''You never told me how you knew about the codex to begin with.''

Kul gestured to Chalker. ''I have to thank Niles for that. You see, he was present when Ms. Riordan's sister made the purchase.''

Matt recalled what Rachel had said about the buy: somewhere at a site in the Petén. He looked at the archeologist, trying to read him, then said, "Jesus Christ. You were the one Aguilar was holding for ransom. What happened—you wandered into the site where Billie and Aguilar were making the deal?"

Chalker threw Kul a nervous look.

"Go ahead, Niles, tell him. What does it matter?"

"I was there before she showed up," Chalker began, a quiver to his voice. "I came in while the guerrillas were tearing apart the site. But when I saw what Aguilar had found—what he planned to sell to those two—I couldn't let it get away. So I offered him twice what they were prepared to pay."

"Half a million?" Matt said.

Chalker nodded. "Aguilar was adamant about the new price. When Billie refused to meet it . . ." He uttered a short, crazed laugh. "He tore the thing in half."

"The missing fragment," Kul interjected.

Matt said, "You had the other half all along."

Chalker worked his jaw muscles. "Aguilar demanded a ransom for my release. He allowed my assistant to make the arrangements. Mr. Kul was good enough to pay it, and at the same time I procured the first half of the codex."

"And you told him about Billie and Neil."

Chalker nodded grimly.

Kul said, "Of course they led Niles to believe that they were going directly to Guatemala City. But I instructed my employees to make some inquiries locally beforehand. Niles went along. And this is where you entered the picture, was it not, Matt?"

Silently, Matt tried to assemble the facts. Chalker and Kul's men showing up in Sayaxche, hiring a speedboat, coming upon the Usumacinta camp at first light . . . "You see what kind of animals they are," he heard Rachel say. "I couldn't let them have it."

"Billie told you to bring the codex down," he said after a moment. "She told you about Chalker. That's why they decided to use T'sup Kin."

The words stuck in her throat. "She phoned me from Tikal. We thought Chalker would go to the authorities.

We thought we could substitute the fake to confuse everyone. But Matt, listen to me, I swear I didn't know that Kul was involved. I couldn't understand how he learned about the codex. I didn't know they were in this thing together until you mentioned Chalker's name at Natalie's. But by then you already knew that Kul was behind it. There was nothing more I could tell you.''

"Except maybe that you were about to pass them a fake. Or that you knew all along Billie's deal had been compromised.''

"I didn't think you'd agree to any of it,'' she said in a rush, the edge of a scream. "I needed your help.''

Matt turned away from her.

"Matt, please! I didn't want to lie to you. I meant every word. About New York, about everything.''

Kul said, "How very touching. The time has come, however, to make good on the deal, Ms. Riordan. The money is of no concern, but I want the codex—now.''

Rachel's hands flew up. "I don't have it. You'll have to wait—''

"Niles,'' Kul interrupted. "Put your weapon to Mr. Terry's head while I repeat my demand.''

"Please, Jules,'' Chalker objected. "It's horrible enough that people have had to die because of this thing. Those thugs of yours killing—'' He swallowed a strangled sound. "I'm not good at this sort of thing. Don't—''

"Just do it, Niles!'' Kul roared.

Matt stiffened as the cool tip of the barrel touched his temple. Chalker's gaze was unfocused. Matt could see Paolo eyeing him from across the *palapa*, his fists balled up. Kim, off to Kul's right, wore an amused expression.

"Now, Ms. Riordan—the codex.''

Rachel, Huatcho and the three *xateros* were out of sight behind Matt's back. No one moved for what seemed to be an interminable time; then Matt heard Rachel get up and walk over to Godoy's mules. Two minutes later she returned with a flat plasticware container, the type one could pick up in the Palenque market.

"Well done,'' Kul applauded, accepting it.

Relieved, Matt felt Chalker ease the weapon away.

"Before you do that, Niles,'' Kul added all at once,

"there's something else I wish to ask Ms. Riordan—*Rachel*. Exactly what is it about this place that she is willing to risk her life to protect?" Kul sniggered. "I thought I heard mention of glyphs and codices as I was waiting to present myself."

In plain view, Rachel offered Matt a tearful, pleading look.

Kul asked if he needed to repeat himself as Chalker pressed the gun to Matt's head.

# 19

## Killing of the Power

"**D**id Billie and Neil really find the page?" Matt asked Rachel the following morning. It was the first thing he had said to her since the confrontation with Kul in the *palapa*, and she showed him a hurt look.

"What are you saying, Matt?"

"I'm just curious to know if it played the way you told me. Or if maybe the page turned up in New York first. I'm thinking maybe this guy Nagel ran the whole thing from his end. Got your sister to do the dirty work, deliver the Agency's money down to Volan, collect a favor from you for old time's sake."

"How could you think that?" she asked angrily.

"That's the least I'm thinking," Matt told her.

No one had gotten much sleep. Kul had split them up, Rachel in one *palapa*, Matt and Paolo in another, Kim in some kind of standing zen all night long, the rifle by his side.

In the morning they'd been moved to the repository, and they were in the clearing outside the mound now, hands and feet tied, mosquito lunch. Matt had been fully prepared to tell Kul about the repository mound, but it was Rachel who led everyone to it. Chalker and Kul were currently inside.

Paolo was off to their left within earshot with only his wrists bound. Kim, the M-16 cradled in his arms, was watching all three of them from the drum-shaped pedestal stone nearest the tunnel. Huatcho and the boys from Bethel were back at the *palapas*. Matt was certain that the two *xateros* had had an easy time convincing Godoy to keep his mouth shut. The muleteer had raved on about the guerrillas and the arms cache, but Kul had been disinclined to believe him or was simply unconcerned.

Rachel said, "Sol would never do anything like that. It was Michael's idea to approach the museum. They gave me the page, and I showed it to Sol to see if he thought the museum would be interested in acquiring the codex. He wouldn't have gotten involved in any of this if he had known that Laurie was in danger."

"Maybe you didn't hear what Kul said—" Matt started to say.

"I don't believe a word of it. Sol's an honorable man. He's one of my dearest friends."

"Like an uncle to you."

"Go to hell!"

Matt smiled to himself, figuring it might very well be his next stop. "I must have seemed like a real asshole, telling you that you'd have to sit on the codex for ten years. Sol didn't give a damn if you got it or not. The delivery of the money was the important thing. It didn't matter that the codex was stolen, paid for in blood—"

"Fuck you, Matt. You're so naive. You think any museum in the world would have passed up a chance at that codex? Look around you, for God's sake—Kul is only the tip of the iceberg. Everyone's got their hands in this business now, from those *arrieros* right on up. Looters and guerrillas, runners and arms smugglers, collectors, museums, even Mexico's Institute of Anthropology."

"Well, I feel a whole lot better now."

"You're a fine one to climb on a soapbox. You're selling the past just as much as everyone else."

Matt uttered a short laugh. "I guess I'd be offended if the circumstances were different."

Rachel lowered her head, holding something back—tears, a string of epithets, Matt wasn't sure. "What are they going to do with us?" she asked at last.

Matt glanced over at Paolo before he answered her. The boatman had been trying to follow their exchange and was now regarding Rachel as though she were some sort of succubus. "I don't think he'll kill us," he said in an offhand manner. "But I suppose that's an option. He's got the second half of the codex. And he's about to crawl out of that tunnel with more than he ever dreamed of possessing. So I figure he'll put some of it aside for his coffers, then hightail it out of here with the mules and leave us to fend for ourselves. He'll have to get to Palenque or maybe Tikal to report the find, and with Chalker to back him up, he doesn't have to worry about us."

A group of howlers started barking nearby. Matt scanned the canopy north of the mound but couldn't discern any reason for the sudden commotion.

Rachel said, "We could just stay here. We'll give our version when the police arrive."

Matt blew a mosquito off the tip of his nose and shrugged. "I doubt it would do much good, but you're welcome to try."

Rachel snorted. "I'm on my own, is that it?"

"You've been on your own from the start. There were a dozen other ways we could have played this, but you decided to stick to the same covert shit that got everything rolling in the first place. I'll tell you something, Rachel, if that's the climate up there—the fucking mindset or whatever you call it—then I'm glad to be out of it. I'll take my chances with revolution."

She stared at him pityingly and looked away.

Matt saw Paolo shake his head in a dejected way.

The howlers were continuing their raucous transit, and there was a hint of rain in the air.

Forty-five almost lazy minutes passed before a drained and sullied Jules Kul hobbled from the mouth of the tunnel. But a look of transformation wreathed his face. Chalker, armed with one of the handguns, was a few steps behind, moving like a somnambulist. He dropped the miner's lamps to the ground and settled himself alongside Kul on the trunk of a fallen tree opposite Matt and Rachel.

"I believe I underestimated you," Kul told them,

breathing hard. "In fact, I'm tempted to say that I find myself greatly in your debt. Did you suspect, even for a moment . . ." he said to Rachel, "Please, as one scholar to another."

She glared at him. "If I told you I did, would you give me credit for the find?"

Matt raised his eyes and laughed. "Here's one you won't be able to keep from the world, Kul. What are you going to do, take it apart and have it shipped back to L.A.?"

"I'm not a greedy man, Matt," Kul said, regaining some of his composure. "The books are mine, but I will give the world the room, in any case."

"You prick!" Rachel screamed, straining at her ropes.

Kim made a threatening gesture with the rifle, but Kul waved him away. "Niles," he went on, "is almost certain that he saw the missing inserts among the plunder the guerrilla leader showed him. This . . ."

"Aguilar," Chalker filled in. With a gesture of discomfort, he pulled the handgun out of his belt and laid it next to him on the tree trunk.

"Yes. This Aguilar claimed to have found the codex in an unknown site, and our guess is that he was referring to Aguaculto. It's remarkable that no one thought to excavate this place long ago. But then, there are few possessed of Ms. Riordan's remarkable intuitive gifts."

"You're nothing but jackals! I'd rather see this place destroyed!"

Matt was about to tell her to calm down when he heard what could have been mistaken for a trilling birdcall issue from the trees behind the mound. At the same time Paolo came alert and turned an apprehensive glance his way. The call was answered in another part of the forest.

"What I suggest we do," Kul was telling Chalker, "is take the mules and drivers with us. We'll leave these three here. I'm certain they'll manage to free themselves, but by then we'll be on our way to Tikal. And if they don't get free, then the *guardianos* will find them. Looters could be blamed for any unfortunate accidents."

The birdcalls sounded again, closer this time. Rachel

flashed Matt a questioning look, as though aware of his sudden vigilance.

"We could send the *arrieros* back up for them," Chalker said. "I won't have a part in any more *accidents*."

Kul appraised Chalker with his eyes. "You're soft for such a young man, Niles. Would you have me include Ms. Riordan on the find? Perhaps we should let *National Geographic* proclaim its wonders to the world?"

Matt saw movement at both sides of the mounds. He counted four heads in a glance—camouflage soft caps, red bandannas, and web gear, the glint of steel. He thought at first that they might be rangers but quickly recognized them as insurgents. One wore frayed polyester pants and rubber sandals, another a loose-fitting black skirt. "This place isn't yours to give away, Kul. Any more than it belongs to the Maya or these ceiba trees."

"Why, Matt," Kul asked with affected surprise, "are you planning to entertain us with a bit of Petén philosophy?"

Matt turned his head somewhat to the left; Rachel and Paolo were agape. "We're dealing in hard truths, Kul," he continued, keeping his voice carefully controlled. "And I'm about to do you a big favor. But first I want you to keep looking straight at me and tell Kim to get rid of the rifle."

Kul looked baffled, then grinned. "One has to admire your brazenness."

"Chalker, listen to me," Matt said imploringly. "Put the gun down on the ground. Do it slowly and don't turn around."

"Enough of this—"

"You've got nothing to lose," Matt cut him off, raising his voice a notch. "We're tied up, we can't do anything. And you've got half a dozen soldiers behind you."

Kul blanched but remained still. "If this is your idea of a joke—"

"Don't turn around!" Matt warned him.

Rachel said, "Listen to him—please!"

Kul nodded his head to Chalker and spoke two rapid sentences in Vietnamese. Kim stood unmoving for a moment, then complied. Matt could see that the boy's hearing had picked up on movement behind him.

"Not the muleteers," Kul said uncertainly.

Rachel swallowed and found her voice. "Matt, what do we do?"

"We sit here and wait for them to tell us."

There were eight of them at that point, and Kul and Chalker were well aware of their presence. The archeologist flinched as the woman's assault rifle touched his shoulder. A second rebel soldier had positioned himself behind Kim. The apparent team leader among them, a tall mustachioed man with night fighter's cosmetic smeared across his forehead, nose, and prominent cheekbones, motioned Matt, Rachel and Paolo to keep silent. As Chalker, Kul, and Kim swung around, the other soldiers mirrored their leader's command, gesturing for the three to lay facedown on the ground.

The woman raised one hand to her mouth and voiced what Matt thought was an excellent reproduction of a tinamou's call. Two of the insurgents were standing over Matt and Rachel, whispering to themselves out of undisguised wonderment and curiosity. Someone responded to the call from far off in the direction of the *palapas*, and within ten minutes twenty or more soldiers had joined their teammates in the shadow of the repository mound.

They came out of the surrounding forest like a feral pack, wary and ravenous-looking, a ragtag group of young men and women dressed in everything from military-style fatigues to cotton campesino garb. Some wore suspendered web gear, boonies and ammo belts, while others looked more like ordinary workers one might encounter anyway along the Pasión. They carried a variety of weapons—assault rifles, sidearms, and shotguns—a few sported wristwatches and silver crosses. Three of their number had been wounded and were borne in on stretchers fashioned from bamboo and canvas. By all indications, they had seen recent action.

One soldier stood out among the rest, a massively built man dressed in leopard fatigues, not tall but barrelchested, with thick arms and legs ill suited to the jungle. His highlander's face was dark-complexioned and hideously pockmarked. Matt recognized him from the Rescate agents' photos.

Aguilar shouted clipped commands to his troops, ordering some of them to retrieve the weapons they had stashed in the *chultun* and sending others out to secure a perimeter around the site. He advanced on the looted temple with angry strides, pausing for a moment to listen to a radioman's report before walking over to take stock of the civilians his recon detail had captured.

His eyes seemed to find Chalker first.

The archeologist was on his feet, motioned up by the woman soldier. Matt watched the two men regard each other, Aguilar narrow-eyed, Chalker's face a mask of fear. All at once Aguilar seized the archeologist's chin in one hand and spit in his face.

"*Chingada!*" Aguilar seethed, and raised a knee into Chalker's groin. As Chalker went down, the woman slammed him in the neck with the butt of her rifle.

Rachel let out a painful sound that brought the rebel leader into an abrupt about-face. His expression mirrored his astonishment; he had at first mistaken Rachel for Billie.

"Cut her ropes, quickly," Aguilar ordered one of the men. He stared at Rachel for a moment, then glanced uncertainly at Matt and Paolo. "Who are you?" he asked her.

Tongue-tied, Rachel rubbed her wrists and looked to Matt.

"Don't just sit there. Tell him."

"Rachel Riordan," she said hesitantly. "I'm Laurie, uh, Billie's sister. Billie Westphal."

Aguilar's cruel eyes softened somewhat. "Billie's sister? But what are you doing here? Is she here?"

Again Rachel turned to Matt, who nodded and said, "Go ahead."

"She's . . . dead. Billie and Neil both." Rachel's voice cracked, and her face went tight. "They killed her," she rasped, pointing to Kul and Chalker. "For her half of the book, the Mayan book."

Aguilar looked down at his boots, not angry, almost heartbroken, Matt thought. He waved a hand, and Kul was yanked to his feet, struggling to maintain his balance while the rebel asked, "Is it true?"

"I didn't even know her sister!" Kul said with a pained tone.

Aguilar took note of Kul's goatee and topknot and made an amused sound. "He looks like the ones on the stones, no?"

Some of his troops laughed. Then, for Kul's benefit, he motioned to Chalker, who was still doubled up on the ground. "You see this slug? This slug bought one-half of the Mayan book. He would have good reason to want the rest of it. He told Billie that she would face great difficulties. She was my friend, a friend to all of us who struggle for the rights of the people. And it is my shame that I took back my word to her."

Aguilar walked over to where the archeologist lay fetally curled. "I told this slug that when I let him go with the book and his life that he should steer clear of the army or the police. I told him I would find him and kill him if I learned that he spoke of our whereabouts to anyone." Squatting down, Aguilar pulled Chalker upright. "Slug, did you and your companions kill her?" he asked.

Chalker made as if to speak, but instead coughed twice and vomited. Aguilar stood up disgusted and ordered the woman rebel to kill him. Without a word she took hold of Chalker's sandy hair and drew the razor-sharp edge of her knife across his throat. Rachel gasped and collapsed while Chalker fell back, bleeding to death.

Matt fought down the lump in his throat and shut his eyes.

"What is your part in all this?" he heard Aguilar ask him.

"I was with Billie and Neil when they were killed," Matt told him after a moment. "On the Usumacinta near Yaxchilan. I was taking them into Mexico."

Aguilar looked pensive. "And the assassins took you by surprise. You were careless to lower your guard."

Matt choked back a sardonic laugh. "Yeah, well, it sounds to me like we both let her down."

Aguilar nodded and turned away. "I am not a fool to think that this slug acted alone," he announced, pacing back and forth in front of Kul, a restless beast. "You see, I know that the ransom money came from a wealthy gringo, and something in your eyes tells me that you are that man." He whirled on Kul unexpectedly. "Are you the one?"

Kul was as speechless as Chalker had been. "You don't understand," he started to say.

"*Jefe*, wait!" Rachel managed.

Aguilar turned to face her. "You said he killed Billie. Now you want me to spare his life?"

Matt pried his eyes off Rachel to find Kul staring at her, dumbfounded.

"No more blood," Rachel was saying. "Please. There's been enough killing already." She looked at Kul. "Let him pay in another way. He's wealthy; he's worth a hundred times what you received for Chalker."

"Yes, yes," Kul said anxiously, cautiously stooping to retrieve his walking stick. "She's telling the truth. I'll pay you whatever you want. Not only for my life but for whatever you have to sell." He gestured broadly to the mounds. "There are wonderful things here, *wonderful* things. And surely as a man of Indian blood you can appreciate their value, their inherent *spiritual* value, the grandeur and brilliance your ancestors brought to the world with their writings and temples."

Aguilar listened to his interpreter without interruption, allowing Kul his moment. At the same time, he ordered one of his soldiers to fetch something Matt heard him refer to as *la caja*, "the box." It turned out to be an ammunition crate loaded not with bullets but with looted treasures. Aguilar showed one of them to Kul, a cylindrical vessel, slightly broader at its mouth than at its base, eight inches high and glazed in rich earth tones. "Come on, man, tell me about it," the rebel leader demanded. "How old? How much is it worth?"

Kul hesitated. "Difficult to say. Late postclassic perhaps, one thousand two hundred years, more or less."

"How much, how much?" Aguilar asked harshly, striking the rim of the bowl with a fingernail. It rang like a copper goblet.

Kul showed him a frightened expression. "Anything you want, anything."

"And this?"

It was a plate with three rattle feet, the inner surface painted in dull yellow and terra cotta, with an outer band of black hieroglyphics.

"Ten thousand," Kul said panicked, "twenty, thirty."

Aguilar said, "You think these represent the heart and mind of my people, the hearts and minds of Guatemala. *This* is what I think of these things!" He grinned maliciously and smashed the two objects against the pedestal stone.

Then he thrust a stub of forefinger into Kul's chest. "We have no interest in the past. Here we look to the future. *Our* ancestors were slaves to an oppressive regime, forced to build these funerary monuments for people who thought only of wealth, the untouchable sky, their own self-importance."

He brought his face close to Kul's, breath to breath. "You find them heroes. To me they were devils who dared to call themselves gods. But my people overthrew them, as they did the friars and landowners who came later on demanding that churches be raised and fields be cleared to satisfy their unholy appetites. As we shall overthrow your Reagan and the tanks and helicopters he sends to Guatemala, his so-called democratic demands that we follow him into the gutter of the capitalistic world."

Kul fell back on the trunk as though struck. Aguilar drew a saw-toothed survival knife from his belt and had it raised to strike when the radioman summoned him.

Matt didn't have to hear to the message to know what had sparked the sudden activity around the mound: government troops were closing on the site.

One of the rebels cut Matt's ropes, then Paolo's, and led them along with Rachel, Kul, and Kim into a forested hollow on the east side of the repository mound. The woman accompanied them, ordering everyone to keep silent.

Matt guessed from the way Aguilar divided his group that the rangers were attempting to box them in with flanking assaults launched north and south of the ruin complex. After moving the wounded into the tunnel entrance, a small rebel contingent scampered across the dry moat to the higher mounds opposite the repository. Prone, Matt looked to his left over the back of the guerrilla woman to where Rachel, Kim and Kul were hunkered down behind the massive buttressed bole of a truncated ceiba. Paolo and the second rebel were off to Matt's right exchanging whispered remarks like two old friends out on a weekend hunting trip.

The forest began to surrender some of its light and heat to a darkening sky, growing deadly still as Aguilar's troops settled themselves into defensive positions. Matt became deeply aware of his own breathing and that of the woman. She seemed to grasp this and gave a quarter turn in his direction. Matt put her age at nineteen; she was round-faced and pretty when she smiled, her cheek resting almost seductively against the battered rifle stock. She asked him what he was called.

South of the mound, the first claymores detonated, followed by short-lived animal shrieks and the staccato chatter of automatic weapons fire. Guns with different voices answered the rebels, and with the ambush blown, skirmish fire opened up to the north and west. The rebels' rifles spoke in controlled bursts for several minutes, but moments later Matt could hear the M-60s enter the fray, clanking out a slow and steady flow of death.

He could also discern intermittent shouts as the battle waxed and waned. The fighting was mostly in the east now, and Matt reasoned that Aguilar was trying to force the rangers into regrouping before leading his own troops in a counteroffensive. The sounds of rifle fire swelled to a kind of crazed rock 'n' roll crescendo that had nothing to do with war. It was pure riotous noise, disconnected from the stillness that lingered in the forest surrounding the repository mound. But the next round of explosions changed all that.

Angry flashes strobed in the east, as though vying with the lost sun for light. An eerie wind stirred the trees, carrying the stink of cordite on its breath. Matt peered out of the hollow as concussive roars began to fill the silence he had prayed would go on forever. The verdant canopy was dancing madly, swaying in the updrafts from roiling clouds of fire and smoke. His body could feel the

impact of each grenade and mortar rocket, his face the
heat of that unsettling wind. The two rebels traded worried utterances; Aguilar was falling back, the battle moving east toward the plaza.

Radiant streamers of white phosphorous erupted in a
pyrotechnic display over the top of the high mounds,
punctuating the incessant clamor of small arms. Matt
could hear muffled pops, deep-seated *thup*s; he could
sense in his chest the *thoosh* and growl of unleashed fire.
Gobs of superheated metal fragments ripped sizzling
through the air, stripping boughs from the trees and em-
bedding themselves into rock and earthen mounds. The
smoke stratified into layers, overhanging the site like
gray-white shrouds.

Matt pushed himself down into the hollow and moved
to Rachel's side; she was balled up against the ceiba, eyes
closed, hands pressed to her ears. Deeper in the gray-
green notch, Kul and Kim shivered in each other's embrace, their faces stiff with fear. Rachel jumped as though
jolted by Matt's touch, her eyes all pupil.

"We have to move out!" he shouted in her ear. "This
shit is going to be right on top of us in a minute."

She stared at him, a lost look from deep inside.

"You're coming with us. It's our only shot."

Rachel put her hands back over her ears. Matt squeezed
her shoulder once and belly-crawled over to Paolo and
the two rebels. "The trail to the river." He motioned to
the forest behind them. "We go straight back as far as
we can, then cut south along the spring."

"They're ready to go with us," Paolo said, indicating
the rebels with his chin. Matt nodded.

He could see Aguilar's soldiers retreating down into
the dry moat and plaza from the tops of the mounds,
surrendering the high ground. It looked for a moment as
though they were going to head east into the hollow, but
instead they moved north toward the high forest behind
the repository mound.

Matt flattened himself against the ground cover as two
rocket-propelled grenades exploded nearby, showering
dirt and bits of tree into the hollow. Looking up, he spied
a dozen rangers coming over the saddle, moving tree to
tree in odds and evens down into the plaza. A handful of

rebels had positioned themselves along the front of the mound to supply cover fire for Aguilar's escape, but they couldn't hold the rangers down. Two more rounds landed near the mound, deafeningly close.

Matt put his arm behind Rachel's back and shoved her into motion. "Kul!" he said, looking back to where Kim had the old man supported on his shoulder. "Come on! Stay close!"

Kul gave no indication of having heard or understood him. He tried to push Kim aside and craned his neck around to view the repository. Two of Aguilar's men were helping their wounded *compadres* exit the tunnel, rounds slamming into the dirt all around them.

"No!" Kul shouted. "The books!"

Matt took a step toward Kul, then swung around to find Rachel on the ground, paralyzed. He shouted for Paolo, who was already twenty feet into the forest with the two rebels close behind. The boatman heard him and started back, and at the same time Matt pivoted and headed for Kul. Kul and Kim, however, were nowhere in sight. Matt took a step forward and was blown flat on his back.

He came to a second later, aware that the explosion had partially blinded him. He rolled down into the hollow and lay still a moment, slowly regaining his strength. Paolo was calling him, *"Matt,"* over and over again.

Matt sat up and waved him an okay. Paolo had Rachel by the arm; the guerrillas were long gone. Matt got on his knees and took one last look around for Kul, stunned to see him crawling on his hands and knees toward the mound, Kim several feet behind him, flat on his stomach.

"Stop him!" Matt screamed. The boy glanced behind him and hurried forward in a crouch. But he only managed three steps before the first bullet found him. It clipped him in the right shoulder, toppling him over through two complete turns. As he came up in agonized confusion, someone stitched a half a dozen rounds across his back, diagonally from shoulder to hip.

Matt bellowed a curse and threw himself back against the throned side of the hollow. Kul, already bloodied from shrapnel or grazing shots, was up on his knees, advancing on the mound, a sacrificial acolyte. Above the stutter and crack of continued fire, Matt could hear him pleading for everyone to cease fire, raving about the treasures their war had endangered.

The two guerrillas pinned down near the mound entrance didn't know who to fear more, the Kaibil rangers across the moat or the deranged, howling madman who looked like a cross between America's Uncle Sam and a god-struck self-mortifying Mayan lord. A rocket fell on the summit of the mound, fountaining up fire, stone, and fragments of the past; a second corkscrewed into its face. But Kul was unharmed and still in motion, struggling to get to his feet, hands clawing at the crumbling surface of the mound as though he meant to scramble to the top and proclaim its truths, to ascend and reveal.

At the tunnel entrance he finally was able to raise himself fully, standing there with his arms wide, shouting his holy imprecations into the face of the firestorm. The guerrillas fled, scattering like heathens from some suddenly sacrosanct mount. Kul railed, transformed in his final moments into the bark god he had chased to Central America, the living text of the revelation.

Then a tongue of orange flame streaked between Kul's upraised arms, headed for the center of the mound, and in an instant the tunnel belched a blinding mass of fire, dust, and debris that blew what was left of Kul clear into the center of the plaza, as though satisfying the gods' demands that sacrificial blood be transformed to smoke.

Another explosion erupted immediately after the first, blasting away the entire front of the mound, revealing limestone and rubble, a short length of stairway. With nothing to impede its course, the third rocket went straight for the heart.

Matt shielded his eyes from the intensity of the flash, the mound, the temple that was, a smoldering ruin in twilight. He staggered through a slow turn to the west and ran for the forest, the rangers' weapons and war cries senseless in his ears.

Paolo and Rachel were waiting for him. Gunfire crackled from the streambed as Matt led them on a jagged course southwest from the mound. A short distance along, someone stepped out in front of them, a rifle raised in their direction.

It was Sergeant Guttierez, the vengeful ranger from the Pipiles *garita*.

# 20

## Auto-Da-Fé

**"I**'ve been thinking about Bali," Jake Welles was telling Matt some weeks later.

"As in *South Pacific*?"

"As in Indonesia," Jake said, opening a map and weighing the corners down with bottles of *habarnero* and *picante* sauce, a cedar salt and pepper trough, and an empty Corona Negra.

They were side by side at the Xibalba bar. Midday, and the place was deserted, Marisol and Elena at a corner table sharing smokes. Six-foot Jake had started a beard since Matt had seen him last, a clean-lined fringe that stopped short of his neck. His face had Colorado color, a high-altitude tan.

"Sumatra, Sulawesi, central Java. There's bound to be good treks. Prambanan, Borobudor . . . And Bali, nothing but beach and temples."

"Extinct volcanoes, I hope."

"Slim women in batik skirts with fruit piled on their head."

"Carmen Miranda goes East."

Renewed violence in Guatemala had forced Jake to cancel the Pasión-Usumacinta trip. El Chichón, "the breast," had taken care of the Yucatán-Chiapas tour. Just before sunset on Saturday, April 3, the mountain had erupted again, burying the highland pueblo of El Naranjo and spewing a column of ash and debris more than seventeen kilometers high. Over five hundred seismic events were recorded during the night and on into Palm Sunday, which the locals were now calling Ash Sunday. At least 115 people had been killed, and the Zoque and other Mayan-speaking groups were still wandering around in a kind of postapocalyptic daze, asking themselves what they had done wrong to warrant such a catastrophe. Was it a warning or a response? And from whom—the Christian god that had ruled them for two centuries, or some more ancient gods who ruled the day?

Camps had been set up for the *damnificados*, the damaged, now homeless ones. Palenque's temples and plazas were covered two inches thick with ash, the glyphs and bas-reliefs obscured for a time, tangible proof of the volcano's fire-breathing wrath.

All this and the considerable efforts of Cosmo Bustamonte had in a sense cleared the path for Matt's return. Lieutenant Escobar had been transferred to Villahermosa, where he'd been promoted to captain. Gossip had it that he had made a deal with the devil.

"We can spend a couple of months scouting out sights," Jake was saying, his ice-blue eyes shining. They were into their fourth round of *cervezas* by then. "I've already got a list of museum contacts—ethnologists, botanists. All we need to do is square away hotel and local transportation costs. Get a brochure together by September and we can begin adverti ing it for next year."

"You talk to Nat about it?" Matt asked.

"She's decided to stay, even without the office. I think it'll work out. We'll get by with telexes and phone calls, like everybody else. She can continue to run the Yucatán trips. And Ángel's staying on. Oaxaca, San Cristóbal, all that will work out fine. We're just going to have to lose Guatemala for a while. Say good-bye to the classic Maya until the revolution's over."

Matt smirked and raised the bottle to his lips. "Say good-bye to Central America."

Reports of the firefight in the Petén had been picked up by several wire services and carried by both *The New York Times* and *The Washington Post*, whose front-page article bore the legend GUERRILLAS CLASH WITH

GUATEMALAN RANGERS IN MAYAN RUINS—
ARCHEOLOGIST AND NOTED ARCHITECT ARE
AMONG DEAD IN JUNGLE CROSS FIRE.

Jules Kul, Niles Chalker, and Rachel Riordan were
thought to have been members of a hastily formed expedition undertaken to reach the remote site in advance
of an insurgent group known to be plundering the district
for marketable antiquities. The Guatemalan government,
while angered by the archeologists' transgressions, was
appealing to Washington for assistance in dealing with
insurgents who were receiving arms from smugglers and
antiquities runners operating along the Mexican frontier.
Raphael Aguilar, the leader of the rebel group, had escaped and was believed to have crossed the Usumacinta
and infiltrated himself among Chiapas state's growing
refugee population.

Jake had brought the articles with him to Palenque,
along with the *Los Angeles Times*'s lengthy obituary on
Jules Kul. The architect's private collection of pre-
Columbian art had been left to that city's Masonic lodge.
A spokesman told the paper that the lodge membership
was considering making several select pieces available
for museum or private purchase.

"It's hard to comprehend. The loss," Jake said.

"Makes you wonder how the Alexandria fire brigade
must've felt."

Jake laughed, spraying beer on the map. "But you got
to see it. You and Rachel. Fuck 'em if they don't believe
you."

Matt took another pull from the bottle, catching a
glimpse of his reflection in the Coca-Cola mirror behind
the bar.

Colonel Reyes of the Pipiles border station had been
more than a little surprised to find him, Paolo, and Rachel when the smoke cleared. Still, their presence at the
site raised questions about possible complicity with
Raphael Aguilar's guerrillas, which were further complicated by the discovery of the three civilian casualties.

They had been placed under arrest and deposited under
guard at the police post in La Libertad after a long day's
forced march from Aguaculto out to the new *petrolero*
road. Huatcho, Plácido Godoy, and the two *xateros* had

beaten a lightning retreat from the site before the first shots had been fired and had reached Bethel on the Usumacinta River without incident. Huatcho had slipped across the border into Mexico and was picked up by *federales* in Tenosique. The codex, however, was nowhere to be found, and no two stories were alike as to the circumstances of its disappearance. Godoy maintained that Huatcho had had the book with him when he crossed the Usumacinta at Anaite; Huatcho, on the other hand, claimed that he had turned it over to the *xateros* in exchange for their assistance in getting him over the border. The *xateros* swore that the guerrillas had accepted the book as payment for allowing Godoy's party to leave Aguaculto alive. There, the codex had either been lost, hidden, or destroyed.

Police officials from Guatemala City and Agents Ortiz and Suentes had tried to sort things out in La Libertad, questioning Matt and Rachel separately over the course of a week. Paolo had been released and allowed to return to Sayaxche. Matt had no idea what Rachel was telling her inquisitors. Suentes and Ortiz would show up, grill him for a while, then disappear, only to return with bits and pieces of information he was left to deny or corroborate. Matt played it reasonably straight, and by the end of the week Rescate had managed to piece most of the story together. The mound hadn't been leveled by the rangers' rockets, but it was going to take the experts a long time to put the pieces back together. No one gave much credence to Rachel's theory that the temple room could have contained as many as a dozen codices, but everyone bought the idea that she and Chalker had been trying to salvage what little the guerrillas had left behind in the way of stelae and inscriptions. Rachel's Polaroids of the fragment were confiscated.

Matt kept his mouth shut about Sol Nagel and a possible government connection linking him to the two grand that had been paid for the original codex. He wasn't sure he believed it himself. He did learn, however, that Alejandro Volan had been found in Tegucigalpa, murdered by an unknown assailant.

"Are you planning to see her again?" Jake asked,

drawing Matt out of his thoughts. "There's time to fit New York in."

Matt spun around on the wooden stool watching spring's first shower, the barranca drinking it in. Marisol threw him a playful wink from the table, then leaned over to Elena, whispering something that set them both laughing.

He had ridden with Ortiz and Suentes when they drove Rachel from La Libertad to the airport in Flores. She had looked thin and hollowed out and refused to say a word to any of them for the course of the two-hour drive. She sat in the backseat with her head turned to the window, watching the thatched dwellings, forest, and banana plots, her eyes concealed behind dark glasses. As the car approached San Benito, she had reached across the seat and taken Matt's hand, holding it for the rest of the ride.

The Rescate agents waited outside the one-room cinder-block terminal while Matt walked her inside. A ticket was waiting, courtesy of the Guatemalan government through arrangements made by the American embassy. She was still silent when the plane from Guati put down, just another traveler in jeans and running shoes among a few tourists fresh from Tikal, fanning themselves in the heat. Lake Petén Itzá was silvery and rain-swollen, in places threateningly close to the airport's tarmac strip.

Matt recalled watching passengers from the capital take the stairway to the puddled field, recalled seeing three men deplane together, a distinguished-looking man in an expensive suit of European design flanked by two others in sunglasses and government cloth. He recalled Rachel saying, "Oh, dear God."

Expectant, anxious, Sol Nagel had seen her as soon as he entered the terminal and called her name across the room, waving, hurrying along. But Rachel had swung around to face Matt by then, panic in her eyes. It brought Nagel up short, flattening his smile. Over Rachel's shoulder Matt saw him motion his companions to hold, all three of them glowering in Matt's direction.

"Matt, I can't go back. Please," she had said, holding on to him.

"Guatemala isn't asking you to leave, Rachel. They're ordering you out. There's nothing I can do about it."

"Then come with me. Don't you see? You're my only connection with everything that's happened, the only one who can corroborate the find. And you're my only connection with Laurie, Matt."

He remembered the bitter laugh that had welled up. "You were *my* only connection with her. But you wouldn't let me help you. You had yourself convinced that I was your enemy before you even came down here. That you had to go it alone, do whatever you had to do to get the book. You've got your slides back in New York. You'll come out all right."

Rachel bit back a curse. "I don't even know if they came out, Matt, thanks to you and your paranoia. Rescate has the prints. I've been cheated out of everything."

"You can blame Billie for some of that, Rachel. Besides, it's like I told you: you found the thing. Nobody can take that away from you."

She gave him a pitying look. "It's not enough."

Matt shrugged. "Maybe I fucked up somewhere along the line, led you into the woods, I don't know."

"I'd undo all of it if I could. Can't you believe that? It's not too late for us." She cast a look behind her, urgency in her voice when she returned. "But if you let me walk away from you like this, it will be."

Nagel was waiting, confident, wearing a patient gesture, tolerating Rachel's small indiscretion. And Matt, staring at him across the crowded space of the small room in the middle of Central America, experienced a kind of supercharged current in the tropical air, a sense that something important was passing away and that he and Rachel and Nagel and Nagel's eyeless escorts were standing at the start of some dark new chapter of America's story, that all the lies and lunacy, the dirty tricks and shady deals, were just getting under way.

"It has nothing to do with us," he told her. "I'm just not ready to go back there. Not yet."

Without another word Rachel had moved into Nagel's embrace. Matt turned his back on them and walked away, easing his way against the flow, as the travelers headed home. Ortiz had promised him a ride to Sayaxche at the end of the road. Farewells to Paolo, to Silvio, to La Perla.

Until then . . .

"Of course you could just come straight up to Denver from Mexico City," Jake was saying. "Spend some time catching up with everybody. I still have to firm up our departure dates, figure out whether to fly into Singapore or go straight into Jakarta."

Matt took a long drink, contemplating a return to the States. Mexico was behind him, but America wasn't in his future just yet.

Jake said, " 'Course, I could just give you the flight information. We could rendezvous at LAX."

Matt lifted his bottle to it. "You'll find me in the transit lounge."

## ABOUT THE AUTHOR

James Luceno has traveled extensively in Central America, and has worked as a travel consultant in South America, Southeast Asia, and the South Pacific.